Unbound Love

Unbound Love

RATNOJYOTI

NU VOICE
PRESS

First published by NU VOICE PRESS 2024
An imprint of Hubhawks Pvt. Ltd
www.nuvoicepress.com

This is a work of fiction and all characters and incidents described in this book are the product of the author's imagination. Any resemblance to actual persons, living or dead, is entirely coincidental.

ISBN: 978-81-970218-2-4

Typeset by Saanvi Graphics, Noida
Printed at Thomson Press
Published by Nu Voice Press

By the grace of Lord Ganesha.

CHAPTER 1
Bestowed Grace

When the mist cleared in the mountains, the *Gompa* was visible. Or at least, its great entrance. Beholding the sight people said, "The Grace is pouring through the clouds, upon us!"

And truly it appeared so. Unique sounds emanated from the various musical instruments—the wind ones like *Dungchen, Dung kar, Gyaling*; the string ones like *Dramyn,* and *Piwang*; and the percussion ones like *Cho nga* or *Lok nga*. The ambience was overwhelming, as if you were being drawn by the source, mesmerized. The Lord blessed everyone—with his eight feet gilded statue installed in the monastery, the grace emanating off his palms.

Tawang, in the North-East of India, was the place where this unique monastery stood as a testimony of the lofty human values. The Tawang Monastery situated in the valley of the Tawang Chu, is at 3000 metres altitude in close proximity with the Chinese and Bhutanese border. Known in Tibetan as *Gaden Namgyal Lhatse,* meaning "the divine paradise of complete victory", it was founded in 1680. This three-storyed, yellow-roofed monastery, belonging to the Gelug school of Vajrayana Budhhiism, was the oldest monastry in India where more than three hundred monks lived.

For centuries, the monastery has stood there drawing people towards solace and being blessed by the one and only Lord

Buddha. No surprises when the Chief lama—the supreme monk—appeared, and everyone knew that the message of the Great Soul had got respoken for the commoner.

The message of love, humanity, compassion, grace, and kindness, with the strange, overpowering music, got the better of Gautam, who was drawn towards the Gompa. He later found about the locals of the tribes who had been there for aeons.

There, in the hazy twilight ambience cocooned by the odour of camphor and strange incense, he contrasted the earthly realities ensconced by the ungainly figures of his friends—Sonam, Palden, and the one and only, Tshiring.

People, comforted by the ascending spirit of devotion juxtaposed with the descending semblance of surrender, would call it "the gracious blessings". The Divine Lord, however, appeared unmoved by the seemingly pure feelings of the devotees. His radiant smile had been on his face since antiquity. After all, it was the "Grace Bestowed"!

CHAPTER 2

Tshiring, the Snow-Girl

Tawang was linked to the rest of the world by a pass at 1400 feet. Mostly, the town was covered with snow, and it was one among the many beautiful places in the region. An exotic area whose pristine, natural resources have been preserved for millennia.

The region was called the Arunachal—a landscape full of diversity that ranged from extreme altitudes to low plains, and snowcapped peaks to monsoon forests. It was a land full of exquisite treasures where rare flora and fauna were offered by Nature in their virgin form. It was known as India's "Land of The Rising Sun", the first region in the country to be lit by the dawn. Geographically, it formed the pigeon-beaked, nose-dive shape of the Indian political boundary in the northeast, with international borders on three sides.

Gautam had made new friends when he went to the secondary school, which was the only one of its kind in the area. Sixth grade was the best year to make new friends, and among these was the lively Sonam, who was always smiling, sometimes for no reason at all.

Sonam soon became Gautam's best friend, and told Gautam about his village, his parents' house, and his family. They were the aristocrats of the tribe, since his father was the *Tsorgen* or the headman.

These things were the centers of Sonam's world. And one day, he would be the *Tsorgen*, for that was the tradition. Given his family status, education, and personality, he was sure to win the confidence of his people, who would choose him to be their leader.

"You should see a *monpa* village, called the *lumpa.* You'll love it," Sonam urged one day.

"Why?" Gautam questioned. "Is it very different from our town, from Tawang?"

"Oh yes," Sonam replied. "Why don't you come and see for yourself?"

One school day, a fine morning in the summer, they skipped classes and made for Sonam's home. The geography teacher had been his usual monotonous self. He kept repeating, parrot-like, what he had to say, and he had surely been saying it for over a dozen years to sixth graders. He was another *Lama,* of a sort, who was not even half-blind.

"Our Arunachal," he droned, "has a very rich heritage. Tawang, the town we live in, has the highest gompa in the country, at an altitude of 3000 meters. It is nearly four hundred years old." He waved his arm in time with his phrases.

"Here, in the late seventeenth century, was born the sixth in the line of succession of the divine incarnate—the Dalai Lama, and the *Avalokiteswara,* and the *Dhyani Boddhisattawa,* who is the spiritual head of Tibetan Buddhism.

"Malinithan, at the central part of our region has the medieval ruins, where the Hindu kingdom once flourished."

He paused for breath, and then continued relentlessly. "To the eastern part of this magnificent region where the Tsangpo-Brahmaputra enters India on its way from Tibet, the ancient Hindu pilgrimage center of Brahamakunda, the Parasurama Kunda is located. A fairy land by any account…"

Gautam looked at Sonam. They were seated next to one another in the back row of a class of forty students. Sonam too, he could see, was utterly bored. So Gautam made a small sign to him. Aha! When the teacher was looking the other way, they ducked under their desks, crept forward quickly but carefully, and ran out of the classroom.

Soon, they were halfway to the village where Sonam lived. Off the road, in the countryside, were curious stone shrines known as *Mane* and *Chorten.*

A Mane was in the shape of a stone-wall, twice as high as Gautam—almost as wide as his arms spread apart, and nearly four paces long. On each Mane was written the Buddhist mantra, "*Om Mani Padme Hum*", meaning "Jewel in the Lotus", with letters carved in the stones. Some of the Mane also had images of the Lord Buddha.

"Why are these stone walls here?" Gautam asked Sonam.

"To ward off evil spirits. Take care to keep a Mane to your right when you walk past."

"Why?"

"Because then," explained Sonam, "the evil spirits cannot catch you."

"I am not from the village, so why should evil spirits want to catch me?" protested Gautam.

"True, but as I am with you, they might try to catch me instead."

"Hmm," Gautam said, "I suppose you are correct." So, he had better keep the Mane to his right.

The Chorten were dome-shaped structures. According to Sonam, devotees walked quickly around them three times, and the Lama offered prayers there.

Gautam and Sonam continued walking, and passed by small, colorful fields with crops such as barley, maize, chili, oats, bean, peas, and millet. Soon, there was the valley, the village, and its houses scattered everywhere. It was the first time Gautam had been to such a place. It was inhabited by northern *Monpas,* who called the region "*Mon Luvak Ful Sum*", meaning the three-Monpa areas south of the passes. This village was made up of separate hamlets and clusters.

Sonam's family house was made of stone, for his father was the village headman, whom the people called Tsorgen Tasi. He was a man of middle stature, with very strong arms and legs, well-built body, and a hardened face—all indicative of a tough life amidst nature's rough ways. A headman's life was even more arduous: hearing, advising, and directing his people. He was the intermediary between the government and the village people.

Hardly anybody in the village had gone to secondary school. Not even the Tasi! Most boys from the village and nearby areas attended primary school, and then dropped out. But girls? No! Not at all!

As they arrived at the house, an old man grinned at Gautam. That was the ailing grandpa of Sonam and Tshiring, who coughed every time he wanted to speak and was too old to move. The only time Gautam saw the old man sit on his bed was when he would pray, his prayer wheel was kept by the bedside.

Just then, like a surprise, he saw Sonam's sister Tshiring. She was full of warmth, charm, and grace!

Her face delighted Gautam. When she smiled, a broken tooth gleamed, and her face lit up. She was the brightest speck in the whole village. She looked beautiful, like a fairy in a storybook, an enchantress who came straight down from heaven.

Tshiring was wearing a blue dress, which fell below the knees. Her jacket, called a *Chuba,* was made of coarse, red-dyed wool, and reached the waist. She wore a round cap over her long hair, which was plaited in coils on the back of her head.

She beamed at him. "So, you are here!" Her manner was so soft and loving. Gautam nodded slightly. How could he say that he had run away from school?

"Come along!" she smiled. "You are Gautam, aren't you?"

"How do you know me?"

"Why not?" she replied candidly. "I know all about you. Sonam has told me everything!"

"Really?"

"Oh, yes! You are from the plains, a *Bengali*. You and your parents live in the town and you have a younger sister." Then she added, "You get good marks in the class-tests."

The last words were a compliment, and he felt flattered. Coming from a pretty girl, they were a sure way to fire his imagination, for Gautam was a boy in the first years of adolescence, when admirers are adored and affinity is raised to the realms of love.

Tshiring's warm smile, grace, and charm were enough to draw Gautam to her. Her hair infatuated him, and she was all color, like that of a carpet she was weaving with her mother at the loom.

She was utterly wonderful.

Sonam broke in, asking Gautam whether he would like to see his livestock. A lamb had been born the other day. "It's so pretty!"

Tshiring came with them, and brought the lamb to Gautam in her arms. Never before had he seen such a beautiful lamb, as white and glistening as snow.

"Just touch it," she urged, "isn't it beautiful?"

He nodded and obeyed.

Tshiring looked at him. "Would you like to hold it?" she enquired, and put the small animal into his arms. He balanced it against his chest and began to fondle it. Then, abruptly, he was pushed from behind! He nearly fell, as he realised that the ewe had not taken a kind view of him for caressing her young one. Hastily, he put down the lamb, which tottered for a moment and then ran to his mother and urgently began to suckle.

Tshiring had something else for Gautam. "Come on, take it!" she laughed. It was a glass of goat's milk, with an odor so strong that it nauseated him but he could not hurt her feelings. He did not wish to say anything that she might disapprove of. He wanted to tell her that the stuff had a revolting smell, yet he couldn't. So, Gautam turned away, pinched his nose, and quickly gulped down the contents.

Tshiring was happy.

The Grandpa awoke from a brief nap. "Tshiring," he asked, "have you told your new friend about the Gompa—the Lord, and the divine incarnate?"

"Not yet!" she said. "Only when he has time to listen. He has come here to run around the village and play about our house. He just wants to have fun."

Gautam felt a little uncomfortable.

"Never mind," nodded the old man, "for he is a good boy—he'll come to know of all those things some day. Tell him about them, when he has time."

"Oh sure." She smiled.

Gautam did not know what to say.

"No, no, young man!" exclaimed Grandpa, seeing his discomfort. "Do not be unhappy, you will learn gradually," the old one said and quickly dozed off to sleep.

Tshiring clasped Gautam's hands. "You see, don't you? Grandpa likes you, and wants you to know of all the great things. Won't you do so?"

He nodded compulsively.

Working in a corner of the house was Tshiring's mother. She looked at them and smiled, although she did not understand one word of their language. Not even broken Hindi. She could only feel.

Gautam knew it was time to go, and for Sonam to bid good-bye at the outskirts of the village. Tshiring's last words echoed in his ears.

"Are you coming again? Tell me when you will be back?"

"I shall come back soon," he declared softly. On the way home, he could not stop thinking of her.

The next time he met her, she took him to see Lama Norbu.

"Gautam!" she cried. "The Lord was born in the mountains, where divinity incarnate speaks from. Wouldn't you like to hear more?" Her tenderness and warmth were overwhelming, and he could only nod. "Come, then, the Lama must be finishing his prayers. He will bless you." She caught hold of his arms and started running, and Gautam was obliged to follow.

The place they went to was a dirt-filled, dim-lit, smoky chamber. The only sound was the disharmony between a man's voice and a prayer wheel, somber and frightening. Before Gautam could make up his mind to turn around and run, he found himself before the desolate figure of a man seated in prayer.

Gautam felt uneasy. The odor was strange and he felt in awe of the dragon masks. He wanted to leave, but could not say so to Tshiring, who put a finger to her lips as if she had anticipated his reaction. Gautam had no option but to keep quiet and wait to see what would happen next.

After the prayers were over, the Lama looked at the youngsters. He was half-blind in one eye, and completely so in the other.

"I knew, little one," Lama Norbu declared to Tshiring, "I knew you would come…now, who is this?" He looked at Gautam.

"My friend," Tshiring answered.

"Hmm...he doesn't look like someone from the community," the Lama pondered.

"He...he's from the plains, a Bengali. But he is my friend."

"From the plains!" Norbu became cautious. "Does your friend know what the mountains mean to us?"

Gautam found his voice. "Why not? These ranges are part of the Great Himalayas beyond, which are the abode of snow. The highest peaks are located here, all are very beautiful."

"Surely," the lama responded, "For the uninitiated, all mountains are the same, here or anywhere else. For us though, these beautiful peaks have something more—the sense of Nature, and the spirit that is more than mere feeling."

Gautam felt distinctly uncomfortable.

The old man continued. "For a great many people trying to visit what you call the Himalayas, there is music in the rustling of trees, a voice in the humming wind, comfort in the balmy breeze.

"For those who have given up the everyday world, there is happiness and peace, and meditation to seek the knowledge of God."

Such things mattered little to Gautam. The air was too heavy for him to inhale, he was overawed by the mysteries, and he felt desperate. From the edge of his vision, he looked for the exit, and quickly planned his escape.

The holy man closed his eyes again. It was the moment Gautam was waiting for. In the blink of an eye, without a word, he turned and ran as fast as he could. Out in the open air. There, he heaved a sigh of relief. Then he sat on the grass and took deep breaths.

He was taken aback by a shrill, almost sobbing voice. "Why did you run away? Why embarrass me?" Tshiring was kneeling on the ground beside him, holding her head. She seemed ashamed by what he had done.

Gautam thought it was best to remain silent for the moment. How could he tell her that it had been frightening, shocking, and such a heavy atmosphere to tolerate? For a moment, he thought about confess his helplessness to her, but his ego, his *manhood,* got in the way.

"Well!" Gautam blustered, "I could not hear any more of that sermon, you know. So disgusting." He twisted his lips.

Tshiring reacted strongly. "That's the way people from the plains are! All so indifferent."

Gautam had little to say in reply to such a decisive remark, and realised he had made a big mistake. Rapidly, he tried to recover lost prestige. "Never mind. Next time I meet the holy man, I shall be more presentable. I shall certainly care for your honor!" The male ego had spoken.

"Really?" She looked at him, judging his sincerity. "Mmm…I knew that. That's why I like you so much!" Like sunrise, a smile appeared on her lips even though her eyes still held a few tears. Tshiring was an enigma—so simple, yet so difficult to understand. Moments ago, she was hurting, now she was jovial again.

Gautam took his leave of her, and made his way down the road to his family home in the sleepy Tawang.

His heart was in a turmoil.

CHAPTER 3
The Demonic Deterrent

In the town called Tawang, where Gautam and his family lived, not many others did. Except for families of government servants, a few traders, and some of people of the Monpa tribe. Only a few loved to stay in the hostile climate. The people who worked in the government offices came nearly from all parts of the country. The rest of the people, the tribals, lived mostly in villages around the town. They had been living in the region for no less than a thousand year.

The habitation came up gradually in seventeenth and eighteenth century when the Gompa was built, in the last decade of the seventeenth century. The lama who set up the gompa, it is said, went to the Dalai Lama—the spiritual head of Tibetan Buddhism—to invite him to the monastery and bless it. But the Dalai Lama was busy. He promised to come later.

"As the land was found by a horse, I am going to give you the blessings of the horse-God named *Tamding,*" the divine incarnate had said.

So, the place came to be known as Tawang—a combination of *ta* (horse) and *hang* (blessing). Of the several stories regarding the origin of the name, this one was most popular.

Barely fifteen miles to the north of Tawang was China, the nation who had extended the boundaries to be able to 'shake hands' with her neighbor, India. The nation that had humiliated

India in 1962 and had taught a very good lesson to the "visionary" leaders in Delhi, the ones who believed more in glitter and hype and less on clatter of guns for the defense of the country. Only when the slogan, *"Hindi-Chini Bhai-Bhai"* (Indians and Chinese are brothers) coined by India was given a go-bye, did the leaders realize the futility of good gestures not backed by strong deterrent.

The Chinese had "opened" the eyes of the Indians. They made clear to their "brethen" across the border that the business of protecting political boundaries was a serious matter. The leaders in Delhi learnt, but at a high premium! Of having had to see the shocking deaths of numerous Indian soldiers, unfamiliar with the local terrain, of having had to fight in extremely inhospitable conditions.

The general masses in India believed that it was an act of aggression by the Chinese and so it was. The visionary leaders in Delhi, who never cared to understand the situation at the frontiers, called it "the betrayal".

There were still some people of a special kind, differing not much by birth but by acquired characteristics, who were indifferent at least in public, to the situation. Baba had said so.

They were the communists in India.

Baba continued saying that the communists thought the war was a "goodwill act" on the part of the Chinese to "help" India learn the importance of defense preparedness. Privately they were said to have rejoiced at the victory of the fellow communists.

After all, communism was global; no political boundary could restrain it. The believers all over the world were one. To his father, the communists were mostly the American-Indians, who lacked in 'human values', especially the Indian breed and more so the Bengali variety.

In addition to his inherent dislike of the ideology and the believers, was the ignominy of having had to maintain a newfound relation with one of the "doomed". A brother of his wife (the cousins in Indian families were brothers, too) was a communist. That angered him even more, but he could do little about. The man was younger to his wife and behaved as a perfect brother. He was otherwise nice but for the most abominable trait he possessed—the fellow believed in the "despised doctrine". He argued at length with his *jamaibabu* on communism and that upset Gautam's father. Within the limits of decency in the ambience of the household of a Bengali *bhadralok* that each Bengali proudly called himself so and understood the least, they had endless arguments.

The arguments ceased over the fumes of "boiling tea". Most of the times the young man had the better part of the exchanges, of the rhetoric that was indeed the hallmark of the believers of the Bengali variety. The hangover however remained within the walls of the house. The jamaibabu outsmarted by the young man heaped all the sarcasm, pinches, on his wife—the first cousin of a communist. She, however, remained nonchalant as ever. She had more important things to attend—her household. It mattered little if the Indian communists sided with the Chinese during the aggression, or if the communists "helped" Indians learn the art of "defence preparedness". Or if the Indian communists knew the volume of water flowing in the Volga more than they knew the volume of water flowing in the Ganga. Her family and her children were more important that the communists.

One day Baba came home very happy. His *sala* had received a job offer in U.S.A. and was to leave India. That made his father smile as he could then prove the fallacy of communism. "They are all capitalists in disguise," he said. "The camouflage is only to fool the gullible." Mother was happy, too. Her brother, she could tell, had gone to "*Aamerika*". If any one of her more inquisitive neighbors queried if it were her own brother, she could snub her saying, "He is closer than my *own* brother!"

For such 'great' occasions even the distant relations became close. That the guy chose to forget them even before he left the shores of India didn't matter.

That event Gautam found was one that made each member of the family happy, and rarely that ever had happened. The young man was ecstatic for he was going abroad, Gautam's father was happy for having proved the fallacy of communism and Gautam's mother for being able to tell her neighbors of a brother who lived in Aamerika.

Gradually, rather quite early in his life, Gautam came to know about them. He seemed have developed loathsome curiosity as well, but they seemed no different in looks. He had seen his *mama* who was a communist. He knew they were believers in some kind of a faith. They were a set of people he understood, who had a religion of their own like Hinduism or Christianity or Buddhism. He was curious to visit their Gompas and temples.

He had visited Buddhist Gompas as well as Hindu temples with his father. He had seen Churches and Mosques. But the place of worship, the temples and Gompas of the communists, he hadn't seen. They were the people who certainly had their temples, he knew. Only what he didn't know was where those were located. Those were the people for whom his father had not a very charitable view. His father called them traitors at their worst and clowns at their best. That interested him even more. He was curious to know about them.

Back in the plains, where the family one spent a vacation at his maternal grandfather's home, he had the chance to see a circus, the only one of its kind in his life. One of his uncles had taken the nephew and the niece, Gautam and his little sister Uma, to the circus. Uma was so frightened.

Just at the entrance was a man with no arms and no legs below the knees. The poor creature lay on a mat begging for money and some people threw coins at him. Uma was so afraid that she clung to her uncle with her eyes totally closed as they passed the poor man. She opened her eyes only when told that she was inside the circus'. There she was frightened even more by the tigers and lions, which appeared lame and weak. A man there surprised him. A tiny man, went on whipping the majestic beasts till they followed his instructions and obeyed his orders, surprised Gautam! Gautam wanted to become someone like the tiny man, to be able to defeat the Chinese.

During the breaks came two dwarfs, with shabby clothes and painted faces, jumping around like monkeys. They laughed more than they made people laugh.

"Clowns!" his uncle said as he comforted little Uma. "Open your eyes to see the clowns. All the frightening creatures are gone."

She opened her eyes and then laughed. She felt happy as one of the clowns asked for chocolates and she give one of them the only piece she had. The one with the painted face bowed and she laughed again.

Gautam realized what his father had meant. The clown! He was "the best columnist!"

The worst of them, whom his father called "traitors", he wanted to see! That was his wish. He, of course, had a hazy view of them in his imaginations. In his dreams, which he saw often, he had the visions of demons and *rakshashas* from the tales he read in Bengali. In his own imagination, he likened "the traitors" to those demons.

"They must be very cruel," he thought, "with swords in hand killing people and throwing children into the fire, with tails wagging, eyes protruding, and teeth as sharp as knives."

He heard that the Chinese ate snakes and frogs. The mere thought of the same was enough to make him vomit. And the Chinese were communists. He wasn't sure if the Indian believers of the religion also ate snakes and frogs—the live ones, the wriggling and hopping creatures.

Or, were they like demons of the stories? Of the tales in Bengali? Those who ate adults for dinner and children for supper!

Those gave him nightmares. The stories of the rakshashas he read and the thoughts that followed were enough to make him shudder.

The result was nightmares.

The saga in the late sixties and early seventies of the last century post the 1962 Sino-Indian war was the one, the family lived through.

The perpetual threat of the Chinese at the frontiers made the Indians very patriotic. At the school where he studied, plays and skits were regularly performed in which patriotic fervor was aroused among the children. Most of them were war-time plays where the Indians fought against the *dushman*. The enemy in the Indian patriotic terminology meant the Chinese. So, catchy dialogues were scripted calling the Chinese *"dushman"* who often outnumbered the Indians by ten to one but had to be defeated at least in the plays, at the hands of a single brave Indian soldier who attained "martyrdom" later.

After the 1965 and 1971 wars, Pakistanis too were referred to as dushman; obviously, dushman number two. This dushman could any day decide to wonder down the snow and 'visit' them as and when they liked, from only about fifteen miles away. The Chinese however had an overwhelming presence. They "took" even the Indian homes at the frontier. The fear of the Chinese was strong enough to keep everyone on guard. That worked as a perfect deterrent for mothers to make their children fall in line.

Even at Gautam's home, when his younger sister Uma refused to take her routine glass of milk, his mother coldly told her, "If you don't take your milk, then the Chinese would take you." She would say so and then point across the skies, beyond the snow through the window. "They are over there."

The Chinese had quietly, very quietly, entered the Indian homes, without any guns or ammunition.

It worked. Without any more argument, little Uma took her glass of milk for she was afraid that the Chinese might take her away. She was too young to know how the Chinese looked like. She had not seen any one of them. But more than the actual ones, the fear was important.

The Chinese had entered Indian homes, at the frontier!

For little Uma, the Chinese evoked the fear of creatures she heard more in the fairy tales in Bengali, or the rakshashas and *khokshashas* (demons) with long protruding tongues and nails, with dragon like faces and a number of limbs and wagging tails.

"*Dada...*" she whispered to Gautam in Bengali. "*Chinara Ki Rakshashas*?" (Are the Chinese demons?)

Gautam played the big brother. He wanted the myth to stay on.

"Yes" he said, "They are demons. But they are alive. They live over there," he pointed out over the skies as his mother did.

But she was still inquisitive.

"If I don't take my milk, are they going to come here?"

"Yes," the big brother replied. "They came here once before to take away children like you. They are waiting to come back."

"If they take me," she asked in a hushed tone "Do I have to drink milk the whole day?"

"Worse!" the brother stretched to appear bigger and added, "If they take you, they are not going to give you milk. They would make you eat live snakes and frogs, as they do themselves."

That frightened her even more. The prospect of having to eat live snakes and frogs was shocking enough to make her take the innocuous glass of milk.

The choice was much better.

So, the Chinese deterrent worked very well. They were much better than the Indian ghosts and demons of the stories.

The ghosts and demons worked at night, after the evenings. Any story about them frightened all, even the big brother. During daylight hours however, the ghosts didn't seem to work very well.

But the Chinese didn't need any such specifics to be effective. They were around every time. Invoking their names worked wonders. They were waiting just across the mountains, the snow-filled ones, the perfect deterrent for errant children and sometimes for uncompromising adults.

When Ma invoked the fear of the Chinese, she made sure that his Baba wasn't around. His father was a man who had great patriotic fervor. He resented the idea of invoking the fear of "foreign elements."

"No foreign element is needed anywhere," he thundered. "All the requisites are available in India."

For him, Indian ghosts and demons were the only choice. Foreign! The Chinese! No! Not at all!

Baba rebuked Ma when he heard the foreign element that the Chinese were being referred to.

"Don't you have any sense?" he asked, "You frighten my daughter."

"I believe she is mine, too." Ma grinned.

"All right, all right, but why should you frighten her with the name of Chinese?"

"Now don't make me a fool in front of the children," her reaction was plausible.

"That you do admirably well without my help." Baba had the last laugh.

So, she took care not to mention the Chinese to make Uma take her glass of milk, to make the errant little one to fall in line, in front of her husband.

Or else she knew, a lesson on child-rearing from him would be on, which she resented the most. She ran the home her way; she attended her children and despised sermons on how to take care of them.

Often when she was bored with his lectures at the end of the day, she said, "Child rearing is a woman's job. And for men, I think they have a lesson or two to learn on that." Her obvious reference to men was clear enough.

That invited a strong reaction from him, "The best thing is to keep quiet and listen…" he continued.

She cut him short, "That's it, the lesson I mean, you have rightly said for both sexes."

She would never stay back to hear his reactions.

While Indian ghosts and demons were the choice of Baba, the Chinese were the choice for Ma, for reasons entirely different—for keeping children in check, to make Uma to take her routine glass of milk.

Baba wanted to keep the foreign elements out, even the fear of them. Ma wanted something tangible, some creatures of flesh and blood, day in and day out, to rein in her children.

Baba had nothing against the Chinese as such, except the "aggression part". No patriotic Indian could have ever forgiven them for that. To him, Chinese were a great nation of the orient whose civilization was as old as that of his. What irked him was that the Chinese had become communists. To him, communists were anathema. Like a red rag shown to the bull; any mention of them made him bitter.

Of course, he had reasons for that, some personal and some not so. He surmised that the Chinese betrayed India only because they were communists.

"Betrayal comes naturally to the communists," he declared often.

And the Chinese, unconcerned with the happenings in an Indian home not much far, not very away, were happy; building roads and communication links, keeping their arms and ammunition ready for any eventuality. If they were to arrive, if and when they had to, at the orders from their People's Republic, even up to Indian homes to pick up children who didn't take their glasses of milk, they did so with discipline.

The Indian army men at the outposts kept watch on them in turns, with binoculars and glasses, hiding behind mounds, with their guns ready. The ignonimity of humiliating defeat, not because of cowardice but because of the myopic view of leaders a decade and a half back hurt their pride and they had to avenge that if need arose.

They were always on guard. As was the practice, Indians could only react and not act. Even at strategic locations and in warfare. If the Chinese acted, as and when they liked to, the choice was theirs, Indians were ready to give a befitting reply.

But the Chinese acted as a perfect deterrent. Of real flesh and blood, living entities located not much far away. Unlike the demons of Indian stories who could no longer be seen! So, the choice of a deterrent as ghostly, ghastly, and lively had to be invented.

The proposition worked very well. The deterrent that had to be demonic!

CHAPTER 4

The (self) righteous Indian

Gautam's visit to the lama, interested his father.

"In my youth," Baba stated, "I tried to become an ascetic once." That was news, a bit of a revelation to the whole family.

"It must have been during one of your vacations, when you had nothing much else to do." Ma sneaked in.

"No, I was serious." He went on, "When the spirit of renunciation was at the threshold, and the hypnotic charm was about to overpower me, I withdraw quietly from the life of an ascetic. Begging for alms was what I could not bring myself to do. The ego was still present in me. When ego persists, one cannot be an ascetic," he declared.

"Does it not sound like the 'grapes are sour'?" Ma enjoyed the unveiling of the mysterious episode.

"Dispassionate analysis can only be done by the unattached. Those who are neck-deep in a flow cannot keep away from the current," Baba replied. "From my youth I have been interested in the teachings of the great men. The *Bhagwad Gita* was the part of my daily readings. I also read the teachings of the Buddha, Jesus, and even bought a copy of the Bengali translation of the *Quran.*"

"You seem influenced by all great individuals," Ma provoked him.

"Except Marx," came the salvo to the "first cousin" of a believer.

"Thank God," she quipped.

"Paradoxes abound in asceticism. A true ascetic is one who has given up his ego. But, on the other hand, it is the ego that separates man from the animals."

He spoke like he was a lama, but with a different tone, dress, and setting.

"Or divine!" Ma incited him.

"Divinity is egocentric. It is the triumph of mania over mind." His will hath no why.

Little Uma had kept quiet for long now. She was shocked to imagine her father—whom she loved very much, in flowing beards and the coloured robes of an ascetic. She was terribly afraid of people in beards, and of people wearing single-coloured clothes from neck to feet.

She interrupted the proceedings.

"Baba! Did you have long beards and a coloured dress when you were a *Sadhu?*

"No, my dear! I was not long enough with them to have either of those things." Baba smiled, and thereby brought back some ease in the air of the evening that had turned serious and sombre.

Uma was happy. She clung to her father by holding his neck with her little hands. She felt happy and relieved that her Baba never had to wear coloured dresses and neither did he have long beards.

Baba was reflective.

He said to Ma, "The communists have missed the natural flow of academics and loneliness. They are no better than the mentally tortured creatures. They have even forgotten childhood frolics. They are trapped in the vicious of what, exactly? For us it was much easier in the villages, in the comforting environs of rural Bengal."

Baba grew up in a village in rural Bengal, the part that was separated from India and subsequently became an independent nation.

The fertile land criss-crossed by numerous rivers and rivulets was the land of immense charm. The villages along the banks were inhabited by people who were, ill-clad but certainly not ill-fed. The fertile land provided paddy that grew in abundance, and there were enough freshwater fish in the water bodies that accounted for the innumerable delicacies the Bengalis devoured.

The only time devil descended on the land was during epidemics, which occurred once in ten, or twenty years, and the havoc caused during perennial causes like flood and storm.

The village was strictly divided into areas of Hindus and Muslims. Yet, there were hardly any occurrences of inter-religious feuds. Each community was reconciled to the status quo for centuries, which they were destined to maintain. They lived in peace and harmony within the ambit of undeclared but accepted truce.

His family was one of the affluent landowners who often flattered themselves in the mould of *Zamindars,* the near *Rajas*, in a bid to elevate themselves into the league of the regal insignia of fancy. They owned agricultural lands, enjoyed the labours of their Muslim tillers, who were their tenants.

Baba often talked at length about his father to his family. A man who had died young, in his thirties, fighting legal battles over agricultural lands with his neighbours and rivals in the village—the Roy Choudhurys, and probably of a severe form of jaundice.

The tale of the villages in the land had the same story repeated over and over again since ages, until the nineteenth century. From then on, it continued with newer and innovative connotations under the influence of the British and within the Anglo-Saxon laws. Basically, the story of a rural affluent family was the protracted warfare for preserving family interests.

The eldest male member was the patriarch, one who controlled the affairs of the family within and from the village. This included overseeing the lands, the cultivation, and the receipts of the revenue collected. Added to that were the annual rituals of the marriage of members. The screening of men for finding suitable match for their daughters, sisters, and even aunts, were accorded top priority. High fertility rate, coupled with the early marriage of boys and girls, produced situations where the procreation of two or three generations continued parallelly, at times even overlapping each other. Often, the proposition came to situations where the father begetting children and the male members of the next generation begetting their share of the population continued unabated—so aunts were younger than sisters and daughters, and sons and brothers were older than uncles.

The chain of events continued over generations and centuries in endless iterations. Each pair expected no less than a dozen conceptions, half of which were certainly miscarriages or still-births. The other half that somehow survived the ordeal to see the light of the day, had their share of misfortune to deal with. Nearly half of the surviving lot perished in infancy due to high infant mortality rates, no proper health care system, and limited knowledge of personal hygiene. Biannual fevers like malaria and typhoid, and the annual occurrences of events like flood and storm also contributed to the toll. Every decade, macabre appearances of epidemics like cholera and smallpox further added to the devastation.

The epidemics wiped out families after families, and in some cases villages after villages, if not the entire population of an area. The people however accepted the happenings as the consequence of divine wrath, attributing them to the sins committed on earth and the will of destiny. They preferred to embody fatalism in its truest form and spirit.

Gautam's grandfather was a shrewd man. He took charge of the household affairs at a very young age. Though he was illiterate, he had an abundance of courage and business acumen. He was a 'man of vision'. With an eye on the future, he sent his young man past to set up a legal practice at the nearest district headquarters, where he could take up the legal battles being fought in the district court for the family.

The third brother, according to the plan laid out by God, was a non-starter. They said that since the major workload was shared by the two older siblings, he had very little to do. He took up *pujas* to the family deity as a part of the daily chores. He was a very simple man, perpetually ailing and had developed mental abnormalities. Some said that was because of his 'proximity' to God. Having had very little to do, he choose the best way to bid adieu—he died, but not before he had started his own lineage of sons and daughters.

The youngest brother, who again wasn't much older than the eldest of the patriarch's offspring, was a bright young man, much favoured, and liked by the man himself. But he probably died of malaria, while awaiting the results of his matriculation examination from the Calcutta University. The patriarch's hope to send the youngest brother to England to qualify for the bar was dashed. He had hoped to settle the most promising of the brothers at Calcutta to join the High Court, and thus widen family interests.

Of the four surviving brothers, the youngest was arrogant, a misfit, a troublemaker, a rogue, and a destroyer of sorts. It was such an elaborate, well-laid out plan of destiny that the saga of a rural and landowning Bengali family felt complete. The same saga had continued in some form or other throughout the society for aeons.

The youngest frittered away the carefully amassed family fortunes, sold land property, and got into legal squabbles for no apparent reasons. He also organized and led violent clashes on the rivals.

The route that fate had chalked out for each family member was complete.

Each brother married early, as was the custom, and soon had their lineage replete with the same old story repeated over and over again—of births, miscarriages, and infant mortalities. Because no one took it seriously, they became routine affairs. The house was perpetually in the care of the village midwife, as every year at different months or even in the same month, births had to be attended in either of the brother's families. The infants were perennially in the care of the siblings, cousins, aunts, and nurses because their parents were busy consummating "the will of God". It was done in the name of family deity whose idol was installed in a separated room—the cleanest and most well-maintained in the entire house.

The grandpa had six children, four of whom survived. Death, as and when descended on the family, surprisingly spared the wives of the brothers despite them being the easiest prey to the "call of God". Somehow, the inevitable didn't happen.

Before he could continue adding his share to the lineage, grandpa died. There was no reason as to why he should have discontinued the time-tested practice of adding to his family. He died when Mr. Simon, famous for the Simon commission, was about to arrive in India. He endured hardships, and sacrificed his health while taking care of the legal battles and family interests.

Gautam's father was nearly a couple of years old then, being the youngest. He never had any memories of his father except the vague ones in which he recalled his father having caressed him on more than one occasion, kissed him, and held him in his arms. There were of course serious doubts about such descriptions. It was known that as the patriarch, grandpa was not supposed to show any public demonstration of love, even to his own offspring. It wouldn't have gone down very well with other members. It was seen as the sign of "weakness", and the man was thoroughly conscious of that. It was believed that Gautam's father was fed those details. Those efforts were made to placate the fatherless child of paternal love and care so that the young one had some kind of a memory of a loving father to cling to.

That was precisely done because it was believed that sorrows and sadness affected personalities. It altered the attitude towards life as well.

So, the rudderless family pulled on, the family fortunes tumbled. It was slow but gradual. Slowly but surely, the slide began. It turned out to be a "free for all" affair, bit by bit. The brothers had their share of the pie. Though the joint family was intact, the cracks had developed within.

The family in due course developed into a centre of intrigue, confusion, betrayals, and downright cheating. The dictum "everybody's business is nobody's business" was brought to reality. The sagging family fortunes slumped further. The joint family was brought down to a level of existence, of a struggle for survival above the one of bare subsistence, not much different from the one the family had mastered over the tillers.

The acts of personal aggrandizement among male members was debilitating and shocking. They however maintained a show of honour for their eldest sister-in-law, the widow of the patriarch. She had responsibility without authority, and whatever residual shades of authority remained, she was without power to execute them.

The great Indian euphemism was in full display.

The cultivated act of according reverence to elders by relation had been perfected in the Indian way of life. So much so, that even those who were out to harm, sworn enemies, or acquired foes; seldom expressed their virulent form in day-to-day dealings.

Despite their well-executed manoeuvres, and their intentions being known, the brothers maintained a show of family unity, as well as care and love towards their nephews and nieces.

The dichotomy of the revelation was artistry of high order—consummated, perfected, and stored in genes for centuries together.

The overriding concern was that they belonged to a family of Zamindars as good as Rajas, who they flattered to deceive. They had a distinct heritage and culture of their own. Years later, when they had virtually become paupers after the partition of the country, those traits were still present. They had a certain sense of delusion in spite of the deterioration that they had suffered.

The delusion of grandeur was complete. They fondly called it 'the family prestige and honour', which meant the virtues and values that kept them flaying themselves till the very end.

Under the circumstances that Gautam's father grew up, there was no particular ambition to pursue. He was said to be a bright child picking up alphabets of the Bengali language. There after he was sent to the high school a couple of miles away, at the other side of the rivulet that flowed by the village. The school fee was two *annas* per month.

He excelled at school—in academics, sports, and extra-curricular activities. He progressed from one grade to the other. With each passing year, he also became a perfect trouble-maker. He incurred the displeasure of the school's headmaster as he organised student movements in support of the freedom struggle led by the Congress party.

The headmaster was called to the office of a British official twice, who was the inspector of schools at the district headquarters, to be warned of dire consequences which meant de-recognition of the school itself. Luckily, the third warning never came as the young man had lesser time for strikes and movements as he appeared for his tenth-grade examination from the Calcutta University just at the stroke of the Second World War.

He joined a well-known college in the city after to qualify as a science graduate. His stay at the city brought him further in contact with freedom movement and his zeal for social reforms was inflamed. He was now on no less than a crusader, a self-styled one. He decided to act on his village first.

At his native village, he was the chosen one. Soon, like-minded young men flocked all around him. They set up brigades to oversee any transgression of morality, and excesses committed on the oppressed and the underprivileged. The privileged and the rural patriarchs, who saw erosion of their authority and dictates, resented these self-styled guardians of the society. But the youth brigade enjoyed their exploits.

There were instances when the enthusiasm of the members got better of their senses. Once, they cut-off the pigtails of some orthodox and bigots among the *Brahmins*, for whom the caste discrimination and hatred was the sole motto. That created such a furore, which put the youth brigade in a very tight spot. The assault was considered blasphemous and that was the height of their action. The consequences of such a bizarre incident forced the brigade to call off their crusade. No one after all could have faced such social turmoil and upheavals. The great crusader and reformer brought his mission to a premature end and returned to the city for the greater cause of the nation, with more experience.

Years later, an old acquaintance once brought the matter into discussion and the whole family listened with eyebrows raised. Gautam's father was however calm and unexcited. He abhorred mentioning such macabre incidents in front of the children. Age and experience had mellowed him. Radicalism had given way to caring and parental concern.

Only little Uma seemed disturbed. She was curious to know what a pig-tail was and how could a pig-tail ever grow on a human head.

"Baba!" she cried, "Show me what a pigtail is!"

Gautam had to pull her by her hair saying if ponytail could grow on her head, pigtails could also grow on someone else's head. She was pacified, but only felt satisfied when Ma drew a sketch of a clean-shaved head, with a pig-tail projecting out.

The young crusader had, back then, found solace in the Indian freedom struggle.

With the dislike of British rule growing stronger within him, he got quite an unexpected call one day.

He was asked to appear before the selection board for joining the Royal Indian Army in the King's commission. The world war had necessitated the intake of recruits in the commissioned ranks. The army authorities had checked out the list of successful candidates in the Matriculation examination from the Calcutta University and had invited them to join the army.

The young man decided to try out his luck and appeared before the selection board without informing his family, for the knew his family could never have approved of such an idea. He was selected on the basis of merit but then something happened and his formal appointment never came through. He later found out that his association with anti-British forces in the freedom struggle had made the authorities cancel his candidature.

That day on he nurtured a grudge against the British, in addition to the dislike of the British rule. He developed personal animosity to anything British. What was never clear to his family and friends was how someone like him, who had the fiery spirit of nationalism, compromise by joining the British Army. They came to know of the episode later.

They reconciled however, saying that even the most incorrigible idealist does wobble sometime.

The next best thing the young man could do was to join the freedom struggle with more vigour, coupled with venom against the British rule, growing stronger with each passing day.

The Indian National Congress had become the platform for the people to organise the freedom movement. No wonder the platform was the meeting place of people of all shades, and of all kinds of political ideologies. All sorts of voices were aired from the platform with all kinds of tones—high, low, baritone, and no tone with pitches varying from high to low and shrill to almost quaking. Communists, capitalists, rightists, leftists, and those with no views were accommodated. The amorphous, heterogeneous, and nebulous character of the congress was complete.

The great Indian truth was exemplified.

It was to be all things to all people.

Like hundreds of young men before him, Baba too joined the platform with not much of a view to adhere. Overthrowing the British rule was the only objective.

The only other movement that had gained momentum in parts of Bengal in the late thirties and early forties was the Communist Movement that attracted the youth of the day.

Baba too had come in touch with the communists. The communists, however, failed to impress upon him with any of their ideals and gave up hope of including him in their fold.

He, on the other hand forgave them, for he thought they were in error. To him, communism was no more than a variant of escapism for some of the Bengalis. It was a short-cut route to nowhere for some who had gone ultra-radical.

He preferred to condone their acts as aberrations till it reached the boiling point sometime during the war. With the signing of the Anglo-Soviet treaty, the British and the soviets became functional friends. The Indian communists suddenly found in the British qualities they hadn't surprisingly noticed before. British became the friends of the communists, and any movement against the British was taken to be against the spirit of communism.

The communists always believed in global terms. Nations had very little space in their doctrine.

In the enthusiasm of newfound friendship, they called the World War, and India's involvement in it, as the "People's War". That was strongly resented by the Indians who felt the British were needlessly dragging India into the vortex of war. The communists added fuel to the fire when they called one of the greatest leaders of the national movement and an ideal for the youth of the country as "Quisling", for he joined hands with the axis powers in an attempt to free India from the British rule.

Baba had all the dislike and hatred for the communists from that time on. In the subsequent years, when the country was partitioned, he became a refugee in his own land. And according to some, the communists had supported the vivisection of the land at least on principle, under "self-determination of minorities", adding to the great human tragedy. He held them responsible for such a catastrophe, in a way.

Besides, he found the ideals of communism in pretty bad taste. He condemned the idea of the Dictatorship of the Proletariat. "How could a dictatorship be of any good to any one?", he questioned. To him, the Dictatorship of the Proletariats was as bad as the dictatorship of the privileged.

During the days when the communists started calling the war as 'People's War', he advised his communists friends to replace their slogan from:

Biplab Zindabad!
Shramik Ekta Zindabad!
(Long lives the revolution!
Long live worker's Unity!)
To the one that could fully explain their attitude:
Biplab Nipat Jak!
Englandeshwar Zindabad!
(Down with the revolution!
Long lives the king of England!)

That kind of sarcasm enraged his friends who believed in the doctrine. He was, however, certain in his belief, and in the erosion of human values in the stewardship of the communists in Bengal.

Nearly three decades later, when the ultra-leftists created turmoil in Bengal, they were put down heavily by the government, resulting in encounters and killings unknown to the land even during the days of the British, he had a point of his own to explain. He found the root cause to the call for dictatorship, and by the average Bengali's rebellious nature of petty dimensions against anything traditional and the general nature of them to opt for short-cut methods. He abhorred the rejection of religion by the communists. To him, the communists had forsaken all forms of attachment to their roots, culture, tradition, and conventions and had become infatuated and intoxicated by the nothingness of a utopia. He opined that the "Religion is the opium of the people" type of slogan no longer carried any meaning. He believed that for the poor communists, "opium had become the religion".

Their constant clamour for the interests of the *Sarvahara* was a hoax. "How could a Sarvahara bring any change to the society at all?" he thundered. In trying to do so, the communists, he believed, had lost everything and had become Sarvahara themselves—of a slightly different kind though. They had lost even their abstractions, their honour, their dignity, their human values and commitment to the nation!

During his student days, as the young man got more involved in the freedom struggle led by the Congress while becoming less interested in his academics, came the watershed in his life and the pinnacle of the freedom struggle.

The Quit India movement launched by the Indian National Congress in 1942 was the greatest moment in the history of the Indian freedom struggle. It reverberated with the clarion call of Mahatma Gandhi to the country—men should unite and fight the British rule, and force them to leave India. To the youth, that was the time to strike. For the first time, the Indian National Congress had given such a call. The people were, in fact, used to the softer movements led by the congress. The 'do or die' mantra suited the people, especially the youth of the country who knew it was the time to act.

For the likes of the young crusader, it was a god-sent opportunity to avenge the tyranny of the British and their rule. They had to act, and act decisively, each according to own methods and within his domain.

The right chord was struck. The core group of the erstwhile youth brigade of the village met and then discussed, debated, and arrived at a decision. To them, the action had to be decisive, to take the British rule by the horns.

They decided to take care of the most visible symbol of the British Empire in the vicinity of their village—the police station.

The police station had to be removed from the face of the earth. It was the symbol of all oppressions and tyranny. Overthrow of the British rule had to begin from the village by cleansing the surroundings.

On the fateful day, four friends met past midnight when the rains had stopped, at a pre-destined place. They were armed with petrol and matchboxes. They then proceeded towards their destination.

Halfway through, they found the eldest member of the squad trembling in the hot summer night. They soon found that it was not malaria that the man suffered from, but the fear of the impending action. Without proceeding any further the other three asked the man to go back and to the village, with the warning that if he revealed the details of the action to anyone else, even God would not be able to save him then. The party was thus reduced to three. They moved with even more determination and resolve, on to their mission of taking on the might of the British Empire.

At the police station, it was all calm and placid. The policemen had not taken any serious view of the movement, as the area seemed not much to have been touched by the agitation. After the early night shower, they had gathered for a nice sleep, while those on guard duty were busy playing cards.

The members of the squad took care to avoid the dormitory where the policeman lay asleep. The constables were all Indians. Moreover, no human lives were to be accounted for in the mission. The Mahatama's diktat on adherence to non-violence had to be followed.

So, they approached the office instead where the records were kept. Very quietly they drenched the structure with petrol, ignited it and ran nearly two hundred yards away. From the cover where they could watch the outcome of their action. When the flames burst to the obvious delight of the members, the bell at the police station rang, and the policeman ran helter-skelter. They knew that their mission was complete.

As their mission was completed, the members of the squad embraced each other and ran in different directions never to meet again. As it turned out, none of the members ever met again in their lifetime, sucked in the vortex of occurrences, as were the destinies of their families and that of the nation in absolute jeopardy.

The members of the squad departed from the scene and the village. They quit their homes, even before those for whom The Quit India Movement was for.

The police soon found out who the culprits or at least who the suspects were. The families of each of them were harassed and subjected to torture. Punitive measures were imposed on the village with special fines on the families of each of the members.

The families had to cough up the amount by selling the agricultural land. The revolutionaries meanwhile were nowhere in sight.

Baba returned nearly a couple of years later, when the crescendo had died down and serenity returned to the land. He was in a wretched state having endured hardships while he was underground. With his academics gone astray, and the consequences of the privations that he had to endure taking the share of the toll, he was a broken man. The British were still there, almost on the verge of winning the war and the nation seemed to be tottering on the brink of disaster, of a sinister kind. Barely a few days after he reached his home, he fell ill—of a severe case of typhoid fever, which probably he had contacted on the last leg of his sojourn in disguise.

When he recovered, the friends and relatives said from the point of no return, his memory was all but lost. His world shattered, his hopes and ambitions of a career thrashed, and he became a recluse maintaining a stony silence. His aging mother and his eldest sister nursed him back to his health at his native village.

Back to his feet after he recovered nearly a year after, he found the world had changed immensely. The World War had drawn to a close with the Allies winning, with the British once again on the winning side. His friends and acquaintances from college had proceeded with their careers and were successful. The political scenario had changed. The enthusiasm and spirit of earlier period had given way to a feeling of resignation. The nation seemed poised for vivisection. Bengal was going through a calamity—The Great Famine.

He stood isolated, recluse, and felt as good as lost.

There was devastation all around. Thousands of people were dying of starvation. The Hindu-Muslim sectarian hatred that appeared to erupt anytime, loomed large over the horizon. His own career was in jeopardy. What mattered was the question of survival against all odds.

Some thirty years later after he managed to survive, he was again at the frontier of a new kind. In free India, now with his own family. The real enemy of a hostile nation, of communists aiming their guns at the likes of him, lay not much away.

Barely fifteen miles away from the Line Of Control, where the Chinese were ever ready to pounce on the Indian Territory, lived the family of four.

Baba had a personal grudge against the Chinese. The story of the Chinese betrayal, aggression and loathsome ideology apart, which were of perilous propositions over the whole of the nation, he had something very personal against the Chinese.

He never forgave them.

After the land was partitioned, the worst human tragedy of the subcontinent descended upon the populace. Thousands were killed and millions were rendered homeless. He had also become a victim of the partition, like thousands who had become refugees in their own land. The erstwhile revolutionary had given up the hopes of building a great nation. He was too busy trying to eke out a livelihood to keep his body and soul together. Petty jobs came his way. All the hopes and aspirations were sacrificed at the altar of the freedom movement and the subsequent partition of the land in which he was uprooted from own land. All that was left was the debris around him—the memories of sufferings, misfortunes, and the will to live. In the search of livelihood, he found himself in the mountains at the frontiers.

Yet, life moved on. He married a girl from the plains adjoining the hills. It was an arranged marriage. His father-in-law was a retired govt. servant on the lookout for a suitable match for his youngest daughter. He was an expert occultist, attending endless sessions of planchette where he got in touch with souls of the departed. Besides, he was a 'reformist' championing the cause of women's education, liberation and the likes, all the while being a staunch religious man with a fair measure of orthodoxy. In short, he was one of the examples of Bengali gentlemen with nineteenth century values—the *Bhadralok*, with all sorts of contradictions present. He sent his eldest son who was a doctor to the war, and his daughters to co-ed schools and colleges in the 1920s-1930s in the small town he lived in. Yet, when it came to the marriages, those had to be arranged ones. For his sons and daughters he and only he made the match, within the traditional system of caste, family, and the locale of the prospective brides and grooms.

How on earth he came to choose the erstwhile revolutionary for his youngest daughter was a mystery. To the daughter who had very little say in the matter despite having college education, that turned out to be the cruel joke of destiny.

She of course had her grudges against her father for being insensitive to her liking and to her husband for being dictatorial and thereby being callous. She had her own axe to grind, to justify the cruel joke.

She had hoped of leading her married life in a city if not in a metropolis. She had a college education and given the circumstances in which she was brought up, she had dreams of a good match. Of a husband who would be very sensitive to her feelings, and God-willing, someone who would rather not apply the mind of his own but be guided by her advice in matters of conjugal life. That however remained a wishful thinking. What turned out was exactly the opposite of what she had hoped for. She was devastated.

Adding insult to injury was his insisting on to take his bride to his workplace to begin the conjugal life. She had natured hopes of some kind of a honeymoon in placid surroundings.

For her the ordeal had just begun.

To the foothills of the mountains, they reached travelling in railway car and vehicles. From there the journey had to be on foot.

The upheaval in her life seemed so nearby.

The newly-weds walked on foot in the mountains accompanied by the porters who carried their luggage. Through forests, resting in between at the villages inhabited by tribal people at night, they continued their journey. "Nearly seventeen miles a day!" she exclaimed later.

On one such occasion she twisted her ankle and the workaholic husband put her up in the nearest health centre under the care of a nurse, and proceeded on to his place of work. He returned nearly a week later to attend to her and after she had recovered, they continued on. This act of his earned him the wrath of the young wife, who called him heartless—the stigma which he had to bear for the rest of his life.

They began their conjugal life in the remotest of the corners of the country and planned to raise a family of their own.

And then, there came the Chinese. Right at the time when the couple expected their first child.

Nearly a decade and a half after the nation gained freedom, the first of the major tests of defence preparedness lay ahead. And an aggressive neighbour trying to gobble up territory despite making promises to the contrary.

The leaders in Delhi believed in their infallibility. They hoped to contain and if possible, repulse the aggressors with rhetoric, when the need of the hour was gunpowder. The result was obvious.

The couple that lived no far from the frontline was apprehensive of being overrun by the Chinese. The expectant mother had to be removed, but not before she had to walk considerable distance on foot. Finally, she was airlifted like many of her female counterparts while the males were left behind to fend for themselves. But the damage was done already.

When the couple met again in the plains after a fortnight, after the husband had fled before the advancing Chinese army could descend, they had the mortification of seeing their first born dead.

Baba never forgave the Chinese for that act of aggression, which had affected his life immensely.

He developed a strong dislike for the Chinese then on. Not much different from the feeling he had for the British. If those differed, those were in degrees.

If the British were imperialists, the Chinese were no better. They were the communists.

The erstwhile revolutionary had his dislike for the British accumulated over the years in full. The arrears he never forgot to pay back, the first chance that came his way. His dislike for the British was very strong. He was contemptuous of their attitude towards the Indians. However, he appreciated their abilities.

"Britons never lost wars in their history," he reflected often. "If they lost battles, they soon avenged their defect to emerge victorious finally in the wars. They lost battles but very seldom lost wars. They always had the last laugh."

British were his adversaries at all levels—mental, emotional, and psychological.

He concluded that the British were the most level-headed of their times, most business like, most professional, and strictly adhered to tradition and conventions.

"How many Rosseau, Voltaire, Montesquieu have the British produced?" he asked. "They could not have ever!" The fact that even the French had not repeated the likes of them again bothered him a little.

"To produce such personalities, you need a society that had to be vibrant, and a class like the intelligentsia which by nature had to be rebellious. And that was precisely absent in Britain. More people in Britain died of natural calamities in the revolutions. Opposition to conventions and tradition was anathema to the British!" He talked to his son who was hardly capable of grasping the facts. But that mattered little. His son had to be groomed and nothing better than parental care and teaching were thought to be effective.

"Could they ever produce anyone like Goethe?" he asked. "But Shakespeare! Baba..." the son joined. "That was a tragedy.

Because they ruled over half the globe by destiny, they could spread his name. He was a great dramatist. The greatest of the English dramatists! If India could also rule over the world, Kalidasa to would have been the greatest of all dramatists in the world ever. His *Meghdottam*, *Kumar Sambhava,* and *Malavikagnimitra* were classics. Pity they called him the 'the Shakespeare of India'. It should have been the other way round."

The son picked up the names, which helped him in the quiz competitions at the school.

Baba felt he had the knowledge coupled with critical analytical ability that made him feel like an intellectual.

"He is all mind and no heart." Ma's reaction was typical.

The son had to recollect his textbooks of the sixth and seventh grade to inform his father that there were other literary figures in England.

"Baba! Wordsworth, Shelly, and Keats were all great poets!"

"Sure! But they couldn't have matched our poets," he cut his son short.

"How many Bachs, Brahms, Beethovens, Wagner, Mozarts, have the British produced?" He reverted to his known territory. For the young son, the names were unfamiliar.

"None," he continued. "Because music does not come naturally to the British. The stiff upper lip does not produce quality music, only devotional songs, and elegies. For real music you got to get both your lips moving." He was very happy that he was able to cut the Britons to size with his analysis.

"The English could not produce any Michellangelo or Vinci. They lacked the supreme imagination and condescending heart to produce the marvels of the art." That conclusion made him extremely pleased, he marvelled at his own analysis. He hoped his son would one day grow up and absorb his analytical ability.

For the son, another English author suddenly appeared in his mind. "Besides, there was another great author in English, Oscar Wilde!"

"He was Irish," his father replied sharply.

"Despite being second graders, they succeeded," he continued.

"The British were no great warriors than the Spaniards, no greater sailors than the Scandinavians, but they won nearly every time."

"They succeeded because they had one thing in abundance—common sense, knowing what to do, how and when to do, and whom to entrust the jobs with. Emotions were certainly not in their traits. They blended all their second-grade qualities to make a perfect mix to emerge on top."

He was very relieved that the British called Bengalis, the "Irish of India". That to him was nothing short of a compliment. At least the British had acknowledged that the Bengalis were a "cut above them".

Like most of the fellow Bengalis, he would have been the happiest man on earth had the French likened the Bengalis to themselves. An average Bengali's notion that his language was as sweet and as developed, his literature and culture as likeable as that of the French, was never confirmed by the French. And that was regrettable. That dampened the spirit of the likes of Baba.

To the former freedom fighter, his son was one whom he wanted to inspire and the process was on. He wanted his son to inculcate the goodness of everything, To the middle-class self-styled upholder of righteousness, that was the epitome of joy and satisfaction.

After the unforgivable act of the Chinese, there was another sacrilege by the Pakistanis. The nation that was born nearly a day before India showed the tyranny of the small. The war that was fought was by India.

Between the two wars, interspersed with events like the elevation of a diminutive but highly acclaimed individual to the top post of governance after the death of a charismatic leader—Gautam was born. To the initial anxiety, transitory delight, and final relief of the couple, a son was born. Small, fair, but suffering from jaundice. The son was born who breathed, and after some very anxious moments, survived. Fortunately that time there was no turmoil, at least in the plains away from the hills and mountains.

Luckily the Chinese weren't around and the Pakistanis were not strong enough to create any upheaval. The couple rejoiced. Sometime after the war, again to the anxiety and relief of the couple, a daughter was born whom they named "Uma", after the namesake Goddess. The former freedom fighter completed his family. What lay before him was to bring the children up to the best of the tradition, cultural and inspiration to become the best of the human beings, at least in sprit and attitude.

While the ex-freedom fighter and now a complete family man nibbled and wobbled at his work place continuing his placid, monotonous job, he certainly added a touch of colour and variety of his own.

He went on correcting the grammar, the punctuation, and the syntax of the sentences of his superiors, which earned him their extreme displeasure. They however hesitated to say anything openly for the fear of further humiliation. Those however resulted in his frequent transfer on grounds of insubordination. The man nonetheless forgave his superiors saying, "They know not what they do." He was confident that one day they were sure to realize their mistakes. For the moment in magnanimity,

on India, and the Americans showed their red eyes. But the iron-lady earned the applause of the nation and the gratitude of the Bengalis all over the world.

For the former revolutionary that was a dream come true. Firstly, of a Bengali nation that soon more or less turned to be chimerical in spirit, and secondly, the conviction that the two nation theory was a fallacy. He recounted how nearly twenty-five years ago he had encountered a prominent leader of the Muslim league who had demanded separate homeland for Muslims, at a meeting in his hometown.

The young man who had recovered from typhoid that had almost ruined him, was a witness to the dreams of his nation being shattered. At the threshold of such epoch-making changes, he had attended the meeting of the leader of the Muslim league whose xenophobic utterances captivated the audience. Soon after the meeting, the young man sought a private audience with the leader. His wish was granted. Soon he was led to the chamber of the leader surrounded by the goons who watched the young man as a non-believer, of faith and doctrine.

"Would Pakistan solve the problems of identity?" the young man asked. "The Bengalis on one side with the aggressive westerners on another side, thousands of miles away with nothing in common?"

The leader looked at him with blood-shot eyes and thundered, "*Amra Phani Khaiya Ek Sange Thakmu!*" in colloquial dialect. The young man left in a hurry without prolonging conversation any further as that would have put his personal safety in jeopardy.

The former revolutionary had his chance some twenty-five years later saying that the plain water did not make people stick together.

"Only if they understood it then", he lamented, "The greatest human catastrophe of the subcontinent could have been avoided."

In addition to the already tense situation during the turmoil, was the question of safety of his kith and kin that had chosen to remain on the other side of the border. In the aftermath of the killings that took nearly a million lives and during that period, the former revolutionary was worried about their safety.

That he solved by resorting to occultism. The method he employed was known only to him, but the results he achieved were surprising to his family members, which was another kind of a revelation. Often the son and the daughter were reprimanded by the mother for making noises as their Baba was in the adjoining room calculating and trying to find out how the relatives were. He often emerged from the room and that happened quite a few times through the two and half a month ordeal, to announce to his family members that all his relatives was safe. His stature grew in the eyes of the family members, as they knew he had the ability to be in communion "extraterrestrial" beings. For his wife though, he was a novice, not much beyond the level of apprentice. She had known her father, a master in organizing planchettes and *yogic* exercise, bring back visions of past happenings to selective individuals. In comparison her husband seemed almost a beginner.

Baba was happy that his relatives were all safe, that the two-nation theory was a failure, that the Bengalis had gained their nation. What appealed to him was that the elusive unity of Bengalis seemed to be in sight. That of course received a jolt within a couple of years when reports reached him that all was not well there. Finally, that culminated in the assassination of the founder of the new nation by the army, aided by the religious fanatics.

The situation was back to square one.

Worse was to follow soon. Reports began reaching that the national emergency declared by the Indian Government in Delhi brought back the memories of the British. The fundamental rights of the people were suspended. Censorship was imposed the press. Political opponents were picked up and put behind the bars. Forced sterilization was performed on the people in the name of controlling the population. The usurpers of constitutional provisions delighted in their acts of defying the edicts, which had put them in their exalted places.

All in the name of preserving democratic values and ideals! In the name of upholding national unity and cohesion!

To the now older revolutionary, the facts were crystal clear. He had seen enough. From the days of the partition when the leaders gave a go-bye to their self-proclaimed pronouncements of principles to accept the vivisection of the land, to mutely watching the greatest human catastrophe of the nation, to immune themselves from the grim situation of death and destruction. He had watched the erosion of values and ideals, the evaporation of lofty principles like that of camphor. The world had come full circle for him.

The refugees from the eastern part had got a raw deal. The democratic spirit soon gave way to sycophancy and pretensions in the new nation. The longest written constitution of the world could not plug the inherent ability of the leaders to circumvent the provisions to attain their personal objectives.

Amidst the turbulence within came the latest straw in the last quarter of the century—the Emergency that rocked the nation.

The 1975 Emergency came and went, like the demonic tales that his daughter read and heard. The middle-aged revolutionary had difficulty in reconciling his priorities and notions.

The enemy barely fifteen miles away aiming guns at him seemed different in no measure from the ones within the territory who disguised themselves as protectors and benefactors.

Equally, the escapism of people of his fellow ethnicity made him sad. The Bengalis had resorted to short-cut methods and adopted the path of political bigotry in the name of progressiveness.

So, under the circumstances, he found a way out.

He chose to retain his own version of self-styled righteousness and look within. His family provided him the solace, the only solace, the only hope of joy and happiness in the otherwise marooned set-up.

The (self) righteous Indian reconciled and virtually resigned himself to the proposition.

The tectonic shift was inevitable.

That made him happy.

CHAPTER 5
Lord's Own Children

Gautam and Uma, Uma and Gautam.

The brother and the sister. The sister and the brother.

In the land amongst ice, ferns and conifers, they grew. The ever-vigilant mother, the "now-resigned revolutionary" father, the condescending teachers and the perpetual deterrent, not far from them, kept watchful eyes. They grew up amidst those surroundings, the all-absorbing ambience.

For Gautam something special was in the locale. For him, someone else—the beautiful ten-year-old—smiled through her broken tooth. Tshiring.

The family settled under the circumstances of not much of its own making. With the Chinese barely fifteen miles away and the doses of initiation and inspiration from the righteous father, the son and the daughter had the lessons of human values to be inculcated according to the best of the traditions.

The lives of great teachers like Buddha and Jesus, the stories of Ramayana and Mahabharata were taught with the weekly tests that followed, which the children disliked and the father welcomed. The father hung the calendar portraits of Buddha, Jesus, and the mythical gods decorating the study room so that they would inspire the children. The children however were too busy and tired after their class tests even to look up and observe the portraits that gathered dust and grew colourless.

The father then nailed the only space available, right above the son's study table with the framed calendar portrait of the tenth Sikh *guru*—the one who had dreamy eyes with a bow across his shoulder and a set of arrows partly visible from the quiver.

"The Guru represented the best of the Indian tradition," he declared. The mother, of course, had other ideas. She wanted to put up a framed calendar portrait of Goddess *Saraswati* over her son's study table. The father gave her a cold look and surmised, "The Guru symbolized the spirit of courage, renunciation and sacrifice of India. I want my son to be inspired by him."

The son, however, never found out a way to be inspired by anyone. Over the years, he certainly learnt how sharp were the arrows in the quiver, the length of the ear lobes of the lord in meditation, or the shape of the fingers of the great one from Nazareth.

The father gave sermons, while the son resented any such discourse but had to listen. The gunpoint initiation and inspiration had substantial deleterious effect.

The son grew more and more wary of his father till he started harbouring intense dislike of him altogether.

The ex-revolutionary now turned into a sermonizing father and felt he had done more than his fair share of his duty of parenthood. He felt thar the values would stand his children in good stead against the probable onslaught of the Chinese and of the demons of Indian mythologies that had acquired human forms in free India.

No one was, however, sure or certain how to take on both sets of foes, not even the father.

But that gave him satisfaction, the mere feel of being able to take-on, the confidence bubbling from the 'teaching and inspiration'.

He was complacent.

The rituals in the land were numerous. Those included festivals of people belonging to almost all the major faiths of the world.

In the snow-filled mountains of the region, the people also had their festivals, the days of celebrations of the faith they believed in.

And then came the anniversary celebration of the birth of the lord, Lord Buddha.

In the land of the lord, the *Sakya Thupa*, the Gautama—the birth anniversary of the lord was a great event, to be celebrated with all gaiety.

For the great majority of the Indians in general and the Bengalis in particular, the mention of one of the greatest sons of the soil evoked devotion and respect.

The sermonizing father in the mould of a caring father had his own way of inspiring the children. One of the ways was to pay reverence to the great teacher in person at the gompas, where incense sticks were lighted and offerings were made before the image of the Great Lord—the *Sakya muni*. Clad in spotless attire, on a fast, the father marched to the gompa, bowed in reverence to the lord while the son followed suit, carrying incense sticks to be lit and fruits to be offered to the lord.

The process of initiation was on.

Yet, in the heart of the young lad, something more important lay. Some feeling that made him uneasy.

Back in the monpa village he knew there was festivity all around. He longed to see her in the best of her clothes. He knew she was certainly waiting for him to come.

He made his way to the village, her village.

The celebration of the event with prayers, offerings, and with happiness around was sublime. For the villages of the tribe, the lord was always with them, in their midst. But his birth heralded an occasion to celebrate, to drown the miseries of life.

He didn't have to search for her. She was there for him. Only for him. She looked bright and dazzling. In her blue attire, she looked superb. Her smile appeared even more enchanting.

It seemed that the lord had special blessings for her on the day.

He was overwhelmed.

The Tsorgen recounted the history of the tribe, where everyone sat.

"Long ago there was our ancestor—the master, who led us into this valley of Tawang from the plains much below. He was Rupati, the prince, who brought us here in the mountains some years after the great lord had enlightened the world.

"Our people were very happy, strong, rich, and ruled by the aristocrats called the *kheys.* They worshipped gods of all forms, of all shapes, of all colours, and of all images. They did so for hundreds of years. It was when there was the magic, the presence of spirits, and the super-natural beings all around.

"Then came the great teacher, reformer, and administrator nearly a thousand years ago who spread the gospel of the sakya thupa—the Buddha. He was none other than Terthun Pemalingpa from the Bumtang area of the Druks. He not only spread the gospel but also established our tribes in the Nyamjang chu valley and Tawang chu valley and called them *Monyul Khyimozong.*

"He made the rules for the tribe. But the desire to get to the magic remained. Then came the teachings of the great soul. He was as great as an angel whose teachings cleared us of all the black magic and the fear of all the secret.

"He carried from Tibet the rules of the yellow sect and made this area the *Ganden Namgye Lhatse.*"

It was something like a fairy tale and Gautam was lost. He was so absorbed that he forgot even her, Tshiring, for whom he had come all the way there. He could almost see the prince leading his men, the dragon-faced spirits and the great teachers, as if they were before his very eyes. It was only when he was shaken out of his daydreams by her that he gained his presence back.

"Come and join the dance," she enthusiastically called him.

But he was not interested, nor did he know which dance it was. He preferred to watch.

There were dances with dragon masks before the pitchers, filled with all sorts of grains—buckwheat, rice, and maize. The seeds were worshipped and then those were distributed amongst the villagers, as symbols of good harvest in coming years.

"Do you know why is this area called Tawang?" Sonam asked Gautam.

"No. Is there something special?" Gautam asked.

"Sure," he replied. "There was one Mera lama in eastern part of the Drukland, I mean Bhutan, who had a dream that he would come to north and construct a gompa. He did not actually know which way to proceed. He allowed his white horse to lead him till it stopped and began to dig up a place with its legs. Mera Lama concluded that was the place to build the gompa. Nearly a decade after that, the present monastery, which is more than three hundred and fifty years old, came into being.

"To name the place, Mera Lama went to the Great fifth and sought his blessing. Since the great fifth was busy and could not come personally, he said, "As the place was found by a horse, I am going to give you the blessing of the horse-god named *Tamding*."

***

One day at the school, Sonam said, "Tomorrow Palden would be coming to my home."

"But who is he anyway?" Gautam asked.

"Well, he is a lama in the making."

"But why is he coming to your home?"

"Because it is his home too. He is my brother."

Gautam was surprised.

"No one ever mentioned that you have a brother, neither you nor Tshiring. A brother who is to become a lama!" Gautam said in pure astonishment.

Sonam looked at Gautam and replied with no excitement, at all.

"He is to become a lama. He lives in the gompa. He is not for family life in the village. His ties with the family have all but been severed. To mention someone as one's kith and kin who would no longer be in one's family but dedicated to the service of god and mankind is selfish."

That was shocking to Gautam.

How could anyone give up one's own brother so easily even in the name of God? He wondered.

"But then why is he coming to you?" Gautam asked.

"That is because he has still not become a lama, but is in the process of being one. When he attains that state finally, he would be out of the bounds of the family. He shall then work for the whole folk, in the service of the lord," Sonam answered as calmly as ever.

Gautam suddenly felt Sonam's voice had grown different, very different, much like Lama Norbu as he spoke all those words. Gautam watched, listened in silence. He was in awe. Of Sonam, a different Sonam!

Palden lived in the gompa. The gompa symbolized the -spread and hold of Tibetan Buddhism in the region. Located nearly three thousand metres above the see level, it housed nearly five hundred lamas. It was the highest located Buddhist monastery in India.

The Lamaism—the variety of Buddhism, the Tibetan Buddhism—spread into Tibet in the eighth century when the great Indian preacher, Padma Sambhava preached Tantric Buddhism in Tibet. In the order of the sect came grand lamas. The third Grand Lama received the title of Dalai Lama.

The splendour of Tibetan Buddhism began during the period of the great fifth that laid his claim to the manifestation of *Avelokitesware*—the Dhyani Buddha.

And then came He.

The Sixth Dalai Lama, Tsang Yang Gyatso, who was born in the vicinity of the Tawang gompa, at a village close to modern day Tawang called Urgeling, in the late seventeenth century.

The most colourful, poetic, intelligent, and handsome person was born in the area. He was found to be in love with the nature and her bounties. He was taken into the fold and initiated into the service, when he was only ten. Probably, he never saw his mother again. Or even if they ever met, it were not as a mother and a son but most certainly as the 'living incarnation of the Lord' and a commoner.

He was known as a man of emotions who gave vent to his feelings, very explicitly, where it was not expected to be so. Stories abound of his colourful life he led, which coupled with other tragic circumstances brought about his gory end.

His wish for the material love, which he missed, was very touching.

The point that he yearned for maternal love was very true. Some of his compositions spoke of his desire to be with his family and the love for his mother.

The sun rays mix in the air
As the sun sets.
As the shepherds collect
Their lambs and sheep in time,
The bleats of the sheep and lamb
Certainly remind me how I called my mother.
Oh white swan!
Please lend me your wings.
Could you not?
I promise you I won't go much far.
Only to my mother to see her
And return.

It was in the holy premises of the great gompa where once the sixth Dalai Lama was reared that Palden—Sonam and Tshiring's brother, was being reared into the folds of Lamaism.

Palden was a couple of inches taller than Sonam, for he was a couple of years older as well. With a square forehead and square jaws, with clean-shaven head, the slender built boy looked every inch a lama in the making. He had strong arms and legs. He was serious and talked less. He wasn't too expressive either.

He was, after all, going to become a lama. Probably, he was on his last visit to his family, after which the ties with the family were to be severed forever. He then would be on his way to become a lama, in the service of the lord, bettering the lives of his people.

Palden talked of his life in the monastery, of the devotional hymns he sang, of the rigours of theological studies. He talked of the colourful paintings of gods and goddesses of Buddhism as well as of human figures in frescos, of those significant in religious history like those of Padma Sambhava and Atish Dipankara, of the decorative paintings of religious symbolism. His talks seemed exotic to the listeners, especially to the young man from the plains.

Gautam listened to him with eyes wide open, to nearly everything that Paldan had to say. Sonam and Tshiring were less inquisitive. They were used to the descriptions. They, for sure, had heard those hundreds of times before. What they enquired were the newer additions to each of the description, which appeared a little different from the ones they heard earlier.

For the children of the village and the visitor from the plains who happened to be close to them, the vacation was the opportunity to go for excursions. The four of them—Paldan, Sonam, Tshiring, and Gautam found it immensely exciting to talk, play—in the mountains, amongst the firs and conifers, away from the village.

For Gautam, it was an altogether a new world in the midst of a totally new setting, the likes of which he had never seen before.

To the seventh grader, life was all revelations. All wonders contained in a book of some kind, each page bringing out new experiences and new treasures to be preserved in memory.

Back at the school, the botany teacher explained all the god-gifted exquisite varieties of herbs in his inimitable style, and of the nomenclature. Those were all literally Greek and Latin to the boys who only looked at each other and laughed.

For the purpose of examinations, they composed rhymes much in the way of nursery rhymes, as the only way to remember the tongue-twisters.

Anaenitum	*Farox*
Acorus	*Calamus*
Alpinia	*Gal-Ganga*
Artimesia	*Vulga-ris*
Barbaris	*Asition*
Crocus	*Sativus Linn*

Those were the botanical names of the medicinal plants grown in the region that had to be arranged in the form of rhymes to remember. In fact, such rhymes were the only way to remember all the mathematical formulae too.

Palden, Sonam, Gautam, and Tshiring made many excursions out in the forest and vegetation around; up and down along the river that flowed; nature seemed to beckon them with all her bounties.

The boulders and rocks were covered with foliage. The rocks laid bare only in some stretches. There were waterfalls. The fir trees were in abundance. They explored the forests, all four of them, but never ventured to go deep inside, for fear of being overtaken by evil spirits. The evil spirits could descend upon them; they could assume all sorts of forms for example, the shape of pythons, bears, etc.

The forests seemed to refresh them every time they went in. The vegetation consisted of entirely conifers and rhododendrons. The rhododendrons were tall. They almost covered mountainsides forming thickets. They had flowers of all colours to bloom—pink, violet, and bright yellow, as delicate as could be.

The explorers came across dead trees, some struck by lightning not long ago. They climbed over the trunks covered with lichen and moss. The foliage was thick and heavy with pine needles, dry leaves, and branches that had fallen sometime back. Those housed the nests of birds chirping all over.

They made their forays into the forests, for the children of the village this were nothing new but only experience repeated. They had come in those domains probably many times with the village folk. For Gautam, those were all so exotic in presentation. He had never seen those before. He was wonder-struck.

What captivated Gautam was the wonderful zone of rhododendrons that were in abundance, in a variety of colours, of shades of orange and red that welcomed him. For him, the first view was fascinating. He could not imagine anything more beautiful; every pace he took, he was absolutely enchanted.

There were other flowers too—the large, pink coloured ones—which the botany teacher at the school called saxifrage (such an evil name for so beautiful a flower). The open spaces were covered with deep reddish- and purple-coloured flowers (another irritating name he learnt later, the primula, it seemed no one could assign any musical name to the beautiful flower!)

The foam of the flowing water of the river that dashed against the boulders and rocks that circled around the cliffy mountain broke the smoothness of the hillsides, the sides of which rose against the skyline. Far across, much beyond them the ridges rose above the forest level, the bare bluffs of rocks towering over all of them.

Far away, like sketches on picture cards, were circles around wooded bays in which foaming torrents danced. The river looked like a track from a distance. The sudden appearance of sheets of broken foam, breaking through foliage, was wonderful.

Up above, along the upstream, the river just before it was to make a giant fall, passed through an open grassy valley where gigantic arums grew. That seemed to be the land of flowers where giant lilies could be seen and so were big red roses.

Any fallen branch, any hollow trunk teemed with life, the insects that could withstand extremities of weather (their life span was no more than a couple of seasons), the ferns and orchids—all filled the space.

Away from the forest, in the village, in the protected areas of the nurseries, grew plants Gautam had never seen before.

These plants grew in cold climates as the weather was the best for those to grow. Palden said the lamas from the gompa knew the medicinal use of the plants and herbs.

The plants and herbs like saffron, lemon grass, and the other medicinal orchids thrilled Gautam—more for their colour and variety than for anything else.

Once Gautam got the feel of the tremendous delight of nature, he could not resist the temptation of re-exploring what had already been explored but those and only those to his liking and satisfaction that he desired. With the brothers not much keen to do so with him, the forays were only his and hers.

He was again amidst exotics.

They went down and up. Up and down in the forests, in the area among the firs, conifers, and the rhododendrons amongst the stones and pebbles. They were happy.

At a distance they could see the cane bridge across the river. It was made of two parallel canes on the same horizontal plane that was firmly tied to two huge trees on either side. On those canes, sagging loops of canes were placed at intervals. On them were placed two pieces of bamboo that served as flooring, very firmly secured least the loops dislodge and come close to one another.

Those were the last days before the hard days of winter, which was sure to bring the share of pain and difficulty. There were the orchids growing in the valley, in the forest, there were insects all over and watchful birds kept constant vigil.

On one such occasion Gautam moved to the interior of the forest, the border of hitherto unexplored frontier, and Tshiring stayed back to survey the mound that had caught her attention.

Gautam tried to climb up the gradual rise of the rock but the rhododendrons had thickened and the going was steep as well. He retreated. He came down looking for her and there she was kneeling on the ground.

With her back arched, attention focused, her eyes shone in very happy delight of having discovered a great treasure.

Gautam stood behind her and watched.

"Hey! What are you doing?" Gautam asked her.

"Sshh… Don't you see, I have finally got it!" She exclaimed with the obvious smile of satisfaction on her face.

He saw a stone-covered figure that Tshiring had just dug out of the mound, all covered with soil. The object was no larger than the scale in length that he had in the geometry box.

The stone figure carved on a single block of stone, he understood and realized was that of the lord Buddha.

Most certainly someone, who could have been a child like them had hidden the treasure there, many years ago.

As soon as she realized what the figure looked like, she ran as fast as she could, as fast as her legs could carry her, towards the river which was no bigger than a big stream.

Gautam followed her. She was there, lying flat on the ground with her face over the stones and pebbles on the bank so that she could reach the river water flowing by. She did it so that the stone-curved figure of the lord was cleaned.

"Oh my god! How beautiful does it look!" Tshiring exclaimed. She was almost at the point of ecstasy having discovered treasure, the treasure that no money could have ever bought.

"But how on earth could you find it?" Gautam asked her.

"I know something which you don't," She responded. "I knew something was there in the mound".

"Do you like it?" She asked him suddenly, with a sparkle in her eyes as she turned towards him.

"Yes, very much," Gautam answered. "It is so beautiful".

"Then take it," she replied, "This is a gift for you. When you see this image of the lord, you will remember me. Won't you?"

Gautam was not prepared for such kind of a sudden development. He hesitated to accept the gift, as it was someone else's labour.

"But Tshiring, you were so delighted having found the image of the lord. I know you are dying to keep it. Then why do you gift this treasure to me instead?"

"It is said, you gift the most loved possession to someone you love the most." She was self-composed.

Gautam still was hesitant.

"Come on, take it. Keep the image of the lord with you. We are after all Lord's own children. Aren't we?"

Gautam saw even greater pleasure and satisfaction in her eyes, and on her face. But he had to do something. He had to reciprocate.

"Tshiring," he said. "Could you please stand here for a couple of minutes, with your eyes closed. I shall be back in a flash."

He ran as fast as he could on to the higher stretches of the land, for he had seen the red flower—the red rose bigger than anyone's palm. He had to get it for her. He came back with the flower. It was more than five minutes but she was still standing there with her eyes closed.

He came back with the single flower of the great red rose and tried to put the stalk in her plaited hair. But every time he tried to do so it came off. Finally, he resigned and gave the flower to her.

And there she was, so very happy, so very proud of him. So very satisfied. She smelt the flower and drew it close to her cheeks.

Down the valley, the river continued on its onward journey, the noise of boulders grumbling, rolling on the riverbed down below was audible from a distance. The sound of clear sparkling water making its way was sonorous.

The cane bridge swayed to-and-fro, the loops making a creaking noise, adding harmony to the melody present in the air.

They sat on the huge boulder, hand in hand, their legs dangling, the huge rose in her tresses that she put herself perfectly well.

She said she would tie and sew the flower in her *mala*, the garland of beads that she wore—so that when the flower dried up, it could still be with her.

They had no reason or place to move away or go.
They had the best of the world with them.
The rediscovery of the mysteries was taking place.
In the best of the effortless and spontaneous flow.
They knew that something between them was through.
That they were for each other.
Was certainly true.

Though he attended his classes at the school, Gautam was lost somewhere else. He attended the routine affairs unconcerned and uninterested. All he wanted to do was go and meet Tshiring.

The father was his usual stern self. The mother kept her watchful eye, the sister busy in her studies. The lad was lost in the nature's delight and in her ambience.

From the father came endless sermons—more vigorous, more particular, and more objective.

Gautam was sucked in the whirlpool of sermons and inspirations trying hard, very hard to reconcile the environs of the home and the soothing comfort of her presence and his academics.

For the first time, he felt pain of some strange nature.

Pain in the heart, in the mind and of the spirit. The eyes, his own, the reflections of which he saw in the mirror spoke of the things that were happening.

He felt like becoming a poet.

"Till one is in pain, one cannot become a poet," his teacher had told in the class. Then, the teacher in the literature class had quoted not out of context, a famous litterateur: "The first poet in the universe must have been the one whose sighs must have formed verses, out of his eyes must have rolled down poems."

The whirlpool, the abyss, the vortex that he was in, the feel of the plight led him to pen his first poem. Gautam the poet was born out of the suppression, oppression, and depression by the sermons and inspirations till the sensation gave way to more delicate outpourings.

The first poem he wrote was the one where he poured his heart out. Rhyming his feelings much in the same way as the poem in the seventh-grade textbook of English prose, the annual examination of which he had appeared some days back: 'Water, water everywhere, not a drop to drink.'

The maiden adventure of the young poet in the realms of human feelings and sensations made him very happy. The trifling problems of arranging the words into rhymes however remained a trouble of sorts. The romantic poets of the bygone era then came to his rescue.

The poem was ready to be penned after all arrangements and re-arrangements in the mind.

Sermons, Sermons every time
Not a moment to think;
Father, Mother and even the little sister
All upon me
In a wink.
'Do this', 'Don't do this', or
'You ought not to do that';
They tell me every time.
As if I had no mind of my own,
And had borrowed thine.

Studies at class and at home,
And nothing else to do;
Or you again get a sermon
On what you ought to do.
Why does no one understand?
I am an infant no longer!
To be fed off the bottle
Of milk and surely water.
Almighty God gracious if you are
Somewhere above in the sky,
For I know not where
If ever you live.
Tell my father, surely you must,
I am lost, and doomed forever.
I hate him for his sermons
And also, for his inspirations.
If he goes on and on with his sermons,
I promise, I take a vow
I shall forever
Be gone.

Gautam was satisfied. He was a poet after all. He felt as if he were a skinny version of Tagore - a Bengali boy's dream. He had become one who could vent out his feelings in verses and rhymes. Having composed such a comprehensive portrayal of his feelings made him ecstatic.

He read his poem a number of times. And then he smelt coconut oil, like the one that came out when Ma applied coconut oil to Uma's hair, over his ears. He knew someone was nearby.

He turned to see. He was right! It was Uma and none else. She snatched the paper and as usual, ran to her father. The happiness for him appeared to be short-lived.

Even that ephemeral joy it seemed, he could not cherish!

"Baba," she said, "look Dada isn't studying anymore. He is writing poems!"

"Poems!" Baba was surprised. He took the paper. Read it a number of times. All the while Gautam stood in front. He knew that the worst was in store for him.

The mother was summoned. Ma came. She read. She left but not before she had a good look at her son. The son noticed in her eyes the pleasure and satisfaction, the fruition of her deep feelings. The coming into shape of her feelings deeply entrenched in her heart. Not so much the satisfaction or jubilation of a mother for her son's achievement and prowess, but something different.

Those words had an obvious identification with her feelings, the words she could never give the desired form. Her son had done that while quite young. The feelings she had over the years pent up but could not express for a variety of reasons. Her own son, her own flesh and blood had at some point of her life given form and expression to her feelings in words, which she had felt over the years of conjugal life.

She had her own resentment against being dictated.

The worst descended upon the young poet.

Not the inevitable that he feared. Not any thrashing, nor the final commandments. Not the usual follow up.

Baba looked at Gautam.

The father looked at the son. Straight, straight into his eyes!

Not a word followed. Not a syllable was spoken as time stood still.

Instead, what came off was the deep, rather the deepest sigh possible.

Without a word the father handed over the paper to his son. The son's composition!

The father looked lost. He looked helpless. For the first time in his life, the son noticed in his father the sense of dejection. The shock, the overwhelming impact of the monumental event, of being let down by someone whom he wished had given shape to his ideals or at least come to terms and be shaped by his teachings, seemed unbearable.

The proposition, the erosion of faith and confidence was quite clear in the eyes and the face of the resigned revolutionary.

The son was, by then, was overcome by a new set of feelings, of sadness, sorrow and the likeness. He was engulfed by remorse for having scribbled the wretched words. The ominous words that had shaken the edifice of his universe. The proposition was absolutely perilous. The catastrophe had truly and finally come.

The individuals were mere characters of the 'divine drama'.

From that day on, the father stopped rendering any sermons, not any more, not any word of those. No more of dos and don'ts. Except of course some oblique suggestions, which in any case were rarities. The efforts to reconcile with the hurt feelings, the injured compassion—the untimely finale of events was somewhat disastrous.

From the D-Day to the rest of his life, not a word of sermon came off Baba's lips. And how the son felt the consequences! Those daily doses, without which he couldn't even dream of surviving, suddenly lost their overshadowing presence.

The polemics over finally, both the father and the son tried to adapt to the newer situation.

Gautam was as good as lost without any such direction. Like a rudderless boat. Like being let loose in a fathomless, bottomless ocean. Not having any idea of how to swim.

But Baba kept quiet so far as sermons and inspirations were concerned. Never again in his life he ventured to do so.

At times in the son's life, he longed for those. The son longed, wished, desired and wanted the father to appear with his sermons. He yearned, almost prayed deep down in the heart of his hearts. But nothing of the kind happened.

Gautam's maiden venture in the delicate faculties of human mind was momentous, rather a calamitous one. It proved to be the perfect hour of disillusionment!

How he wished he had not written the damned poem. But it was too late. The faithful day had become the D-Day for the father and the son.

Days and nights went by for the rest of the life. But it was never the same again.

Was he lost? Wasn't he? Gautam longed for an answer because the thin line had vanished. The thin line showed no sign of resurfacing again.

He looked to the stone-carved image of the Lord.

Lord Buddha with his eyes almost closed in deep meditation, sitting cross-legged appeared in divine benediction.

The son looked to the lord for solace.

He was after all, one of Lord's own children.

he forgave them as they were in error. Frequent transfers in the hills however meant that the whole family had to move from one place to another and in the process, the academics of the children got affected. He nonchalantly took everything in his own stride. He said that it was sure to make the children self-reliant and strong enough to be able to face the adversaries.

For the former revolutionary, whose spirit fast evaporated more so after the ultra-leftist of the Bengali escapists resulting in blood, both in Bengal and loss of innocent human lives; there was a new source of rejuvenation.

After the creation of Pakistan in 1947 and the unfolding of the two-nation theory, the euphoria of the Bengalis on the other side of the great divide was over even before the impact of the enthusiasm could be felt. The martyrdom of some young man in the early fifties for their mother-tongue and culture in the otherwise military dominated bigotry in Pakistan, sowed the seeds of a rebellion.

The Bengalis, irrespective of constraints of faith, had one thing in common—the innate urge for freedom and rebellion from the share over teacups to that of nation states. From the late sixties the signs were apparent that the Bengali dominated East Pakistan had very little in common with the orthodox western part. Their identity in doldrums, the Bengalis protested, resisted and revolted.

And then all hell broke loose. The Pakistani let loose the army—killing people with impunity, raping woman, and then bayoneting their private parts, killing even the infants. The Devil's dance was on. That continued till the rag-tag motley bands of fighters were joined by the Indian army to liberate the region, which came to be known as Bangladesh. The premium was of course very high. Nearly ten million refugees were thrust

CHAPTER 6

Rosa Macrophylla–The Big Red Rose

The winter brought with it the usual quota of snowfall and the snowflakes. The first drippings of the flakes through the air heralded the onset of winter, and the ground was soon covered with heaps, as delicate as butter and as hard as rock. From powdery snow to sharp as glass snow.

The winter had come early, a bit too soon and with it the snowfall was to continue for nearly half the year. The roads, the pavements, the housetops, the trees, the bushes were all snowy. The hillocks, the ground, the ravines, the gorges, and the slippery water formations were all white and glistening.

His friends Palden, Sonam, and the one and only Tshiring captivated him.

Palden was all set to pack up and leave his home. He had completed his stay. He was all set to be initiated into the service of the lord. He was to leave his family for good, to be absorbed into the fold for greater service of mankind.

Before Palden left at the beginning of the Winter, all four of them, the Lord's own Children, decided to take their excursion into the forests again. It was probably their last adventure together, as the very next day Palden was to say good-bye. It was the best time as the winter had set and it was the last time you could go trekking. With more snowfall due in winter, it was unwise to tread the snowy ridges any later, the ravines, without knowing the terrain fully. More than anyone else, the brothers and the sister knew that Gautam was only learning from them.

They made their way to the forest, covered with snow. The trees stood as if they were banished from the world. No leaves, no flowers—they stood alone in the mass of snow oblivious of their good old days.

Palden was to leave for the gompa and all thought it was best to spend time with him in the forest. Amidst the first of the winter snow that aroused passion and excitement, they were all for the spirit of it.

They roamed, jumped, hopped around, and ran on the ice. They hurled the powdery snow—so soft yet so sharp, at each other. They had fun.

They were all covered with powdery snow. For Gautam it was all magnificent and he wanted to explore more. They were all at the edge of the forest where the steep rocks began their ascend, perched with snow, and with crevasses and ridges and ravines full of snow. They all stopped.

But Gautam wanted to explore, to see and look beyond.

"Come on," Palden shouted, "Don't proceed, you idiot. You will be in trouble."

Gautam saw before him the sea of snow, it was sublime. He knew he had no reason to listen to Palden. Palden had that air of dominance, he threw his weight around. He had a big brother attitude—always admonishing, cautioning, telling the dos and don'ts as if he were a lama already.

Gautam went on. He wanted to defy Palden, and look beyond.

Then it happened.

Suddenly, Gautam slipped as he stretched himself while he tried to climb the rock midway, with no place to gain foothold. He could only grasp the powdery snow and he knew he was falling below.

That would have been his end. He knew he was going to die in the crevasse covered with snow. The ravine had the softest bed of snow, all white and glistening, ready for his death.

In a flash he remembered the faces of Baba, Ma and Uma as spontaneously as he shouted, "I am dying!"

Then like an angel, it came in the way of the free-fall. The root of a dead tree!

In his frenetic search for a grasp, somehow and suddenly his fingers touched the root. He firmly grasped it. First with one and then with both his hands.

He could at least cling to the support. But despite his best efforts he could not raise himself. He hung precariously from the rocky projection of the slope.

"Tshiring!" Gautam shouted in desperation. "*Mujhe Bachao*!" In the moment of crisis, no other name came on his lips.

Gautam saw Palden take a few steps and then stop.

Sonam came running to the edge of the rock.

But Tshiring ran all along, as fast as she could to come to him.

Palden shouted at the top of his voice, "You fool! Do you know what you are up to? You will get killed for that stupid fellow. Stay off!"

Sonam tried to stop her saying, "Wait! Let's see how we can save him." But she was rushing on.

Palden shouted at the top of his voice again, "I am running back to the village to tell the people. I shall get back with people and the equipment at the earliest. Till then stay on!" Saying that he turned and ran, and was soon out of sight.

Sonam looked at Palden once but was too scared to leave his sister alone. He confronted her, "You silly girl! Have you any idea of what you are trying to do? You could die!"

"Have you gone crazy?" she shouted back, "Your friend needs your help. If you help now, he might survive!"

"Nonsense!" cried Sonam, "How can we help him? It needs strength to pull him back. Moreover, ropes are needed, too. Wait for people from the village to come and help."

"By that time", she cried back "He won't need your help anymore!"

Gautam saw Tshiring and knew she was the only one who could help. He felt that he coundn't hold on to the root anymore and the white deathbed was waiting down below to greet him.

"I am dying," he shouted, "save me Tshiring!"

Without a word Tshiring came running. He heard her approaching steps. Within a few minutes, she reached him.

She lay headlong on the rock, trying to reach him, by her hand. She also tried to throw her long clothes down so that he could at least grasp one end of the same.

Sonam hopped and jumped below. He tried to guide her. But his shouts distracted her attention.

With great difficulty, over a span of some minutes, and after a few unsuccessful attempts that seemed to span over decades, with the fear of impending death looming large every second, he caught hold of her cloth as she moved forward.

Then Sonam joined her. The brother and the sister did all they could as Gautam raised his head over the rocky projection.

He knew he was safe, saved by her.

But then, it was not all over. Curtains were not over yet. Something had remained.

While he tried to breathe after the ordeal, she tried to steady herself. Then, she slipped.

She was exhausted. An inch of imbalance, one second of complacent satisfaction resulting in carelessness was enough for her. Her *chouba* was already torn and she slipped further, losing her foothold. With a couple of rips, she fell. With a thud!

On the floor of the ravine, with an all-pervading yell.

Snow fell all over her. Covering her. She was not fully visible from the top. They could only see movements below the heap, hear her yell, and notice the desperate efforts she made to get up. Those were stronger initially and grew milder as time went by.

Sonam was shocked. Gautam clutched his hair. What he had feared didn't happen to him but to her. She lay on the perfect bed of ice covered by snow all over.

Gautam had nothing around to bang his head onto.

Sonam cried and shouted but no one listened.

Soon people from the village arrived with Palden—the rescuers with ropes and shovels.

The experts got down with ropes fastened around their waist, down to the ravine and after some difficulty, cleared the debris to pull her out.

But she didn't respond to her name being called.

She was carried off to the village. Then she was rushed to the health centre where a lone doctor attended his patients with his staff.

She was unconscious.

She didn't gain consciousness.

She didn't at all.

She didn't at all ever after.

She was lost.

She died.

With one hand sticking up as they found, her other hand had clutched the garland of beads at the spot where the dried red rose bigger than anyone's palm was.

The dried one she had sewed to her garland of beads.

The fingers of her little hand clutched the dried big red rose in the garland that she had sewed on to.

All the while when she as struggling in the heap of snow,

all the while when she was being carried for treatment,
all the while when she was losing herself;
Dying.

The doctor removed the garland from her clutch—the dried red rose, bigger than anyone's palm.

"Rosa Macrophylla," the doctor said.

Only Gautam knew why she had done so. The faith, the trust, the confidence she had in him. She embodied in herself the overwhelming love, the compassion, and the outpourings of grace of a lovely heart.

She knew he could have made an effort to save her. But he had not. He hadn't even tried. In trying to save him, she had gone down. She had sacrificed herself for him.

But he had failed her.

He was devastated. He was marooned. He was as good as lost. He was a scoundrel, selfish, and coward.

The image of the lord in the stone with the eyes almost closed in deep meditation, never looked at him. He could not look into the eyes of the lord either. The lord had saved him from further ignominy. He didn't have the courage to look into the lord's eyes.

He was no good to live. He was lost on all counts. With her memories cast all over him, of the episodes over-powering him with her spell and magic charm, he felt he could not have lived any longer.

The more he thought of her, the more he felt her presence, her smile. The smile with one broken tooth visible and the rest shinning.

His existence was blurred. It had become of very little consequence to him.

He was on the edge of the precipice himself. Waiting for his turn to fall into another ravine.

Of despair, of loneliness, and no use of leading his life.

She had sacrificed herself in the spirit of negation for someone she loved.

All the memories came rushing to his mind... of the ambience of never ending attachment, of love, of friendship, of endless emotions... undefined but of substance...the grace of the lord ... the lord with his endless grace... eyes closed... as if in a trance!

The trance named Tshiring. He thought at once of her, of when he had met her, when she had captivated him. All the memories came back haunting to engulf him.

CHAPTER 7

The Snowfall and the Snowflakes

"Mist in the air, mist in the eyes, snowfall and snowflakes—when these come," the people said in the mountains, "they come together."

When the snow fell, a sudden overflow of emotions engulfed Gautam's heart and mind, and he tried to understand Tshiring.

Tshiring—the person of his dreams and bounties. She who had innocent eyes, expansive delight, and an enchanting smile. All these seemed to beckon Gautam, and it was when the snow fell and he touched the flakes that he could almost feel her. She came often in his dreams and every time he felt snowflakes, he saw her monpa dress adorned like a butterfly around her petite form, her tresses braided in serpentine coils.

It was the damned snow that had covered her when she vanished.

"Gautam," he could hear a whisper, "I am here, all around you." He would turn to see her, yet she was not there.

"You are gone, Tshiring!" he called. "Yet every day in winter, when the ground hardens and snowflakes can be touched, I know you are here. Beyond my reach, my touch, my senses, yet present in the mist that is in the air, in the ground, and in the eyes."

Gautam could inhale her fragrance all around. There were other things he associated with Tshiring as well. The taste of rancid butter, smoked tea, her distinct robes, her very fragrance as of a ten-year old—all came to his mind, his senses, and even his taste buds.

Those tangible human residues kept him out of touch with the everyday realities, such as the odours of dust and fur, the taste of a Tibetan tea, hot smoked meat, and cakes of roasted barley flour. Even the barking of a dog, cloaked in his fur of silver, white and black, even the sight of dingy, makeshift shelters proudly venerated as homes by their owners, seemed distant and unreachable. Such realities were no friends, for surrealistic actuality superimposed itself on Gautam's mind, in very uneven visions.

It was then that Tshiring stared at him, the excitement of her all-pervading presence spreading, and the piercing gaze of injured innocence transcending physical realities. Gautam knew she could find a firm pathway to come to terms with life and death, an avenue to provide a communion with him. That was possible for her, and for none but her.

Tshiring had had her small hands joined in prayer, her head bowed in reverence to the Lord, her prayer wheel in motion, seeking divine benediction. It now seemed that the Lord had answered her, because of the warmth, love, and nurture of her wishes. He must have granted her desire, Gautam knew, to be in communion with the Lord who was the epitome of affection and care, the embodiment of truth and novelty, the manifestation of sacrifice and renunciation of human beings. Indeed, was the Siddhartha, the Gautama, the *Manushi* Buddha, and the Sakya thupa, as people of Tshiring's clan and tribe liked to say.

Like all of her family, clan and tribe, Tshiring had immense faith in the Lord. It was devotion, trust, and absolute surrender of the self. From birth, she had been initiated into believing in the omnipresence of the Lord in matters both spiritual and mundane. As a youngster, the mundane and earthy ones were important, for she was as yet far too young to fathom the depths of the spiritual.

She would say, "May the Lord bless you" and "The Lord wants me to be with you" as spontaneously as if she had a vision of the Lord giving his blessings. After Tshiring had vanished into thin air, she must have then had a more comprehensive view of the Lord.

She remained an enigma for Gautam. He did not know how to address his tempestuous feelings and anxieties for her. Tshiring had an inimitable sprit of the negation of self in favour of someone else, of the one she loved.

CHAPTER 8
Cathedral Beckons

The thoughts, the smile, the broken tooth all seemed to be around Gautam, all the time. He could hear her voice, calling out his name, urging him to go and play among the conifers, in the snow, throwing the powdery snow at him; it was so real that he almost felt the chill.

His friends at the school were suspicious of him. They chose to maintain a distance. The teachers kept an eye on him too. They were not much convinced of his wellbeing, in health and in spirits.

The parents were in a dilemma. They had their share of anxiety and parental concern.

Gautam, however, did not find cause for any such concern. In fact, others seemed to be more concerned about him. Overtly or covertly when they expressed often their apprehensions in hushed tones, in low voices, in a softer cajoling approach to him, he knew something was wrong. He felt embarrassed when they did all that. They all seemed to be so unnatural, so unlike their real selves. They were pretending, presenting themselves in forms and attitudes, which were not exactly theirs. He felt a little uneasy.

He saw nothing wrong in his talks to her, in his dreams which others called nightmares, in his exchanges with her. Surprisingly those frightened his friends and tormented his teachers and parents alike.

Gautam couldn't help it at all. Those were so spontaneous. The ice, the powdery snow, the snowflakes, the conifers, all seemed so natural. More so, those appeared so commonplace. To be with her was in his nature.

He not only enjoyed the occurrences, he loved those.

The parents were worried beyond any reasonable doubt. They were very concerned. Uma was frightened. She was not too sure of all that was happening. Why her dada behaved in so grotesque a manner—so unlike his frivolous self. Not for once did he pinch or punch her. She was very concerned as well.

Everyone seemed to be convinced that the boy was unable to come to terms with reality and with his self. All of them thought that the 'shock' had been too severe for the boy to absorb.

Baba said one day, "I am not at all sure of him getting well. With each passing day the boy seems to develop newer complications." He looked grave. Ma looked at him but kept silent. She wanted him to continue.

"I am convinced things are not going to work out for him here, anymore, and any longer. I had hoped that things would improve. Time, I knew, was the greatest healer. But I am afraid it is not going to work for him here." His words were experience personified.

Ma nodded as she mostly did. "Can't we do anything for him? Say, like removing him from here. That might work wonders."

"Work wonders! I doubt it very much. If he does not recover in our presence, where on earth could he feel any better? Where do you expect him to improve?" He asked in a voice that invited suggestion.

He deliberately avoided using my instead of our as he was, it seemed, in need of solid suggestions. The present and future of their son was at stake. Afterall the son was their's and he was magnanimous enough to concede that.

Rarely did he ever need any suggestion of any kind. The decisions had to be his and all others had to follow suit. For the moment though, the issue needed more parental touch and resolve, not just only that of a father alone. He was wise enough to understand that.

"Well, if we put him at a boarding school..." Ma was cautious.

"He could then possibly have good education, new friends, and a new environment," she looked at Baba for assurance.

She seemed to have struck the right chord. Only the consequences were not very forthcoming. Some bureaucratic delay was inevitable.

When they met again to discuss the next morning, he had given sufficient, proper and sound thoughts to the proposal. She looked at the man at the helm of the affairs for the final decision.

And the decision was soon announced.

"I have decided," Baba declared, "it would be best to put him at a boarding school. The best one would be the St. Mary's school, where some of my friends have put up their sons and daughters."

The school he mentioned was located some three hundred miles away, amongst the tea estates of the plains.

Ma was happy. She could now relax. At least there was something concrete, and something decent. Her son would be away from the 'haunted surroundings' to a hopefully more placid and friendly place. Moreover, her son could have good education, a good English education at that.

"If he is put up at a boarding school like the one the Christian missionaries ran, Gautam would have good education despite his being away from us. He would be in a completely new setting, removed from the troubled one here." She convinced herself of the proposition before she could tell it to others.

She needed those convictions to assure herself, in an attempt to gain courage and confidence for the uncertainty that lay ahead.

Baba then put the final stamp. "What is equally important, rather more important, I feel is he would be a *swabalambi*. When he would have to live in a hostel, catering to his needs, his meals, his studies, his dress—their dress code is very strict, pressed uniforms, and polished shoes, he is sure to develop that attitude." He was counting and recounting the gains.

"Self-reliance is something that is prerequisite in any one's life," he concluded.

He went on referring to the gains of living in a hostel run by the strict discipline of the missionaries where a boy could grow up to be self-reliant, and gain more confidence.

He was also trying to convince himself of the move of which till date, he was sceptical. To him, no education was better than the one the children learnt living within the family. Now having had to make a move out of sheer desperation, he needed to assure and reassure himself of the gains. Whatever his ideas might have been, whatever he had harboured in his mind for so long, had to be replaced by the new one, however strongly he might have despised that earlier. That had to be carried out.

More than anyone else, he needed to reassure himself of the infallibility of the decision taken.

"I am sure if Gautam is put at the St. Mary's boarding school, he could overcome his inhibitions and grow up to be a nature young man one day."

Baba was reassuring himself. He was making sure that any apprehension that he had, any misgivings he had nurtured were put to rest finally by his own newfound strong convictions, discovered afresh.

"Moreover, if everything goes well, he could appear at the Senior Cambridge examination and might get good results."

That was meant precisely for Ma who had to be comforted.

It was a foregone conclusion that certain hollowness was sure to descend on the family, especially for her. The sudden emptiness due to the removal of the most important member in the family for her would cause a temporary sense of loss and sadness, and that looked imminent.

The words of conviction worked. His words mattered nonetheless. Ma tried to assure herself even more. The proposition that her son could be out of sight for the rest of her life, pained her. Except, of course, when her son would be due for vacations but like a passenger. That was the most important issue. The pleasure of watching her son grow before her very eyes was something which she in no way was ready to give up, no treasure in the world could equal that pleasure. That was priceless, invaluable. Given any other alternative she would never have accepted such kind of a suggestion.

The exigencies of the situation had however forced her to accept such a choice. In her heart she felt pain. Deep down inside she cursed herself for having offered such a suggestion.

She had hoped that he would reject any such ideal, as he was averse to any idea of sending the children away for academics. Yet, to her utter surprise, the man had agreed. She now had to bear the mortification of living with that proposition.

The only consolation was that he had presented the proposal as if it were his own. That somehow relieved her from having to bear the consequences at a future date, in case of any eventuality.

That left a void, a room for discussion, debate, and counter—charges later, if need arose. If everything worked well, there would be no cause for any problem. In case of things not working out, she was in a comfortable position of laying the blame on him for being dictatorial, rash, and for having some kind of a "single-track brain".

This strategy apart, she was at a loss. The pain of having to live away from her son, the mere the thought of that cast a spell of gloom on her.

She knew, when the children grew up, came of age, and matured as man and woman, they move away. That was reasonable. But to send them away before the day arrived was sheer torture. She was pained to let her son go away. She knew she would not be able to watch the best period of his life for her, the growth of her son from adolescence to teenage and beyond. That pleasure, that warmth, that self-satisfaction she could not experience anymore; that was the reality she knew, but could hardly do anything about.

The departure was to be premature—out of the house, out of the house, out of the family, and who could say with certainty, out of her life as well. Except for very general and casual bonds of love and affection.

She tried to look calm and happy though. She imagined her son in the attire of a *sahib*, in a suit and tie. One day, her son might unfurl the national flag on Independence Day and Republic Day. The young civil service officers who unfurled the tricolour in the sleepy towns were the only visible symbols of the rule of Delhi in such remote and obscure places.

The comfort of the dreams of a time to come, the dream of her son rising to dizzy heights, inspecting the guard of honour was on the credit side.

The loss, the bond of family ties being weakened, the unit

family becoming quieter then on, and the maternal joy and satisfaction watching her son grow up before her very eyes almost being lost forever, were on the debit side.

She knew it could be the beginning of the end. Her son might complete his secondary education and the higher ones away from home and might go on for a career too, all away from home.

The fruition of family ties; the ties between parents and offspring in her family were to remain unfulfilled. The bond seemed to loosen if not be severed, all together.

Yet, she agreed or rather had to agree. The situation demanded that. The fact of good education being imparted at the missionary school and that her son had to be removed from the debilitated setting had to be addressed.

The welfare of her son was the top priority; her petty maternal prejudices had to be disregarded.

So, she agreed. They agreed. Efforts were soon made to seek the boy's admission at the missionary school and the hostel. Once it was confirmed, the news had to be broken to Gautam and convince him of the availability of better education there—the debilitating setting could never have been the point to be stressed upon while the boy was to be convinced.

Gautam was called and Baba informed him.

"Gautam," Baba said, "I think you need better education. The school, no doubt is good as it is, and the teachers are very kind and caring, yet I think you need better."

"But" the son replied, "It is perfectly all right here. I mean the school, the syllabus, and the friends…"

"Yes," the father said "But it could be better. What you lack is self-esteem and reliance. Those are the most important things. If you are self-reliant, you can gain confidence and then only can you achieve what you desire."

"Baba, I am becoming self-reliant. I care for my studies, do my homework, and I am gaining confidence was well," Gautam replied.

"But your friends, your teachers, and we are not very sure of that. There is something seriously wrong with you here. I hope you understand that," the father was blunt.

Gautam kept quiet. That was true. To others his condition seemed disturbing, to some even perilous.

"So, I have decided to put you at a boarding school. The very best one in the region, where gaining admission is a hassle. That has however been sorted out. You must prepare yourself for the stay there. When you learnt to live alone, caring you your studies, your dress, your behaviour and your attitude all by yourself, you can be self -reliant.

Baba patted Gautam on his back.

That was it. The father talking to his son. The talk of senior Cambridge, of a bright future awaiting the young boy somewhere down the line only through the strict discipline and perfect self-reliance at the missionary school, were told. He learnt.

He did not have much of a choice, either.

He had to be moved to a new setting. That was necessary. That was important. That was imperative because others thought that he couldn't have lived here with the memories haunting him.

In a new setting far removed from the reality, from a world in which he could only have hazy dreams, from a world in which the self in him was supposed to grow bereft of strength, where his communion with the snow-flakes was thought to have a deleterious effect on him. He was to be removed to a newer one that could make a man out of him.

So, he had to leave. He was to be a man with a bright career, in the discipline, care, and academics of the convent. He had to grow big, as much as he could.

So, Gautam was asked to pack up. For the first time in his life, he was asked to do so, in the preparation for future. Not once or twice but several times he missed some item or other. He missed his tooth-brush once, his comb the second time, the handkerchief and the pair of socks kept together in a packet the third time, the extra pair of shoelaces another time.

Under the watchful eyes of Baba, the first lesson of self-reliance was being learnt.

Still, he missed something. The post-cards with addresses written on them already. What he had to do was to write "*Aami Bhalo Ache. Tomra Kemon Aachoo? Porrashona Bhalo Cholchaey*" in Bengali (I am quite well. How are you all? My studies are fine here), and drop the cards at the nearest post-box available. The father wanted the son to write in Bengali to him from the English convent because he believed that it was the only way to keep the ties between the son and the parents alive.

Yet, he missed those post-cards, a dozen of them in a bunch. He forgot to put them in his bag. Baba would have made him unpack everything and make him repack his baggage again for the post cards; for if the first lesson of self-reliance was not being learnt in a proper way, how was he expected to fare in future!

Ma saved him on that occasion. She collected the bunch of post cards and put the bunch in his bag, right under Baba's nose. After all, a mother could also exercise her discretion.

All said and done, Gautam was ready for the move, or rather, made ready for better education. He was initiated into lessons of self-reliance, from which sprang confidence that was the vital asset for a career—away from home, away from the watchful eyes of Baba, away from the loving care of Ma, and away from the pranks of Uma.

For Uma, it was the saddest moment. She knew her brother was moving away to an alien land, from where he could only write to her. She would be alone then on, totally so. Despite all his intimidating gestures she liked him. She never had a cake or an apple or a *rasogolla* without making two unequal halves, helping herself to the smaller one and keeping the bigger one for her brother.

She was sad. There was none to be around to shoot her pistol, the toy pistol her father had bought for her during the *puja* festival. Her painted watches, black plastic goggles with green rims for her and blue rims for her brother, toy pistols, toy cars—an Ambassador for her and a jeep for him, would all remain untouched. No would play with her now.

But she understood. Her brother was not keeping well. So, he was being sent away to the place where he would grow into a big man and one day return as a big-officer.

Gautam had to leave the place of the horse-blessings with mist in his eyes, in his heart, in his feelings: never to return again, never to be in company of her again.

Never to be in company of her again. Tshiring, who lay at the foot of the cliff, some four feet below, with her garland on, the one that had the dried red rose sewed and stitched—the big flower, bigger than anyone's palm called the Rosa Macrophylla.

He felt as of the dried flower wished him all the very best for his endeavour, and his efforts to gain his manhood.

On the appointed day, the whole family moved off for the ceremonial transplantation. The ceremony comprised of putting the boy at the school, where education, discipline, and growth of self-reliance were the top priorities.

To gain his manhood, to have a disciplined education, and to have a decent upbringing, Gautam was led to the convent. It was the English medium school run by the Christian missionaries in the plains, in the perfect setting of serenity amidst tea-estates.

Compared to the desolate corner amidst snow and conifers where the rest of world seemed distant, where the radio was the only means of communication to be in touch with the national and international happenings; where the pass at fourteen thousand feet was the only link with the world; where the day began at about noon and ended in the evening; the new place was different and the difference was pronounced.

It was in the plains that Gautam's life was to begin in new form and setting. Between two sleepy towns in the plains connected by roads with the tea-estates on one side and human habitation on the other, lay the school.

The railway track with steam engines dragging trains along, more goods trains than the passenger ones, with few buses and even fewer care plying along the otherwise deserted road was a different presentation of sorts.

On one such misty morning after Christmas, when the session was to begin after the vacation, everyone greeted the other with "Happy New Year!" wishes and received greetings in return. When even the stern faced Fathers and Sisters looked relaxed, and the air was beginning to get tense for the inmates of hostel because of the renewed rigours of academics and discipline of the session that were to begin afresh—the whole family landed at the convent.

The ambience was exceedingly charming. The parents were enchanted by the sight, the son was in trepidation, he didn't know what lay in store for him, and the daughter was wonder-struck by the school, the church, by the buildings and all of it.

While the sprawling grasslands lay on one side of the road marking the extent of the residential school, the other side was marked by the fencing—the boundary of the tea-estates, the plantations where the air smelt as if it were the tea-pot of the world.

Perfect setting for perfect education.

Far down the road the vehicles approached, the buses plied between the sleepy towns, touching the boundary of the premise of the institution on their way. The *pooh-poohing* engines, the smoke of the steam engines dragging the shanty boogies of a few goods trains and odd passenger ones, which swam through the air in wavy formation, added the only polluting share to the environment. The institution stood head-high in the air, everyone who passed by had to look at her.

She was after all, the spectacle of the area.

If the place Gautam came from—the snow-covered regions, the snow laden terrain where the powdery snow fell all along, was shrouded in mysterious and magical isolation; the new place was the one with the colours of grandeur sprayed all over.

From a distance, the Cathedral was visible. It stood like a cliff overhanging a valley, overshadowing areas beneath like a huge mass of ice with a faint vision of a cross.

That added further touches of majesty to the location, like the regalia; the institution appeared to master all that she surveyed.

The experience was new to Gautam. To be confronted by a huge, tall cathedral, the church within the school, the school itself, and the hostel—all felt alien to him.

He saw the cathedral and wondered if he were on the edge of another precipice, if he would be the next one to be swept off. The arresting grandeur was more intimidating than charming and the portends, ominous. He was afraid that he could be swept away by a violent gush from the edge of the cathedral like an avalanche that gushed down the mountains, from the snow-capped peaks.

Uma tried to gauge her own appraisal. Her little eyes had not seen grandeur of such eminence, the church, and the school the sprawling lawns, the huge figure of Jesus on a cross, curved on wood. She was captivated by the charm and that was evident in her eyes.

There were holy men in charge of the convent. The senior amongst them was Father Mathew; everyone revered him. Father Andrews who very young and in charge of the boys' hostel assisted him. Besides, there were a few Brothers.

The nuns under the guidance of Mother Superior looked after the academics with Sisters in control of the girls hostel.

The Fathers wore robes from neck to root—all white with a metal cross in a chain round their necks; the cross dangled in front of them, the grace of divinity was needed for everyone. They wore boots.

Uma surveyed them with her little eyes. For the first time in her life she had explored the domains beyond snow and seen a holy man of a different faith, so closely. She drew comparisons. For her the holy man didn't seem to differ. They seemed to be the same in all faiths.

She whispered to Gautam as they sat facing Father Mathew, "Nothing is different here, dada."

"What"? Gautam asked, "I find everything totally different here."

"Oh no!" She exclaimed, "I am talking of the *sadhus* here."

"How?" Gautam asked, "How are they no different?"

"They wear robes from neck to foot. They are all like our sadhus."

"Explain how are they all same."

"Look, they are covered from neck to foot."

Gautam agreed.

"They have beards and ours have as well."

Gautam agreed again.

"They have boots on while ours have *kharram.*"

"So, their sadhus are like our sadhus." She was supremely confident.

Her fear of a fully covered body with beards and heavy presence seemed to last forever.

"But then," Gautam argued, "the colour is different. Our sadhus have coloured robes and they have white ones on." He was trying hard to pull apart any semblance of similarity.

"But white is a colour too!" she finally put to rest any doubts. She had once and for all put all of them on the same plane.

The only difference she understood was, the sadhus had to be theirs and ours.

Gautam agreed. White was a colour too. The colour of powdery snow and ice with bright reflections when sunlight fell. Indeed, white was a colour.

Some colours he had learnt had meanings of. They said that white was the colour of purity. If white was the colour of purity, then snow could be the purest of all substances. He wondered who assigned meanings to colours. He knew that rocks underwent change of colour and properties called metamorphosis, as he read in his sixth grade textbook. What he wanted to know if colours too underwent any metamorphosis of meanings!

Did saffron signified renunciation, or white?

Did white signified purity or red? The red, like the one of Rosa Maycrophylla. Who could answer that?

He was not sure, at all.

He was not sure of what lay in store for him. For better or for worse? The rescue, the recovery from what to where? Only time could reveal.

He had to grow as tall as the cathedral, to gain his manhood. The cathedral with its lofty summit appealed to all, but Gautam was appalled.

For others it symbolized the all-embracing joy to be in the presence of the sombre and the solemn—the perfect, absolute, and real transport of feelings to be in communion with the lord. For him though, in the majestic isolation high-up in the air like a cliff, like a rocky projection—the cathedral of the towering presence appeared to stand, to throw anyone it chose off-balance, to transport anyone it liked, to deep ravines. He often dreamt of falling from the top of the cathedral in his sleep. Every time he dreamt of falls from the top of the cliff of the cathedral, he woke up with nightmares.

The bliss of the cathedral was elusive for him, neither perennial nor even ephemeral. It did not even seem to be transitory.

To him, the cathedrals with even greater heights, touching the sky could not have provided the solace of any kind, let alone the bliss the Fathers talked about.

Gautam began his stay and study at the boarding school. His journey to manhood and self-reliance began with vows and promises to his parents, the parting kiss from his mother, and the sad waving of hands, *tata-bye-bye* from his sister.

The academics were rigorous and the strict discipline enforced at the hostel made the stay no happier, but more troublesome was the steadfast adherence to ritualistic proceedings and the reference to the kingdom of God in heaven.

To others the visible symbols of bliss, divinity, and satisfaction were the likes of the lofty cathedral, but to him not even the kingdom of God could provide the solace.

Everything said about the kingdom seemed illusory to him. He wondered if the big red rose also grew there.

The kingdom of heaven, in heaven; was nowhere in sight for him. It is for him just another story-like, myth-like proposition. He felt the kingdom was possible within and not without; nowhere in the left side of the chest just above the centre of the rib cage for when he felt a pain, a certain numb feel, he knew it was all because of the red rose. The red rose, bigger than anyone's palm, the dried Rosa Macrophylla, lying in a trench dug out of ice and earth at the foot of the white robed cliff—all glistening in the sun-rays with all white reflections was the colour of purity.

For white was a colour too.

CHAPTER 9
Angel Mary

Life seemed to fall in proper places gradually for Gautam with new friends, new acquaintances, new syllabus, new teachers, and new classmates.

The days of acclimatisation was a testing time, full of trepidations, the transition from the hurricane to the more sedate proceedings, from episodic to more staid ones, from near nothingness to attempts at coming to terms in life.

The teachers took care in the class; the nuns oversaw the proceedings. The Brothers enforced strict discipline at the hostel—the 'big brothers' who were the least brotherly. One of them had a cane like strip of rubber to swing around. He made whipping with that improvised equipment of his to affect brotherly concern, a habit. At night when lights would be put off and only the dimly lit one on, the Brother would come out of his dormitory with the whip in his hand, swing at all the mosquito-nets, the quilts available on each bed received his care, make sure everyone was asleep. That seemed to be his only job around.

The boys awaited his arrival with silence. Greet him with motionless postures, lying absolutely quiet to show "all was quiet on the sleeping front". The whipping and the swinging over—the ritual complete, the Brother would leave. Once one of the boys tried to overdo the act and tried to snore. The Brother promptly awakened him and reprimanded for that was an act of indiscipline and a very unchristian way of sleeping. The poor fellow had to cross himself there and he had to vow, never to snore again.

Then there were stern disciplinarians in the study hall where the inmates assembled in the evening after the play-time was over, when study-time began. Any attempt to talk to each other, with even academics as their subject was frowned upon. Everything had to be channelled through the Brother—another burly fellow whose only job was to shoot and thunder, with a cane in his hand. The black board was never used for nobody approached him for any suggestion. His only job in addition, was to shoot missiles of all forms at the boys whom he could not reach.

Father Mathew sometimes surveyed the whole scene. When he approached, there would be pin-drop silence. Even the friendly brothers appeared normal.

Father Andrews was a young man. He was fresh from the theological college, still in the process of initiation to the service of the institution. The Brothers didn't give him much of a room to interfere. After all they had been serving the institution since long and brooked no interference. The young Father with a smile on his face understood everything but said nothing. He was a traditionalist, allowing each one his due. Seniority had to be respected. That was the code and he had no objection to that.

During playtime everyone had to play. If someone didn't like to join, he had to report. When someone was sick, it had to be reported to the Brother who would then call in the doctor who looked more like a self-styled practitioner than a doctor.

If anyone violated the code of the Brothers, he had to withstand another round of whipping on the palm, or on the back, or on the calves of the legs; the choice of course would be left always to the boy.

The teachers were strict in their classes as well. No foul language, no slang, no swears, no curses; all were taboo. No language except English was to be used. Most of the students didn't speak English at the hostel or at home, so it was free-for-all at the class. The punishment for any of the offence was nearly the same.

Gautam had his share of punishment on two separate occasions. The first time he had to write "I shall not speak bad words" and the second time, "I shall speak only English" four hundred times on ruled exercise book. Any mistake or any clever-act was liable for further punishment and everyone took care to be very particular while serving sentence; more than when they completed their home-tasks.

Anyway, they had very little time for home tasks, as they were busy serving sentences or living in perpetual fright of the brothers.

Despite such strenuous efforts from the teachers, the English hardly improved. The free-for-all continued with newer variations of the language being added each day, each hour, which even those who spoke the "Queen's English" would dare not dream. The teachers were happy that at least efforts were on for bettering the English.

Indeed it was. English in full improvisation. Free for all. The innovations were at their exhilarating best. *English-o-fying* the Indian languages—Bengali, Assamese, Hindi, and even tribal dialects. It was quite an experience, quite alarming variations for purists. The perfect Indian curry—the culinary delight.

The English had to be bettered and so the bettering was on.

The Mother Superior once walked past the gathering of students —an elderly lady with her glasses on, she overheard the English and said, "Good Lord!" The class teacher Ms Verghese in her inimitable Malayali accent said, *"Ids a pidy thaad the Bridish left some thirdy years back. They did not hear your English. They would have then fled the land without yeany agitation or moment."*

For the inmates of the boy's hostel, life was dull and unexciting. It was the routine that had to be adhered to.

In the morning hours, after the breakfast was over, the dress had to be kept ready and tidy, the shoes polished, books and stationery arranged. There was not a moment to relax. Then the moves in queues to the church, when everyone's dress was inspected by the Brothers who led them to the divine presence for prayers and then to the best part of the extra-curricular ones and the colour.

There were two groups in the boy's hostel, the groups placed apart. One set of boys resided in the better part of the hostel who belonged nearly to all faiths found on earth—the Hindus, the Christians, the Muslims, even one or two odd Buddhists and Sikhs; those whose parents paid for their upkeep, food, boarding and academics. Those were the boys who paid their way though sometimes quite exorbitantly.

The other group who lived a distance apart, was the one that comprised of the second-generation converts. The parents of those boys were mostly tea-garden labourers who worked on the tea plantations and had converted to the faith; because proselytism was strong in that part of the world. The church paid the expenses for those boys. Those boys were allowed to study and live in that part of the hostel where amenities were less, where even the sanitary and living conditions were worse.

Even the dining and living halls were different. The menu two was surprisingly different. While the inmates living in the better part ate mostly rice and curry, egg, fish and meat sometimes, those living in the not-so-better part of the hostel didn't eat rice. They were served rather a sort of porridge that smelt like barley, and mostly vegetarian dishes.

Not surprisingly those boys maintained a distance from those who were actually better off. That in turn was reciprocated.

Segregation was in vogue even in the presence of the divine. The tradition of the great land fully maintained. Rarely, if ever, the two groups interacted and even when they did, those ended in fights, exchange of blows was common. But those were resolved before the authority could get any or much inkling. That was "peaceful co-existence" displayed to perfection! However, the result of the fights on the field mostly ended in favour of the less privileged group. They usually won the better part of the episodes for they carried their "conviction of the lord" in greater measure, in fact they were of much better build physically, and were relatively older.

The only part of the routine obviously for the inmates of the boy's hostel therefore lay in and during class hours, which brought renewed vigour and fresh lease of life every day.

There lay the colour.

The girls nearly outnumbered the boys in the class. Of all ethnicities and groups; they came from different background as well. All in school uniforms with skirts that touched the knee and went beyond, of pomegranates shaping off their chest. They were the welcome change—rather the most important change of the day.

The teachers came mostly from Kerala, far down the south. With their accent all lovely and musical (they were all females and to teenaged boys all females sounded musical), they made the class even more charming for the boys. Young, warm, and vibrant so unlike the nuns, they added the remaining touch of colour to the class and to the lives of the "lost" inmates of the boy's hostel.

For seventh and eighth graders, life was at a crossroads. With their voices gradually becoming coarser, sometimes even they were excited to hear their own voices. The gruff and deep sounds surprised themselves as they felt the changes. Even the hair turned black from being brown all over the body to some special ones at some special places—curly and lovely. The shorts, especially knickers seemed to get shorter everyday. All seemed to be at the threshold of strange, pleasing and inciting changes.

Their classmates, the girls, seemed very lovely and charming. To the inmates of the boy's hostel, even the teachers seemed lovely and nice. After all the only chance of seeing the females and to be in their company was the six hours of class they could attend six days week. Given a chance they would have opted for holidays as well. In fact, some of them enrolled for the music lessons after class hours and on Sundays, to be in the august company.

All those, of course, failed to excite Gautam. For him those were all momentary distractions from his perpetual marooned state. The memories of earlier episodes didn't seem to fade off as readily as was expected. More over the sudden removal from the protective and pampered setting to an entirely new one, where one had only himself to cater to his needs didn't appear to be a very smooth transition.

All the "self-addressed" postcards for his parents where he had only to scribble three well-rehearsed lines didn't reach them—not a single one. Because no vernacular was allowed and only English had to be used.

If English was used, strict censorship was imposed.

The reason being that the "quality" of English had to be improved. In reality, the strict censorship enforced was to make sure that all the letters could be read and that was possible only if those were written in English. Though most of the letters sent by the boys never reached their parents, the greeting cards and "best wishes" reached them from the authorities regularly.

The only and the best, the most pleasing change was therefore the six hours of class with a break for lunch in between.

The thrusts of teenage desires on the upswing—the intense liking to hear, overhear and join the discussions on hitherto forbidden topics, the first trespasses on to secrets that reverberated with the changes in the physical and emotional levels of the boys; were provoking.

For the "cursed" ones from the boy's hostel, the only chance of any kind of exchange with "beauties" was at the class. Being unsure and not much initiated in the art of conversation with their female classmates, they choose to remain huddled in groups, mostly occupying the benches from the middle to the rear, while their counterparts from nearby towns—the day-scholars carried the day.

The consolation for them was to watch the legs sticking out of the skirts of their class mates. Often, they indulged in lovely games of "counting hairs" on them. Most often the girls were completely unaware that they were being subjected to such intense scrutiny.

Even the teachers in their colourful sarees and blouses looked exquisite. They were tall by the Indian standards and they looked beautiful. What excited the inmates of the boy's hostel was the portion of the body that they could watch and observe. In fact, the teachers were the only grown-up-the women around, their classmates were only girls. The portion of the body, bare and natural, that made appearances often while they teachers were busy teaching, excited them. The portions in the middle, between the waistline, and around the navel upward till the upper garment covering the rest were exciting.

From the backbenches those were a treat to watch, with the teenage sensation at the explosive best.

In such a setting when the life settled down to plain, staid, dull, sequential chores except for aberrations, the heart within him yearned for love. The "exciting" legs sticking out of the skirts inviting to explore the higher reaches, the rounded navel above the waistline, the ridges of the rounded breasts, the shades of undergarments, all failed to sustain the excitement, after the initial flashes. The pumping organ within the rib cage was in turmoil, and Gautam felt it.

There was nobody to talk to him, no one from the females. They were mostly "taken care of" by the more charming counterparts. Neither could taking seat at the back satisfy him. He was too shy and timid and "too lost" to be paid any attention.

His attention of course was drawn to the individuals very similar to his own disposition at the class. The girls who viewed the boys as creatures from a distant planet, those who lived in the "care of the church" at the girl's hostel under the spiritual and moral tutelage of the nuns. Those included girls from the northeastern corner of the country. That group was in the 'care of the church' for their upkeep, academics, and hopefully of a future. The future was teaching at the school run by the church, possibly in a corner of India, like places in the north-eastern corners of the country.

For him, they seemed to be of interest. Shy, unsure and timid as he was, they seemed to be ideal match for him. He longed for them. The imaginations cut loose and the desire got upbeat.

The desire for love and being loved—the companionship of females—the smile of the girls was the "need of the hour". The earlier flashes only inflamed the excitement, they were however distractions which could never have been soothing.

He therefore the search for hearts that had beats like he had, nothing more, nothing less. The frequency, like that of the pendulum he learnt at the class, had to be the same.

Then the angel appeared.

They called her Mary.

She called herself Angel Mary.

The records showed her as Angel Mary Pertin. She was a tribal—an *adi* girl, someone from the same region Gautam came from. The rugged terrain of Arunachal.

She appeared to him as someone who could fathom his feelings, the beats of his heart.

Not very tall, she was fair, with her mongoloid features very prominent. Yet surprisingly, she had dimples that shaped extremely well on her cheeks, when she smiled.

And there was a mole, right at the centre of the dimple on her right cheek. The dark black spot on an otherwise bright cheek! She seemed to be the girl he was looking for.

There were other attributes as well. Shyness, simplicity, and the elusive grace, all were evident.

And she sang the devotional songs beautifully at the church, mostly as the lead singer in the chorus. She could play the guitar. The songs she sang at the church mesmerised Gautam. Here was one he felt he was looking for. She epitomised the charm he had dreamt of.

To provide the balm much needed, much required, and much desired. The longing became intense, forceful, and strong every moment.

The songs she sang were splendid. Gautam would hear only her voice, in the chorus. There were other voices and tones also. Yet to him, only her voice seemed to standout. It was clear, soothing, and of excellent tonal quality, in perfect devotion to the praise of the lord, in perfect unison with the meaning, every syllable she uttered.

From the fresco, the virgin Mother smiled with all her benevolence, all the tranquillity, with the infant Jesus in her arms, radiating charm. May be the grace was on him, Gautam thought while Mother Mary smiled at him, there was another—Angel Mary, who grew in his heart. All the while he figured out the profile of her lips and if the profile matched the one in the fresco.

"Mary," Gautam asked one day, "How wonderfully you sing with all warmth, affection and love in devotion."

"Oh, really!" She answered. "Do I? I love to sing."

She smiled. The profiles seemed to match.

They were classmates. During the breaks when everyone deemed to chuckle and frolic, she kept a distance, much aloof, much sombre. He drew close.

"Mary," Gautam asked. "I presume you are from the mountains. Where exactly do you come from?" The conversation had to begin somehow.

And she talked, of her village, of her place, the hills, the rugged terrain, the forests, the greenery, the winding, roads—all gradually, hesitatingly but surely. Sure enough, she did.

They met during breaks; after prayer on sundays and talked. That was the turning point, the watershed. From that day they met, with urges growing compulsively and gradually the spontaneity became an integral part.

At the hostel, where the afternoon play-time had become more boring than ever before, the young Father added the cherished variation—the spice to the routine proceedings.

Father Andrews—so very young, tall bespectacled, fair complexioned was on a learning exercise. He was the most loveable of all men and women in white robes. He was probably on probation. In fact, Gautam felt a little uncomfortable, a bit uneasy to call him Father. He was a bit too young, to be addressed as Father.

Father Andrews had his lessons of motorbike riding. Father Mathew who was older and experienced, gave him the lesson. Father Mathew was the teacher, Father Andrews was the learner.

Gautam wished Father Andrews all the very best in his endeavour. The young Father smiled.

That way Gautam tried to cheer him up. The young Father tumbled a few times —rather every time initially, as he tried to mount the bike, trying to come to terms with reality, each time he attempted to ride and drive.

Gautam also was in turmoil and stress—a seemingly perpetual state, searching for hope. Trying to make way through snowfalls and snowflakes, falling off cliff-cathedral, and then of Mary. He was also trying to come to terms with reality.

Then, one day, the bespectacled Father somehow steadied himself to be able to mount and start the kick-start one. Gautam knew he had to steady himself, deep down in his heart, to shake off his inhibitions and gear-up.

Mary and Gautam met. He talked. She listened. She nodded. She smiled. She replied.

Then she talked. In short sentences, in syllables. In more and more words.

They got closer, becoming more and more so.

In the senses, in feelings, in emotions!

He felt the warmth, of her feelings, of her fragrance, of her radiance, of her gaze. He needed the balm and she provided the same. He couldn't have asked for anything more, anything different. She came. She saw, she felt. She responded.

She told how her grandfather was converted to the faith. How her father had struggled to have both ends meet. How she had the privilege of gaining selection to the institution.

Her likes and dislikes.

Beyond the seemingly innocuous revelation she was not willing to speak much. She was reluctant to speak of more personal problems, and her family. Then at the time when the spirits seemed to get better if not high, she revealed in characteristic understatement, the state of her family.

Her father was a boozer—a first-rate drunkard and her mother had to toil hard for the upkeep of the family. She had been ill and breathed her last when Mary was but a child, but not before a nun had been kind and promised the bed-ridden woman that her daughter would be put in the care of the church. That was the only solace the mother got before her death as she had fears that leaving the child to the 'care' of the father would be as good as leaving the child father-less or even far worse. She however died with peace in her heart, as she was sure that the church would take care of her daughter.

Mary told Gautam of her complete faith and trust in the lord, her unending faith in the values. The natural flow of compassion in her was clear enough.

Gautam felt the charm had returned to his life again. This time of a different kind of sensation, a different kind of yearning, a different kind of longing, of the surprise element of teenage passion for compassion.

Back at the hostel, life was as usual. For Gautam though, it did not seem to matter anymore. No particular dislike for anything to abhor. The proceedings had become bearable.

Every evening the boys gathered to play football and cricket. Limited over variety was the order long before it had become the national craze.

Meanwhile Father Andrews had completed his lessons of both motorbike and car driving. He rode on his bike with the authority of someone at the charge.

He drove the car, too. At the steering wheel he looked confident, calm and very sure of himself. He drove past Gautam, the dust following the car to the villages nearby where church services were required.

Gautam was also sure, confident of the exercise. He was growing beyond his contradictions. Not very far in future he believed he should also be driving along. It could be with her, he thought.

It was her charm that she radiated each time she met him, that he thought he was the only one to feel only one to be able to notice the glow. She trusted him.

She believed him. She believed in him. She exuded the belief and confidence in him. He felt elated. Thrilled, as if he were on the top of the world—of the feel of complete trust, confidence and faith someone could have had in other.

Gautam was overwhelmed.

The bud was visible, of teenage love.

For her, the gospel was the truth, the lord was the embodiment of all that was good. For him though, she was the truth, the manifestation of all good.

The affection was contagious; it was infectious in reciprocity. The more he felt for her, it was responded with even more force. When she did so, Gautam felt the upsurge of similar sentiments. The presumption of the feeling of "being lost with no one to care for but the lord" she had, gradually evaporated.

The stay at the institution became very pleasing, very comfortable, and very lively. The same setting with the same chores, the same routine not so long ago appeared different, with changed spirit.

The life it seemed had undergone a complete overhaul. Gautam felt the change. That perennial source of delight called love could change the "doomed" existence into a loveable one; he had read in literature. He could now experience the hitherto unknown, unfelt and ungauged feelings.

The ninth grade was long over. The tenth grade was drawing to a close. He could hardly feel that. Time seemed to fly so fast. The existence was not drudgery anymore. It had given way to some very pleasing notion-the heart-warming one.

His first year of stay was a miserable one. He could count each day, recount the experiences of one day and multiply with the number of days for the year or the month he desired to get the sum total of experiences.

His last couples of years—more so the last year that of the tenth grade was one he could hardly have bargained for. How could a full year—twelve months—three hundred and sixty-five days simply vanish into thin air?

The secondary examination approached and more than Gautam, it was Mary who was worried, not for her but for him. She knew his career was at stake and that was important.

"Gautam" she said, "Now that the classes are over, I believe we should not meet at all till the examinations are finally over." Gautam knew she was exaggerating. She could hardly have reconciled the consequences of the proposal she was so unforgiving to put forward. "But why?" he asked. "Why on earth should we do that?"

"Because the examinations are hardly three months away and you need to study." She was stern.

"You too have your examinations. The same one, if I am not wrong."

"Sure. But more important is your career. Any distraction could put that in jeopardy," She sounded exactly like the Mother

Superior. "Exactly so. But not meeting could be a greater distraction." Gautam was persistent.

She thought for a while and came up with a mid-way solution.

"All right then. We meet once a week. On Sundays at the church, after the prayers." She paused and smiled, "From now on, all my prayers would be for you and your examination." She was back to her normal self again.

Gautam gave in. He had no other way. She smiled at him and made him easy. The concern was real and genuine.

And he knew it.

So, it went. Gautam passed with the desired result. The result of his labour or her prayers—only the lord could answer. She passed as well.

The story at the school—the institution that had begun on an anxious, uncertain note on a misty morning ended with a note of a different kind. Not in years merely though, but in moments of love and longings. Now was the time to decide and shape for a career. Launching oneself for a prospective career was on the cards.

Mary had to enrol at the college located at the nearby sleepy town while she still could be in the 'care of the church'. The college in fact received substantial grant from the church.

For Gautam, he was free to join anywhere he desired. His parents wanted him to join a better college for a build-up, in preparation for a career-oriented course. He felt otherwise. Leaving the place could and necessarily meant leaving her. He could never have done that. So, he too joined the college where Mary had enrolled despite strong objections from his parents. He somehow pacified them promising to show as good a result they wished for.

Gautam took up Science with a view to pursue a career that would be rewarding in terms of prospects—like seeking admission at a professional college for a technical degree in the future.

Mary took Humanities, not knowing what to do in future. She did not have much of an objective but as one in the care of the church, she had very limited options. She could carry on with her academics to graduate level and then take up teaching as a profession. Perhaps again at a missionary school, somewhere in the remote corner of the region, in the northeastern corner of the land where a life of obscurity was the rule.

CHAPTER 10
Romance Is Music

The college brought Gautam and Mary into an new world altogether. With not much the rigor of the academics to be taken care of, they came in close touch with each other. They were finally freed from the preying eyes, the watchful eyes, and the stern eyes.

What they had long felt were the joys of love, more at heart, in the longings, to be in each other's company. The shackles were now freed. They were in each other's proximity.

For the first time they were in close proximity, sure and certain, when for sometime, for nearly one year the academics took the back seat was the "second fiddle", as he called it.

It was here that, far from the intimidating gaze, far off from the constant vigil of the teachers, the regular harping on the academics, far from the restraints and constraints, that they met.

Under the clear blue skies, under the shade of the trees, on the grass—he lay straight, relaxed, while she sat, his head on her lap. She caressed his hair, tousled it. Ran her fingers through. The teenage love had finally blossomed.

Beneath the clear, open sky, surrounded by the soothing ambience of tea plantation, the love on earth grew stronger, of teenage desires and aspirations. She moved her finger through his hair, dropped her silky hair over his face. Allowed him all the fragrance, and occasionally ran her palm over his face. That was her prerogative.

Though when it came to be his turn, everything was taboo. The closest thing he could get in touch with her was when she touched him. She knew and knew perfectly well, where and when to draw the line.

"Man," she generalized, "was not to be trusted beyond a point". She was a perfect puritan. The only allowance was, he could peck her cheek.

He could peck her cheek only when there was an occasion for it. Apart from the special occasion, the general ones were during Christmas, or Good Friday, the festivals he enjoyed, the puja, or Diwali and Holi.

The grace of the lord seemed to shower only on those special occasions. He would wait for hours till the moment came when she would close her eyes at the point of impact—the nose, his nose touching the mole in the centre of the dimple on the right cheek.

Nothing more, nothing beyond! A kiss was no question.

The peck was all she allowed. That also, if he stayed away from the drinks—the first taste of freedom had ushered in new tastes for new acquaintances.

"A perfect victim of nunnery," he called her in disgust.

"A perfect example of male lascivism," she said and smiled.

She had the smile that cooled down any adventure-some, that could have otherwise spelt 'disaster'.

He did not have the courage to trespass. She never allowed that to happen.

"Why are you so persistent in touching me? Is that what all you want?" she asked.

"It is only the sacred things that are worth touching!" Gautam quoted. All the while he meant was, the unexplored frontiers that were worth surveying.

"Do you really mean what you say?" She had doubts in his pronouncements.

"Faithfulness is to love what consistency is to the life of an idealist." Gautam rearranged the quote to suit his needs, as he was about to peck the right cheek again, while she covered her face and pushed him.

"What's wrong?" Gautam asked, having been denied what he felt was rightfully his after such an intellectual deliverance.

"Those words," she paused, "I have read somewhere."

"Come on," he told her, "Why do you ruin my chances of caring for the little mole?"

"Not now." She blushed, and then smiled. The smile that she had, delighted his heart but downed the passion.

"When one is in love, one always begins by deceiving one's self, and one always ends by deceiving others. That is what the world calls a romance," he replied feeling sore and cross for having been denied his legitimate shot.

She twitched her brows and said finally, her neck bent. "I know. Why do you quote Oscar Wilde? It is all his."

"Yes," he said, "Did I ever claim that the words were mine?"

"Oh, come on. You are wild with Wilde. Why can't you say something of your own?"

He wished to hear more of the sort from her.

"I know, Gautam, you could do so and hopefully you would," she said looking very meaningfully at him.

And he was inspired.

When such inspiration came from one's ladylove, it assumed alarming proportions. It seemed to be the Sermon on the Mount, as important as the commandments—ten, twenty or one.

Teenage imagination was firing up, he felt it.

Gautam was in search of the originality if it lay within him. Wild was Wild and he could not have got the best of the world piggy riding on anyone's back.

Mary wanted something different. And that was all he cared for.

And indeed, he tried something different. And what better than a poem to write, for her. He wrote one, slipped it in her book and asked her to open it and go through—the treasure. He was not sure if it was a boon or a curse.

His first poem had ended in a catastrophe.

He was anxious about the fate of the second.

She opened the book, unfolded the paper. There it was.

She read as her eyes gradually widened in some sort of a panoramic vision before her, as she glanced through.

He felt like his heart was in his mouth. The fate of his composition was being decided. The moment seemed to last forever. Midway through he cursed himself for having ventured into unknown territory, which had put him in such a quandary.

Slowly but surely in a sonorous voice she recited:

I attend not on your beauty
But something else;
I crave not just for your physical charms
But your longings.
The captivating beauty,
The delicate mannerisms.
I feel the yearnings in my heart
Being fired.
With new waves each passing day.
The throbs in my heart
I hear
The beats of your love like a sonnet.
For if I do not get drenched
In your wholesome love,
Of what fruition and use

Would my life be?
Come and shower me
With your love.
My life-boat
Would then get ashore.

She read it a number of times till he saw her eyes glowing.

"Who was it meant for?" she asked to reassure herself.

"For you, who would I write to?" Gautam was hurt by the query, substantially.

"It's fine," She was pleased." I shall keep the treasure." She folded the piece of paper and drew it close to her chest.

She closed her eyes. He knew it had touched her. He went for the mole, right at the centre of the dimple in the cheek to stamp the peck.

She did not object. She allowed it.

The second poem was not a disaster after all.

"Why don't you write more often?" she asked. Her eyes had brightened again.

"For you?" he asked. "You seem to be hell bent on making a poet out of me."

"There is a saying in Bengali, in the particular variation of the dialect I speak of the language—'one cannot flog a donkey to make a horse out of it.'" he quipped.

She laughed. Laughed her heart out.

"But I see the potential of being a poet inside you and I really mean it." She widened her eyes and pressed her eyeballs to emphasize her point.

So, she could see the potential. Great revelation indeed!

In the soothing ambience of tea-plantation, the placid setting of the shade of the Banyan, the longing grew, the love blossomed, and the poetry flowed.

With the small of tea-leaves all around, the men and women at work collecting tea-leaves in their baskets, up and down the stretch of land in distance, the pair was busy, in love.

The teenage love was busy making new waves, new ripples.

The third poem in his life was equally 'enchanting', as she thought of it so.

The love-language and the blush
Tell your saga.
Why do your yearnings then invite the d-Day at this very hour?
For if our love-saga be in
The hearts of the people,
We bear no complaint
If we find a place in their memories
Of millions in love
How many do live up to it?
If we don't get into the bottom
Of our each other's heart
Of what significance shall
Our love is?
Even if we fail to reach
The goal:
We bear no grudge
If the world says
'The perfect duo in love'.
Certainly, shall our lives be brightened!
If the love-God says
'The perfect ones.'

She collected the treasure again and kept it close to her.

The situation was certainly not so poetic and placid for Gautam and Mary. Things in fact had got worse. Their love-saga was the talk of everyone else in the college.

Proximity between a boy and a girl—both young, was not very encouraged in the land, more so in the puritanical setting. And when the closeness went beyond the level of tolerance, it was frowned upon, despised and if required; punitive measures were called for.

It was no exception in their case also.

Her friends did not take her too kindly for having an affair with a non-believer. Her mates at the hostel who like her, were in the care of the church, were very cross with her, and sore over her love with a heathen. Her mates at the class who came from the same tribe as that of her, resented the idea and swore to avenge the humiliation, on Gautam for having whisked away one of their kin.

The nuns at her hostel, the guardians of moral and spiritual values were very upset, for her having loved anyone at all.

Things had gone worse.

The head of the institution, the Principal of the college, was informed and complaint lodged.

Gautam was summoned. As he entered the chamber, he knew something not so kind was in the offing. The bald man with gray hairs or whatever was left of that, with a gray moustache, looked at him.

"I have got something important to talk to you," the man said Gautam looked at him with expectant eyes.

"I have been informed of late, that you are not doing well at your studies. May I know the reason?" he asked as he pretended to look through papers that seemed very important.

"I am grateful to you for concern, Sir," Gautam answered. "But I am doing well, rather quite well in my studies. Sir, I have topped the class in the last examination". He was stating facts, which he knew that the principal knew very well, too.

"I do not think so," the Principal replied, "I think you can do much better than that. For the moment," He paused, "I am told you are concentrating less on your studies and more on something else. You are getting carried away by teenage distractions."

The last sentence was said while he was going through the papers that lay in front of him, in deep concentration.

The Great Indian euphemism was in logical use again.

"I demand a reply," the man looked up.

Gautam was silent. He didn't know what to say. All he could somehow mumble was," Could you please be a bit explicit, Sir."

The man was not much pleased it seemed.

"I see and sense a growing arrogance in you. That is very evident in your words." The middle-aged man was getting impatient. "You cannot make the institution a place for your affairs. Do you get me?"

So, that was it, then. The institution being made a place for affairs as if no one else had ever done that.

Gautam kept quiet. Sometimes keeping quiet he knew worked well. Moreover, he had nothing much to say either.

The voice softened. "Think about the whole fuss you have made." The man said.

"The mess that you have put yourself in, lands me in trouble. You know, the institute runs on substantial grant from the church and any adverse report from them could hurt you. For the present, I have taken up the matter in my hands. I take you to be an intelligent young man. I am looking for you to excel in the examination, which in any case is not very far. Why don't you concentrate on your studies? If you promise me to keep yourself engrossed in your academics and not run around the trees with that girl, I can assure you, I will take care."

The sermon was over, and it was more of an advice, a suggestion than a commandant. Some helplessness creeping, some resignation peeping in the statement.

Gautam kept quiet. He understood the implications. Silence, he knew, meant agreement. The Principal knew that also. The agreement had been reached with no one saying so in the open.

Great tradition of the Great Land!

Gautam walked out of the chamber.

The situation had to be understood. The man didn't want to hurt his student but was under duress to do something. The strategy had to change. Gautam told Mary of the situation that had placed her in a precarious position; she knew well but was not ready to admit.

The only recourse left was to keep low, keep in touch through someone. And it couldn't be anyone else but Ronald.

Ronald Lego was his name. He belonged to the same tribe that Mary came from.

He was a strongly built young man who could grip anyone by the scruff of the neck. Someone like Gautam, raise him over the head, swing not less than half a dozen time and hurl to a distance of not less than ten metres.

For someone of his strength, physique and stature, he was surprisingly calm and decent.

He was the only who took a fancy for them, liked them, both. While the whole community seemed to be ranged against Gautam and Mary, he was the only one who sided with them.

"You are very fortunate," he told Gautam, "You are in love with the best girl I have ever seen, ever met and by God, and she loves you too!"

"You seem to have met quite a few of them". Gautam pricked him. "Sure!" he said. "I had been in love before, with a girl who ditched me. Ditched me because of my physique. She believed

I had brains much smaller in proportion to my stature." He giggled.

That was Ronald, to be able to make even serious issues as the one, so disarmingly presentable. He made Gautam laugh.

When Ronald laughed, others had to. His spirit was infectious.

Perfect explanation indeed! Brain smaller in proportion to physique!

He looked straight at Gautam. "Man, you love the best girl. More importantly, she loves you more than what you do!" That was his strength again. Back from the laughter he could again pick up the issue with clarity and perfect analysis.

That was enough to upset Gautam.

"Ronnie!" He said, "You are being uncharitable. How do you make it out that she loves me more than what I do?" Gautam was offended.

"Nothing to take offence. When I was love, I loved the girl more than she did. I knew it by looking at her eyes. I loved. I was a fool. Despite the difference in the degree of affection, I loved on. I had hoped for the best," Ronald reflected. "The consequences were shocking. At least it appeared then. Now of course it has evaporated."

"But how about your conclusion on our love, on who loves more than whom?" Gautam was persistent.

"Very simple. From my experience I can say that. Take it for granted. She loves you more than what you do. I have seen that in her eyes and I know that for sure." Ronald passed the judgement, "That is the criteria of sustainability. If the women loves you more, the love survives; if it is the other way round, bad things are in store."

Professor Ronnie, philosopher Ronnie, Father Ronnie—all in one!

"I am all for those who love their loved ones deeply, and dearly," He went on. "I am with them, come what may." He clenched his fist.

Ronnie smiled and patted Gautam on his back. Even the friendly pats did not seem very pleasing off those heavy hands and fingers. "You are so lucky, so fortunate. The best girl possible loves you. I know the guys who are up against you. I have made things very clear, to them. Should I get to know anything, of things they contemplate doing, I shall break every bone in each guy's body." He was firm.

So, Ronald become the best friend Gautam had at the college. Gautam told him of all that had happened, the caution, and the cold warning from the principal.

Gautam hinted at the possible intermediary who could keep touch with Mary as well.

"In that case", Ronald suggested, "do you mean, I could be the intermediary?"

Gautam looked at him, expectations rising.

"Now my friend," Ronald paused, the anxiety in Gautam's eyes was very apparent.

"I would gladly do so if you promise me something,"

"And what's that?" Gautam felt his heart had come to his mouth.

"If you promise to make me the witness at the wedding as and when it comes through." Ronald looked at Gautam who could not believe his ears. "Hey, man! The wedding I mean." After the element was surprise over, Gautam joined in the laughter.

He wondered if people who had hearty laugh and could laugh their hearts out were people with very clear heart and conscience. Their laughter was so natural and was not at all contrived.

Gautam was overjoyed. Ronald had agreed to do that what was the need of the hour.

The meetings became rarities. Gautam and Mary rarely talked in the class. At the teashop as and when they met, away from the preying eye, it was not more than for a couple of minutes.

But the messenger did his job well. His smile brought the only change in their lives.

If the meeting were curtailed or scrapped, the messages grew longer. The conversations had gone rarer and the letters became longer. Poems longer than ever before appeared with short touching reply. The messenger was busy.

"In addition to the joy it brings to both of you," Ronald said, "I am doing this for personal gains as well." He finally let the cat out of the bag.

"I believe if I help a couple in love, the next time I am in love which could happen someday, and though I have taken care, I mean tried hard enough to increase the size of my brain to bring to a level proportionate to that of the body; I need the grace of the lord! I hope to have his grace by this service to you. I hope no one ditches or deserts me again. God almighty should be kind." Ronald was child-like in his clarity of thought and expression.

"But Ronnie," Gautam teased, "It is not the God-Almighty who should be kind. Rather your lady-love who should be kind."

Ronald laughed his heart out, again. "They mean the same thing," he answered.

Gautam called Ronald for his excellent service as the one-the cloud messenger—the *Meghdottam* for he could bring on fresh air, an air of hope, of relaxation, of cheer, of love.

Moreover, he came from the region, very high on the mountains, where he said, he could touch the clouds; the misty fog as it passed by.

"The title is all right. I not want to spend the rest of my life being a messenger all through. Pray for me that I too have someone to send my messages to."

The appeal was very touching.

Gautam told him, "I wish you all the best, the very best for the second part of your wish. For the first part, I mean the prayers—I am not very good at it, I can't, or rather don't. For the praying part—Mary is the one who could do it for you. After all, it is her messages also you carry. Moreover, if someone's prayers are answered any time in future, it would be hers."

With the approaching examination, the maturity gained over the years, the career prospects in sight, Gautam felt he had also become very analytical and practical.

The change of seasons perhaps, or
The Dawn of maturity?
The ripening of teenage aspirations!
The signs of crossing the line?
Becoming an adult?

CHAPTER 11

Transition Interferes

The examination drew closer. Gautam became more and more concerned because the result of the examination could pave way for the career he dreamt of. To secure admission at the technical institute.

Mary seemed to be equally concerned. In spite of her examinations, she prayed for him so that he could secure admission, on course to a career worthy of his 'talents'.

The "cloud messenger" brought her news to him and conveyed his. Examination came and went, as did the annual rituals, as did floods in the plains, or the torrential downpour in the mountains.

Gautam passed with marks he desired, but deserved less.

And Mary, too.

Not only Gautam passed his examinations but also obtained the much-cherished admission. He got his heart's desire—got the much hoped for, the much-longed chance to pursue the higher education in an Engineering College.

Far, far away in the metropolis, in the mainland India.

Ronald left for the hills in search of livelihood. He had very little options.

And Mary? She was asked to join the school that was run by the order in her native land—the hilly terrain of the "earliest lit dawn". She was asked to take care of the education of the young children in the rugged hills.

The day he left, for Mary was scheduled to leave a few days later, they met for the last time in the setting of the shade of the Banyan tree.

The cooling shade of the giant tree.

The smell of the tea leaves in the air.

The men and woman at work collecting tealeaves in their baskets with monotonous regularity, all seemed as normal as possible. Only the love that had grown was destined to be drawn apart. If it was to be with ever-growing affinity or with lessening intensity, no one could tell.

Each felt the uncertainty, the trepidation.

Yet, no one could spell out, for fear of being the first one to do so.

There were tears in her eyes. The eyes that were always full of delight looked out of place. The smile with the mole in the dimple on the right cheek was missing. Instead there were tears that she could barely control. The dry smile was more contrived.

"So, you have got your heart's desire," she said, "I am left in obscurity."

"Not at all," Gautam replied, "When I get you as my own, only mine, that would be the fulfilment of my heart's desire."

That appeared to be the only solace. The solace for the moment and could be for the rest of the life, both knew.

"I can only pray for the same," she said.

For the first time in his life, he wanted and wished to pray. In the hour of reckoning, the moment of separation, the only hope, faint though it was, laid the hope he saw in her eyes (he learnt that from Ronald, the feelings to be read from the eyes). The expectation was that one day he might lead her, from obscurity to fulfilment, of union, of love, of satisfaction.

She was too self-conscious and too self-respecting to speak in any such words that could make her look helpless.

"Wait for me, Mary," he said, "wait for me till I come back. Promise me that." He could only mumble.

She nodded; her head bent.

She understood.

The kiss, for the first time in his life came his way. The parting kiss though. That felt cold but not dry, and tasted salty. Her tears seemed to have gone down to her lips. The taste that was for him, the salty one! It remained with him for days and months together. He could feel it, almost taste it again when he thought of her, and remember her. The taste grew saltier, more than ever before when the feelings came.

He wondered if the silent tears ever tasted salty.

He joined the college—the Engineering College in the city, in the pursuit of a career.

The parents were happy. Baba had retired and settled down in the town where he had a plot of land, with Ma and Uma, the sleepy town, Silchar.

In the one and half room of a house he could construct off the sum he received on superannuation. Baba seemed content.

The life of an ex-freedom fighter was destined for seeking peace with himself. He knew his vision of himself like that of the nation he had dreamt of was never going to be fulfilled, not at least in that life of his.

But he had not changed much. He settled at the place, Silchar. Non-descript and obscure as the place was, the only mention of it was in the record-books that showed the first polo club in the world ever being formed there in 1859, by the British army officers. The club long ago had ceased to exist. (The second such club ever to be formed was in 1862 in Calcutta that survived to the day.) For Baba, such *exalted* status mattered. Whoever expressed inability to locate the place got snubbed.

Some of his old colleagues and acquaintances from different parts of the country had also retired and settled in their respective native places. If anyone ever wrote to him about the exact location of the place, he would reply in his own way.

In the address he added **24d 50s N, 92d 51sE** after the name of the place. He would then suggest the inquirer to look into the Oxford school atlas of their sons and daughters, those that were gathering dust. Keeping oneself abreast with the nation's geography was sure to increase the longevity of the retired people, he *politely* suggested to them, his way to deal with *sheer ignorance*.

Sure enough, he was irrepressible.

Most of his old acquaintances took those in their stride. They were familiar with his ways, not all though.

At least one of them for sure wrote the address on the envelope, Silchar (24d 50sN, 92d 51s E) that came by the return mail.

The local postman was confused. He wanted to know why the highest temperature and the lowest temperature of the town were included in the postal address (the national news telecast carried the highest and lowest temperature of the towns and for him, the degrees meant temperature).

Baba explained to him, the latitudes and longitudes so much so that, the poor fellow got more confused.

The fellow got wary of Baba from that day on. He would make sure while delivering the mail, that Baba was not around; almost tiptoed in and out of the house, least another round of degrees and minutes came his way.

Fair enough, the old man was his usual self. If he was not *the* centre of the universe, he lived *there* for sure.

Gautam began his stay in the city nearly four decades after his father had left, at the height of the freedom struggle. The world had changed in a big way. The second city of the erstwhile empire had changed.

For Gautam, the hustle-bustle of the city seemed strange. Everyone appeared to be in a hurry. Of seeking as much as they could for themselves, of career, of attending chores for themselves and their family. Hardly was there any time for anyone to think for others.

It was an altogether different world. Where everyone seemed to be in touch with international happenings.

The preparations of the Olympics to be held at Los Angels in a couple of years' time interested them, like the speculation if the Soviet bloc would boycott the same. The World Cup

Soccer was on view. How Paolo Rossi netted the winners for Italy. How and why the artistic Brazilians failed.

How U.S.A. under the strongman viewed Asia and India.

There were events within the country that were the topics for discussion.

It was the year 1982. For the first time in the history of the world, a communist government that had been in power was returned. Five years of governance by the communists in Bengal had seen some changes though. More importantly, people had voted them back to power.

Quite an achievement! India had once again led the world in setting examples! Communists suddenly were tuning the torchbearers of democratic values. The communists, (especially the Bengali variety) were going gaga over it.

The communists who throughout the world believed in people's power tried to woo the common man to gain their votes. Great turnaround for the believers of the utopia! Great metamorphosis for the believers of the strong-arm of the state!

Like so many other faiths before it, communism had been Indianised.

The *Indianisation* of the Great Utopia had taken place, in the Great land!

The communists came in generations. The initiation to the ideology took place while they were infants. For someone born in family of a communist had to be a communist. Like someone born in the family of a Hindu, or a Christian or a Muslim. No special baptism was ever required.

The ideals of revolution, dialectics, proletariats, were their possessions.

Gautam had a mate at the college—Ranjan, who was the youngest son of a communist "revolutionary". His father was a refugee from the eastern part of Bengal that had been separated during partition. The man was from a family of landlords. He had taken to the ideology by choice, very early in life. The man had struggled to spread the *gospel* in the land. To remove him from the "surroundings" he was sent to London for higher education. He however came back with a degree in law and more convinced of the doctrine. During the last days of the British Raj—the man was in frenzy. In his youth under the direction of the party, he supported the vivisection of the country and the creation of Pakistan as the exercise of the right of self-determination of the minorities. Yet, when the nation was born—the nation of his choice and the land partitioned; he chose to come to that side—the majority side and not remain on the other side. Surprisingly, he chose to abandon the land, the cause for whose separate nationhood he had championed.

That he belonged to a family of landlords, who were prudent enough to own real estates on both sides of the divide, saved him from a life of despair and perpetual gloom that had become the integral part of lives of his fellow refugees. With not much to care for a living and livelihood, as family fortunes were enough to take care, he jumped headlong into the works of the *party*.

Like as in so many other revolutions, the leaders of the proletariats came from aristocracy in the land, as well. The party in any communist set-up was stronger than the government (the difference however remained in India, a democratic set-up; the difference altogether vanished in true People's Republics).

The youngest son of the revolutionary leader, Ranjan was the "big brother" at the college. He decided on matters of running the college right from the day he joined. He had the right pedigree, right from the process of admission to the allotment of accommodation, his recommendation was invaluable.

He was a potential leader in the making. Academics was not his priority anyway, revolution and concern at all levels of administration and the party, (the meetings were quite frequent) his participation was necessary. He held his own *durbar* to decide on party's actions, which often meant marginalising "political opponents"; violence if required was resorted to. (It was justified for greater cause). A glorious future awaited him, most of his mates thought so, in the governance of the nation someday or at least in the party hierarchy not very far off.

For the less fortunate, the academics were the only way to future, to eke out livelihood, hopefully as engineers. For them, Ranjan was one amongst a select few. He was already on a pedestal.

The communists in India in general and more so in Bengal, the Bengali variety were a class apart. The call of the revolution, which they called "Biplob" in Bengali, ended over their teacups, the cooler their tea became, the milder became their call for revolution. The vision of changing their land vanished with the smoke rings of the cheapest cigarettes (they were too cultured to smoke *bidis*) often off a single stick that nearly half a dozen revolutionaries shared.

Everything the communists did had to be scientific. The socialism was scientific. The returns of the power were scientific—the share of spoils of power.

The party was as strong as the government; in other parts of the world ruled by the communists, the party *was* the government. Since the government was the largest investor, the largest employer, the returns were also the largest. Those were scientifically shared. They had the great and inherent strength to stage-manage everything.

For the first time in India, strikes, agitation, *bandhs* and *hartals* were organized which were state-sponsored, leading to huge losses to the nation: all for "greater cause".

Suddenly, rank opportunists, capitalists were talking of the leftist ideals, while they carried on with their preferred jobs, all the same. Scientific realisation downed on the Bengali society. With the progressive elements in power, the "Bengali Renaissance" was very much on the cards, for the first time in free India.

Away from the great happenings of epochal significance, life in the remotest corner of the country went on as usual. Separated by nearly a thousand miles was someone, in the obscure part of the land trying to find the date month of the existence, for each day seemed to be the same.

Truly, *India lived in many centuries, at the same time.*

Seated in the confines of her school in the remotest corner of the country, where the torrential rain fell for most part of the year, when the cold waves gripped her, in the dimly lit chapel when the classes were over, she longed for someone.

The one who was almost lost in the shine of the metropolis, in the brilliance of all what he saw, in the glow and glitter of the city-life where no one belonged to anyone and everyone seemed glued to own petty existence.

Where the snobs took delight in the erosion of values,

Where the moderns called their brethren from remotest corner of the land, Gaelic.

He felt and longed for her warmth, her tenderness, and her affection. Separation had indeed made the bond stronger.

The cloud-messenger was then nowhere to be seen when the need was extreme, when he felt they were again the victims of age-old ploy of destiny to pull them apart.

The meghdotam was absent.

Only the Post-Dootam was the recourse left. If the cherished one, the cloud messenger was absent, the other one the Indian postal department was certainly alive and kicking.

Any meeting between them was out of question. For her it was beyond any reasonable rationale to leave her place for any period, leave aside her duties. For him the academics were the top priority. If and when he had to assert his independence—both financial and social, to harbour any dreams of any kind of union, it had to be through academics that could place him in a good position.

She too was dreaming. Dreaming the same way! Where and when? When would her fate lead her? When would the Lord grant her the wish she had always prayed for, the union with the one she loved? She had immense faith in the Lord. She knew the union would occur someday, only the time and place was the discretion of the Lord.

For the Lord she knew, had great respect for family life. The family was a great institution in the Jewish home where the Lord was brought up. Family to the Lord was as important as the great kingdom.

A poet of self-satisfying desire, a poet for satisfying her, for poetry could reveal thoughts and feelings, which prose, could not; in rhythm, the impact seemed more and more lasting.

Moreover, his prose contained narratives, which she could hardly identify herself with. He tried once or twice and the response was not very encouraging. The matters of heart seemed to be more in tune with her, than the matters of mind.

The changes and the variations of prose of someone, young in the city-life were difficult for her to absorb. She had not had the influence of the *visual impact.*

So, Gautam continued to 'pour' his heart out, in his poems.

And she liked those, she desired. She wanted him to write to her, she said those were priceless.

She wanted him to write and she wrote, "reading your poems hundreds of times over and over, again and again never wears them down. Had those been narratives, those might have withered away." (In any case she had to read that trash hundreds of times and that was her only solace, he felt.)

Great revelation indeed!

So, he wrote and sent those to her. Some of those he collected from the pages of his near-torn notebook of his romantic days, which he had not shown to anyone. He rearranged those, added new feelings to infuse fresh lease of life in them as he sat, dreaming of her; jotting down the feelings.

In this alien land, I see the star-lit sky.
How I despise the loneliness,
Can I ever accept this gift? Bright gift of nature!
Can I ever enjoy the vision? Without you?
The anguish I find rise in my heart,
Alone as I stand here; ruminating
The blissful moments spent.
Are you awake there to share the feelings?

While I am here alone?
Pangs of separation haunt me
Every moment spent here seems wasted.
I get lost in your thoughts. Do I shed tears in solitude?
Essence of which I had known for long but experiencing now.
When you are not near why don't you leave something?
Maybe your attire, for in the desolate moments of loneliness,
Could provide the required fragrance of your presence.
My life has is very akin to the trees that shed their leaves.
Very ones that comforted people, now beg for sympathy and compassion;
In the dampening cold and frost of the season people call winter.
All that was bright and colourful, has gone.
The very continuance of glee and delight
What people called spring. It is but winter now, cold and gloomy.

The letters Gautam sent were in coloured envelopes—long and broad, with bright shades and hues all over, with even brighter message inside depicting the state of his mind and heart.

The replies he got were in the standard envelopes of the size as available at all the post-offices across the country.

There she wrote of her duties at the school she worked in. Teaching children the language, the grammar, the rudiments of arithmetic, and of course of her social service at the village. She engaged herself in that service to overcome her loneliness, for she had a perpetual void in her heart, in her mind, in her day-to-day life, in her existence. His poems she wrote were her treasured possessions, which she had kept in absolute order, in chronological order as she received the letters. Those she wrote, were her *only* possessions with worth that was invaluable (any way no tangible value could have been attached to all the rubbish he wrote).

Those declarations made Gautam write even more. Even longer poems, monotonous, repetitive ones for her; her *had to* write for her, rather than for himself. The adulation he received, that he flattered to deceive—he was made to feel as if he were a skinny version of Keats, or Wordsworth or Shelly or Coleridge or all of them put together, were fabulous.

He *had to* write for her.

She wrote, telling him in her own inimitable way of *God's* will, rather *invoke* the name for some special reasons, for she was though strongly a believer in God's will, a woman after all.

She cautioned Gautam in her own way, of the *glare* of the metropolis, of the *distractions* that might come his way, like women all over she would prefer understatements and euphemisms to plain statements.

She was afraid, fearful as any other women of the siege or the state of it that was within and not without. The state of concern, the perpetual concern and fear of *losing* him!

She was afraid, she could lose him to someone else in the glare of the metropolis. The distractions was the term she preferred and the likes of which she warned him, of. Those *encounters* she feared could come his way.

The more he read her letters, the more serious he became. The words, the sentences, the syllables, the phrases, all in understatements and coated in euphemism, were all directed towards that catastrophe, arising out of the innate fear, the fear of losing someone—the protector, the benefactor.

Or else why did she make all those projectionist overtures, the latent meaning in her undertones were so potent, though oblique in reference to morals, strictures, cautions against laxity, vices and the likes.

The feel of insecurity, the siege was very evident.

Or did she get the inkling of something different? He *knew* about women and the sixth sense. Was she then cautioning him on his acts, the transgression of morality, which in fact he did indulge in? Could she see what he was *doing*? Or did she know what was he going through?

The glare of the city had definitely caught up with him. As in any other professional college in the country, the place was the meeting ground of people from nearly all parts of the country. The students coming from those different parts resembled virtually the ones from different nationalities except for their writing "INDIAN" in the nationality column of the admission forms.

The dress, the culture, the food habits, even prejudices of different communities, religious and ethnic groups were as different as if they were nationalities apart. The talk of national integration was very often stressed to press the fact that the process was still on.

Amidst the entire conflicting proposition was the bright feature that they were all young. Young and vibrant, the young men and women came from different social strata and economic background. Some lived the life of opulence while others—the majority had a lifestyle markedly different.

The one common feature though was the urge, the eagerness to get close to females, to "IMPRESS" the few who were the fellow students. There were quite a few in the class and a sizeable number of females in whole of the college. They provided the outlet for what the males called "Relieving the sensation". Some of the colourful lot, young and beautiful in jeans and tops revealing shapely curves were the *prima donnas*. There were lots of sighs when they walked past. They carried with them the air of "not-so caring" attitude. Even those who were less charming had that attitude. They were aware that they received more than their fair share of attention and publicity.

The handsome, athletic, boys with enough money, time energy and attention to spare, vied with each other to rope in the females, the prettiest of the lot.

Then there were guys, those who let their energetic, smart and handsome mates the go and settled for the *next best*. Those who looked sedate, serious and reserved amongst the females were the ones they hoped to "impress upon".

The gifts were exchange amongst the pairs. The *gifts* of love had their own role to play in *cementing ties* of heart. Some of the guys, who tried to impress upon their ladies, discovered innovative ways.

In Amul chocolates they found the desired message; the words *gifts for someone you love* written on the cover became their perfect message of heart.

As was said "Media is the message", they believed in the infallibility of the dictum.

Those in some cases led to serious *heartburns* and *heartbreaks*. When and if the lady simply unwrapped the packet, helped herself to the chocolates, discarded the cover that carried the message, it signalled the end of the day for the venturesome males.

While the males—enterprising, young, innovative, discovered new ways of wooing females, not all of them were so lucky. The lopsided ratio of the distribution, the uneven distribution of the sex ratio in the college didn't allow that.

Those were the guys who booed, jeered, and made catcalls.

For the whole lot of young men, getting out of their teens into the shoes of manhood, life seemed indeed pleasing. The protective environment of homes and families no longer to inhibit their activities, they felt free to do what their hearts desired.

The first celebration of freedom was by taking to drinks. Nearly all of them took fancy for liquor, which became the passport to manhood—emerging in full form and spirit. The middle-class prejudices shed; they tasted the elixir of life.

The life had indeed begun.

Along-with the taste of liquor came the desire for exploring other "horizons" that needed to be treaded upon. For lot many, barring a few, that had remained a mystery. Titillating, inciting, provoking the passions. To them, the select few who had for even once tasted "blood" were the new *avtaars*.

The second phase of the celebration, therefore, began by visits to the brothels. In the great land, sex had been a taboo, especially in the middle-class families where even the discussions were considered blasphemous.

So those, mostly the young man who had almost no meaningful encounters with the "unknown mysteries" that life had to offer, choose the easiest way—paid sex.

Paid sex was therefore the only way left! The porn films were the tutors.

And the young men took their time, to arrange and rearrange their emotional, mental and moral values to take the plunge. The taste of the illicit, the illegal the mysterious excitement had its own appeal. The young men coming out of their teens knew it. They enjoyed it. Those who had experienced such encounters earlier shared their secrets! That infused growing excitement in those who contemplated following suit but could not muster enough courage to do the same.

Gautam too was in the grip of such provocation. The loyalty, the fidelity on one hand weighed upon him. The call of the urges was on the other hand even more arresting.

Finally, he decided to explore the mystery. The excitement of passion got the better of him.

The evening—the fateful evening, he could not forget.

In the dimly lit lanes that smelt of something sinister, the smell of strong country liquors all pervading, the men strolling in and out of the *kothas,* the rows and rows of dingy rooms, each of which had a number of girls, women in *choli-ghagra* with bare midriffs and laughter and swears, all the foul words possible being mouthed, he landed in a perfectly alien territory!

Before he could even grasp for breath, he was whisked in. Before he could even know and recover himself, he was done in; losing his entire pampered male ego, along with his cash, in a flash.

He had heard of rapes being committed, he read in newspapers and in the news bulletin and knew it was the males who committed them. The Hindi movies provided the stereotyped rape scenes. Though he had sympathy for the victims and hatred for the perpetrators. Deep down inside he had a belief that it was the males only who could do that and it were some kinds of a rule that *only* the males, who had the ability to do so.

That night after, he realised that it was possible the other way round, as well. The experience was more of a nightmare than being an enjoyment. The episode had shaken his *manhood* and all his prejudicial notions about male superiority came crashing down.

That was the *real* nightmare. That he could not forget about. The very live encounter with the erosion of his male ego. The rosy picture he had imagined of the experience before he made the plunge was destroyed. The feel of the exclusive right of males in the very last domain of existence on earth which he had so believed till then, evaporated with that shocking experience.

Revelations never ceased to dawn in his life.

Each one of them came at juncture, which had *lasting impact.*

The episodic events in his life seemed unending. The mini catastrophe he encountered caused a lasting impact upon him. Was he a man or a machine he wondered? That such a violent and wrecking event could befall a *man* he hadn't thought of. His personality took a beating and he found a certain change of ideals and buildup of his personality that appeared different from what he was till that event.

In that period of solitude and loneliness when he was only with himself, he remembered her. Were the golden moments spent with her the eternal elixir he thought? Those incredible times, the mere thought and reminiscences, seemed to have a calming effect. The contrasting experiences churned the hell out of him and he longed more for her. The soothing calmness that the mere thought of her brought about provided the perfect antidote to the calamitous episode.

Was Mary then aware of what he was doing? Or else how could she write in veiled terms of the distractions? Why then did she ask him to restrain himself? How and when did she then acquire that sixth sense to perfection?

The secrets, which in no way he could reveal! Not to anyone! How could she than anticipate those? It seemed from her letters that those were vivid and clear to her. He was surprised beyond any reasonable doubt that she had acquired the ability to see what he was doing.

He wondered.

But he hated the sermons. Her sermons!

The sermons, it seemed, had become an ingrained portion, an integral part of his life. From his boyhood to adolescence to teenage, and then to the *initiation* into manhood, the sermons were there for him.

And he had to take sermons from least of all people, Mary! He felt his personality had eroded. If he didn't *take care* then, he knew he might end up losing his *existence*.

Sermons appeared to have become the curse of his life.

In anguish he chose to write to her. His emotions vacillated between the extremes of anguish and anger. He decided to pen the longest poem he had ever written.

He checked if anyone had ever written any poem as long as he had, to any one's fiancé. He verified if anyone had ever written any such poem from any college in the country. At least he was Sure of the fact and satisfied himself that his was the longest poem ever written to anyone's fiancée from any Engineering college, in the whole of the nation.

That made him happy with a sense of satisfaction. The sense of achievement of at least having done something *worthwhile*, having poured his heart, his mind, his emotions into it was flattering.

He wrote, first in anguish, then in solitude, then in remembrance and then in plain passion. At the end of it he was a satisfied man.

My letter I think, was of the dreams of love, in life,
The desires I had spoken of,
Unfortunate I am your letter has crushed them.
What ideas were those?
That had troubled you, I know not,
Or why on earth should my feelings
Meet such a fate? Your ruthlessness
Aspersions cast on love?
Desire persists of enchanting love
Hope, expectation, reciprocation, confidence, belief and trust,
I crave for,hope, it comes,by morning tomorrow.

Life-sojourn so difficult, debilitating solitude, destroying loneliness;
Life has become loveless. Send the fragrance, then
For you leave behind only memoires.
Let no distance be such not traversed by life.
Let no memoirs be such, not escaping the bounds of heart.
You come in my thoughts drawn by my longings?
Else, what remains then of my life?
The fragrance you bring along
Are but my reminiscences.
Let the fondling be so delicate
To appears as though of your own-self.
I have kept, your remembrances safe.
Fully assured shall I be If I know, I hear
The sighs and yearnings in your heart, too.
Let no one shatter the dreamy ambience.
The lips are sealed though my heart dances to the tunes
Of your beckoning difficult it is to pronounce
The feel of pressing environs, time for 'love-making'.
Why then, do you test my patience?
For if I commit any mistake, could you ever forgive me?

He left the poem untitled, as he always did. She didn't want the poem *meant* for her to *titled by* him. She wanted to name the treasure all by herself. And he agreed to it as it saved a lot of time and energy.

The writing over, he sent the same and felt relieved. He had nothing to write more. He had poured his heart, his mind, his emotions and his desires there in. He was happy.

The time for niceties was over anyway. The nation it seemed was in the grip of frenzied violence in the northern part.

Life after all was not all poetry!

The only relief was the Olympics of 1984, where the petite Romanians lost to the mechanical smile of a girl for the title of the best overall woman gymnast. The 'radical' students—those with leftist leanings, called it another of the imperialist designs. Those were the guys who condemned the *imperialists,* but went to those countries for employment and education and for settlement. For the rest of the young man, all the women gymnasts looked beautiful and that mattered.

In Bengal, the communists and their variety of Bengali communism took string roots. The parameters were re-defined, the contexts and even the contents were modified to suit their ends.

For quite some time, there had been violence in the northern state of Punjab. People being killed—mostly innocent ones, unwary travellers, people who had nothing to do with politics, in bomb blasts at market places, offices, buses and trains. People being pulled out of buses, lined up and then shot point blank because they believed in a particular faith, surprisingly in the name of religion of the ultras.

People had not learnt from catastrophes in the land.

Then came the calamitous event, when the seat of the religion was cleared off the ultras by the army that had far-reaching and perilous consequences for the nation.

There were several protests by people who felt offended. The politicians took sides as usual, trying to benefit from the human miseries.

Then came the national disaster, when the leader of the nation was gunned by the security guards.

What followed was absolute hell. The tragedy of the late forties being repeated on the streets, in small measures though.

Only this time there was no British to lay the blame on. No excuse was possible.

Men pulled out from trucks, young man stoned to death, young and old—mostly males, who were beaten up, torched. While those who started the carnage clapped and whistled. It was devil's dance on the streets. Their crime—the victims belonged to the same faith as of those who killed the leader.

While Gautam was a witness to the national events, as a student in the city, where people kept themselves abreast of all national and international happenings, far up the hilly terrain and the mountainous tracts, someone passed her days, in abject isolation.

In the devastation, the carnage, and the butchery—the more he saw, the more he felt for the solitary isolation of hers. They too, the two of them belonged to the two different faiths. Beliefs hadn't come in their way of love.

Or were they too young and immature to understand the difference? Was therefore their love to get lost? He wondered.

Indeed! The land had strange features!

The great Indian dichotomy was evident. Talks of lofty ideals and not living up to that. Staunch believers of what the great religions stood for and doing exactly the opposite of what the teaching said, all again in the name of religions.

With such events—the macabre and ghastly, around, one was sure to feel absolutely lost. Gautam felt the same way. The pangs of separation, the yearnings, the longings for the loved one suddenly grew, strongest. That was when he found it difficult to be at peace with himself. The urge to be in physical proximity with the loved one grew stronger more than ever before.

He was coming to her, he wrote. He was dying to be with her, to be in her proximity. She replied in her usual restrained way, that she was eager too.

The best time she said was during the vacation that she had—during Christmas holidays when he too might have his, she added. For him though holidays or no holidays, the separation was unbearable. He could bunk his classes in addition to the few holidays he had. He *had* to be with her.

Nearly more than after two years since they had last met, when the world was so different, when the air seemed altogether different, he set out to meet her.

In the tracts of forest, he setout, the hilly terrain, where she would be waiting for him with expectation in her eyes, tenderness in her heart;

In the name of love.

By the grace of the Lord!

CHAPTER 12

Catastrophe Befalls

Gautam to the hills again. Though not among the conifers, but to the forests. Through the rugged terrain, the hilly tracts, through the monsoon forest, up in the hills to her.

She had come to pick him up at the bus stop, where the only bus that pulled along somehow, the only bus that made a couple of trips during the day from the nearest town; stopped.

The bus stopped near the chapel, in the village. The chapel had a cross atop, though not of the same dimension as one Gautam was familiar with. The cross visible through the mist, through the fog, atop the chapel—just visible as if hanging in mid-air supported by nothing else, but *divinity* alone.

The old man, the caretaker at the chapel, who took care of the guestroom and the compound as well, looked with suspicion in his eyes at Gautam. The features Gautam had—it was quite clear that he was a plainsman, one from the plains; was sure to raise such feelings. Whether he was a believer in the lord, was the moot point. The question to be asked, to be queried about.

When they met at the bus stop after more than two years, she was almost on the verge of tears. The moment the mist and the fog cleared, she saw him, Gautam, standing in front of her; she broke into pleasant sobs. Gautam fared no better. For him it was like locating his fairy queen—long lost in the forests, among the clouds, in the fog, in thin air.

They wanted to embrace each other, hug each other, and hold each other in arms as tight as they could, but there were people around. Any public display of such emotions and that too between a plainsman and a tribal girl, a Christian and a seemingly non-believer (for he had no metal cross in chain around his neck), near a church school—between teacher and an outsider, was to invite trouble. Besides, none was sure if the other would have liked it. Each one was unsure of the other. Each had to find out the changes in the other. For that moment they choose to keep their feelings to themselves, strictly.

To him, she seemed to have grown more nun-like, the months of isolation appeared to have made her closer to God, and *removed* from humans, from human feelings; cold, mysterious, and recluse as much as the misty cold air. The strange ambience added more to the portrayal.

She appeared to have grown taller or so it seemed, and had definitely thinned down. He thought that it could have been both; or that having thinned down, made her look a bit taller. The cheekbones, the eyes, the raised nose she had unlike her other Mongoloid features and the dimple on the right cheek appeared the same, exactly the same. Only her eyes were no longer bright; with dark shades were visible beneath her eyes. And surprisingly, the dimple on the right cheek with the black mole at the centre for some strange reason, looked not at all charming. The dimple that used to deepen when she smiled earlier looked flatter. He was surprised.

He had grown fat though. With his dark beards, short hair and flab in his body around the middle, he had become a man—she told him.

"I would get all right, here," he said, "in your presence. I am sure to thin down, as the city varieties of food won't be available here. Moreover, the foreign liquor won't be available either.

You know I cannot take country liquor. But I can assure you, you are sure to gain weight because you won't feel lonely any more."

Mary listened at him with a bit of astonishment in her eyes.

"The city has changed you, Gautam", she said, "You talk the language of the city-people."

"That's what I am now. But the love for you still burns in my mind and in my heart, dear," he answered.

"Really?" she said, "I don't believe it". She was in fact happy to hear that. That was clear from the smile that appeared on her lips.

"If you don't believe, feel here," he pulled her hand and placed it on his chest.

"Don't you feel the beats? Those are for you," he said.

That comforted her. Those words, sentences, she had read in his letters, in every letter hundreds of time, and yet when those came off his lips she felt reassured.

"Do you think I have come all the way to trek the hills?" he said.

She smiled. She knew. Understood.

"I have come for something more. I have come for you, Mary," He went on, "As a matter of fact I shall be getting my degree and moving out of the college within a couple of years. Till then you have to bear with me. Till then, please keep in good shape. The moment I land a job, I am not going to wait any longer. Come what may, we are going to be man and wife."

Gautam repeated the words he had rehearsed for long. The tone and tenor of his voice appeared very similar to the ones he heard in the movies, in the city. He found his manhood in full force as he said that, as if he were some kind of a saviour.

She listened to him with her eyes widened, a little. As if trying to fathom the depths. It was a declaration of some kind from him, which she had been waiting to hear.

With smiles, blushes, she responded. The radiance and the warmth emanating—all the visible signs of "Mary of the earlier days" coming back.

She ran in, to the dimly lit altar to kneel before the lord, pray and thank him for all that had happened.

The Lord after all had not disappointed her. Her prayers had been answered.

They decided to spend their holidays together. They planned to visit the place, not very far, which was a place of tourist attraction. The archaeological exploration had discovered the site of a medieval kingdom—the ruins of which lay scattered, around.

That would be the last time would be together, before he returned to the city for his academics and she to her school, her work place.

The plans for future had been drawn—the outlines. The rest, the details they hoped to do while they were together, with no one to poke and interfere into the couple's affairs amongst the ruins of the city—kingdom they had set out to visit, during their stay.

There were a few tourist lodges to accommodate the visitors at the place called Malinithan.

They reached the place in the evening and checked in at the tourist lodge, sure enough separate rooms for each one of them on different floors of the building.

The tourism department, ran the lodge. The facilities were not much provided for as it happened in most of the government run organisations, in spite of the buildings and other structures.

The hospitality business in the country was also government controlled!

The next day, they actually visited the site. The location was exquisite.

The ruins of a palace, the statues of human figures probably kings and queens, the statues of Hindu Gods and Goddesses, all lay scattered.

For her, the experience was new and exciting.

For him, it was refreshingly more earthy, away from the hustle and bustle of the city where he had so far lived, spent his days and time at the college pursuing academics for a "professional career".

With the stone sculptures, depictions on stone of the great epics of the likes of Ramayana and Mahabharata, for they were the only epics known to the people then curved on stone lay there; the place appeared gravely solemn. The authorities had tried to preserve the ruins from further ruination, to resurrect the long-forgotten episodes. The works of art of the people who lived through the depictions, adding their own touch to the saga told and retold over centuries, the serene exhibition of their art form and imaginative faculties were sought to be preserved.

The people who lived, at least half a millennium ago had tried to live through their imaginations.

The young pair tried to dream through the ruins, of life, of the cherished life in future, together.

All forms and figures were on display, the stone carvings, the arches, the pillars, and the images that showed detailed workmanship of high order.

Then, there were the figures with the depiction of erotic forms, the *mithuna* figures, of males and females in deep embrace, in passion, of lovely lips and swivelling hips, caressing the breasts and fondling body parts. Those depictions of human existence, the fruition of desires, the process of continuance of life through ages, of procreation and preservation of human life; were all protected.

Mary blushed at the sight of the stone-carved figures. She just didn't want to look at those figures that she found not to her taste, the transgression of moral values that she could not allow. She egged Gautam to move away.

"How violent!" she glanced at them and turned her face away. "How could anyone depict such intensely private and undesirable postures for public display?" she could not restrain herself.

"Private, yes. But undesirable! No!" Gautam replied, "For the present just look at them as works of art."

"Nonsense," Mary retorted, "For union, one needs to invoke the divinity within".

"Just don't try to harp your version of divinity on everyone, Mary," Gautam snubbed her. "These depictions are the greatest truths of life. That's what men and women have been doing over the centuries, over the millennia."

Yet Mary kept her eyes shut, her head and face away from the erotic figures. All the prostration of him that those depictions added serenity and acceptance of the truth of life fell on deaf ears. She was stubborn. The decadence seemed unpardonable, even an innocuous glance appeared to be a moral transgression, the laxity of which could not be allowed.

"Vulgar and shoddy," she told him with her eyes shut.

"Let's forget all these," Gautam drew her aside and spoke in her ears.

"Let's talk of the present. I must say you look splendid."

That eased her up. "Oh really?" She said. "I never thought so," she sounded her innocent self.

"Oh yes. Certainly yes," He said, "In your white shirt and green *glaaley* you appear so beautiful that I don't know what to say." He remarked all the while, looking at her rounded bottom that shaped up in passionate curves, biting his lower lips and pressing his eye-balls and squeezing his eyes.

"Let us move from here," Mary said, "You don't sound too convincing. Let us not stay here for a moment, any longer."

She pulled Gautam by his arms and moved away.

"Restraint. What you need to learn is restraint, Gautam," she said.

"I am tired of puritans like you. Sick of upholders of morality like you. You could better be a nun. Why don't you go and join the order?" He blurted.

"I would have joined the order anyway, but you came along and robbed me of my earnest desire," she smiled again.

"Well, since that didn't happen, it is not going to happen anymore." He said with confidence. "Now for the atonement of laxity of moral values, I must do something." He said as they walked through the ruins.

He knelt in the ruins, amidst stone-carvings, in front of a worm-out, half broken stone image of the Hindu God, Lord Shiva, in his war dance—the *tandava* (that was the one nearest where they stood), held her hand softly and said in a perfect voice.

"I, Gautam take thee, Mary to my wedded wife, to have and to hold from this day forward, for better or for worse for richer or poorer, in sickness and in health, to love and to cherish, till death us do part, according to God's holy ordinance; and there to I plight my troth."

Mary laughed. Roared in laughter.

"Don't be impatient, sir," she said as she laughed.

Gautam put his hand on her mouth trying to keep her mouth shut. "With this Ring I thee wed, with my body I thee worship, and with all my worldly goods I thee endow." For Gautam rehearsed lines came very handy.

He picked up, a long blade of grass and rounded it in the form of a ring and tried to put that onto her finger.

"Not here, not now," she said, "You are irrepressible, Gautam. I want this to be done not in front of the stone carvings, that too of the God-destroyer, but in front of the people. Not mere the blade of grass but the actual ring." She withdrew her hand. "Do you get me, Sir?" she smiled.

Gautam looked sheepish. "Well than, where is my gift?" he asked. He attempted to peck her cheek.

She brushed him aside. "You don't seem to be in the right temperament. Let us move away from here," she said.

As they parted company to spend the evening and the night, Gautam suddenly caught hold of her. He caught her by the arm, bent her arms behind so that she could not free herself, bent her body, pushed her and kissed on her lips, almost biting the one that he had longed for years.

Both were flushing red. She from the impact of the shock and embarrassment and he, from the burst of passion that seemed to grow with each moment that passed.

The sudden shock over, she recovered from the act she least expected and said, "Why don't you restrain yourself? When the time comes, you shall have your due."

Before she left, she told him, "We are meeting tomorrow here for the last time before we part ways. Our plans have not as yet been chalked out. Tomorrow, we must do it. Only I wish and hope better conduct from you." She left in a hurry, not even saying good-bye, leaving him there.

Gautam didn't care to listen. He was already hot. Red hot with fumes coming off his ears, his body; he was uncontrollable. The more he thought. The more he wanted.

"Bloody puritan," he said as she moved out of sight, "I am not going to leave you."

He felt his manhood coming alive. Not the sentimental talks, nor innocent pecks, no more mere holding of hands that had been the case for years. He was coming to terms with his newfound independence, on the would-be-acquired assertiveness that lay in penchant for his manhood. Come what may, he thought, it had to be at any cost; no premium was too high for that.

He was mad with desire. The kiss on her lips, the touch of her breasts was enough to make him a bull—the snorts he could hear. He thought of her, and more than ever before, he felt he was getting hotter.

The next day as they went, she didn't speak very much, other than what was required, mostly in syllables. Though he tried to ease things up, she didn't give herself. She kept an *honourable* distance from him.

Thrice he tried to draw her close, by the hand towards him, taking her hand and placing it on his chest. She calmly withdrew each time. It was clear she was not going to allow him any more liberties. That made him angry. And deadly hot as well. She was colder than ever before.

The excursion nearly over, she talked of returning to her home in the village some two hundred miles away the next day, to visit her father. A man who in the best of times wouldn't have remembered her in good taste and her half-sister—a primary school droop out, Martha, in her early teens.

Gautam listened to her in silence. He had to do what he desired and that night was the last night available to him.

Meticulous planning followed by execution of the best possible way had to be undertaken.

"I have something to tell you, it's very important," he told her, "I want to finish the same tonight. Tomorrow I shall have to leave as well. Before we part, we must draw up our plans for future."

To those words she looked at him. "All right," she said, "Well then, I shall call you in the evening," Gautam said.

Gautam was determined to go ahead. He was all fired up. That had to happen in the evening.

To make matters easy, he went to the nearby village that was near the place, in the neighbourhood, for country liquor was available there in plenty. Despite its nauseating small and intimidating taste, he somehow gulped down the country liquor made of putrid rice—the concentrated juice of what was called the roxy.

The liquor was so strong, he felt like vomiting it at once. But his manhood *was at stake*. He could not do so. Then gradually, bit-by-bit he got the kick—hotter than ever before, he became, to do what he wanted. The more he thought of her, the more excited he became.

Full of smell, his legs unsteady, his steps staggering, he showed up at her place. She opened the door, expecting him and would have slammed the door on his face had he not pushed her in. She tried to stop him, reason with him, but to no avail. He closed the door.

He caught hold of her and threw her on the bed jumped on top her. She called him a betrayer, a defiler, a *Satan* defiling virginity. That angered him even more. She tried to raise an alarm but he closed her mouth. Her cries, imploring had no effect whatsoever. He was hell bent on doing what he had *always* wanted to do.

She was a very simple girl in the service of the Lord and the Lord she knew would grant her the wish, answer her prayers.

The distance then was the only problem, she felt. More than the distance, what troubled Mary was the mere *thought* of it, than the actual one.

So, the postal department had to rescue her.

The postal department collected the mail and delivered all through the nation. In the northeastern corner of the country the communication, the transportation, the terrain, the climate, all played their role in no small measure.

The system was well laid out. In the rugged terrain mishaps were not very uncommon, but those were some due to human failure.

If Mary wrote a letter and sent it through her village post office, it took a couple of months to reach Gautam and when he wrote it took nearly a month to reach her.

But the letters reached and that mattered. But by then, the world had undergone much change and that mattered certainly.

The letters become longer and longer, the postage going up and up. The number of course dwindled. For him, there were other distractions, other avenues for relaxation, and other areas to focus attention apart from the rigours of the academics. He studied at the class and back at the hostel. The examinations were frequent—the semesters seemed so close to each other.

For her, his letters were the only solace, the only balm, and the only comforting feature of an otherwise mundane and dull existence.

Gautam once again imagined himself in the mould of being a poet—a poet of no small or petty volition—an idealist who believed love could be platonic (or rather was compelled to believed that due to the force and impact of her love). He chose to put his feeling into words.

The shirt was gone in a flash. She tried to protect herself by her hands covering her breasts. Then the *gaaley* was gone, torn. She desperately tried to hide herself in the cover of her under garments. When she lost that, she fainted.

Then he did all what he had wanted to do. In that hour, fully dominating his manhood.

The catastrophe had befallen, finally.

Not just once, he was too intoxicated to count the number, but surely more than once. Though he was over-powered by liquor, he still could feel the sensation—as they said, of *'heavenly pleasure'* while the creature on which it was consummated lay withering in pain, motionless, numb, and almost unconscious.

All the while the calendar framed portrait of the Lord moved to and fro over the bed (she had the habit of carrying the portrait everywhere she went, for divine blessings!)

Then as he withdrew, he examined his own chest. It was blood all over. The cross—the metal cross in the chain she was wearing had cut onto his chest, rather shoved in, deep into the skin, and blood was profusely oozing out. The cross too was smeared with the blood, the shiny metal fully covered by the blood.

There was blood on the bed-sheet, blood smeared and dried on the bed.

She was also covered with blood at different portions of her body.

Only he didn't know which was whose. Whether it was his or hers. He was too tired and exhausted to examine.

Leaving her in the state of semi-consciousness, he left her. He somehow managed to stagger back to his room and fell on his bed.

He had fulfilled his desire.

The following day, he woke up or rather was woken up by the *chowkidar* of the lodge. The fellow had thought something otherwise had happened, as Gautam was a sleep past mid-day, in the afternoon.

He then remembered all that had happened—the episode of the evening and the night. Of what he had done to her.

He gathered himself and recovered. The first thing he wanted was to go straight to her, ask her to forgive him and if she desired, the wedding could be arranged even before the holidays were over. In any case, he was to do so after sometime—in a couple of years.

He ran up and to her room. But the space was empty and no one was there. He rushed to the reception counter. The man at the counter was helping himself of country liquor!

"Could you please let me know when Ms Mary Pertin left?" Gautam asked him. The man looked at him with pupils dilated. "Let me see," he said.

He ran his finger through the pages and read, "M-A-R-Y P-E-R-T-I-N, Yes sir, she left very early this morning around 6 a.m." He closed the register and looked at Gautam with expectant eyes.

Gautam handed him a ten rupee note. The man bowed his head and raised his hand in acknowledgement and then dozed off, his head dropping forward.

It was then his turn to be shocked, shell shocked. It was worse than a holocaust. The world seemed to come down on him, come to an end for him. He wanted to bang his head against the walls.

He seemed to be again *on the edge* of a precipice.

He wondered in the ruins. He stood in front of the statue of Lord Shiva, who seemed to be in his war dance—the tandava nrtiya—pose.

The destroyer amidst the ruins!!

The ruins of his life, his spirit, his vision of the world he dreamt of, the world in which he thought he would get the bliss he had searched for, the happy union with the woman he loved and hoped to live with forever; lay there.

For the lovers who had come amidst ruins to start life, to see and *dream* of life, were ruined, the ruins had *overpowered* them.

He picked up his bag and baggage, jumped on to the first bus he could find, then to the chapel at the desolate place where she worked. But she hadn't been there. The old caretaker looked at him with suspicion in the eyes and said, "Both of you went out together a few days back. Now you are here asking her whereabouts. Tell me what's wrong?"

Gautam had no answer. He tried to explain the things he didn't know. The explanations which somehow, he managed to put through. He asked the old caretaker, if the man could tell him where her native village was and how to reach there.

"Well, I don't know", The man said, "The only thing I know, it is located somewhere in the higher reaches of the eastern district of the Dibang valley. That's what I know. Nothing more. She never told me anything beyond that. Better you wait here till I come back with more information." He left.

Beyond that Gautam couldn't gather much information. For the first time in so many years he felt marooned. The second *or* third time in his life!

He moved from the place over-come with grief, remorse, not waiting for the old man to return.

He was the perpetrator, the defiler of her chastity, her purity, in the God's eyes. Instead of living up to her expectations, he had trampled them. The curse of his own undoing loomed large over someone he loved so dearly.

He was inconsolable. For the only time in his life in some years, or could have been the second time, he felt like praying.

There were a few places to look for her. She was gone and he didn't know where to. She appeared to have gone to her native village and again he didn't know where it was located. The best he could do was to kneel before the God, imagining him in the tandava dance, or the stone image of Lord Budda—eyes closed in deep meditation, and speak his heart out. The confession.

But was confession enough? It released him from the bite, from the sting of the conscience, but what purpose could it serve? That what was done could not be undone, and that had been done, however hard might he try, he could never undo.

His self-confession seemed to be another way of working out, another example of escaping from troubles to safety. To shun his responsibilities, thrust his deeds and off-load those on the God. It appeared to be another defilement of divinity.

Did she then, he was afraid, commit the unpardonable thing, like drowning herself but that she could not do because she knew swimming and he knew those who could swim, could not get drowned. Or did she take some other recourse, the less painful ones, like the overdose of pills.

He even imagined her face, lying in the coffin, fully attired with her arms over her chest, mourned by the church members, the coffin being lowered into the final resting-place.

He shuddered to think all the frightening scenes and yet, those kept coming to him in appalling visions.

But then he reasoned out she could never have done that. She was a great believer in the gospel. She knew the cowardly, the dastardly acts were never forgiven. So, she could never have ended her life that way. Possibly, she didn't want to meet the defiler, so she might have preferred the anonymity, he thought and that comforted him. She should be all right then, he thought.

She would then surely return to her place or work someday, he reasoned. So he decided to abandon the search that was leading him to nowhere, and returned to the city—where he had to complete the rest of his education, for obtaining the degree.

He was broken at heart, devastated, because of her defilement. Moreover, no atonement, no redemption was possible. More importantly, there were no whereabouts of her. She lived through his feelings, his sighs, his dreams, and his nightmares. Like the snowflakes and the snowfalls that had once engulfed his mind, the ruins too had taken their share of the peril. Of those images—of the Rosa Maycrophylla, the tandava form of the lord, the God-destroyer, the image of Lord Buddha in deep meditation with eyes closed, the virgin mother holding the infant Jesus in her arms; he had all the visions coming to him.

All those whirled at break-neck speed around him; he was drawn in the vortex of the whirlpool of his doings and undoing.

His ideas, his dreams of a happy family life, in union with her, the warmth and happiness, he craved for, what she prayed for with much more strength and devotion, came crushing down.

Never again, he knew he was to be happy ever. His life was so ominously eventful. The first poem in his life was a calamity. It had been the harbinger, the forerunner, of a peril.

The second or rather the second sequence, the second series had culminated into another peril.

He vowed never again to vent his feelings, if he had them; in any verse, in any rhyme or rhythm of any kind, for he knew another round of perilous occurrences could be lurking somewhere, if he ever attempted or choose to do so.

CHAPTER 13

'Professional' in the Making

The rest of the days to be spent at the college, Gautam thought would be absolutely depressing and gloomy. The 'best of the world' was not within him; what was he to search for without? He thought that the period of nearly two years that he was supposed to spend there would be in a morbid state, if not actually in a moribund one.

He had not totally given up hope of receiving any communication from her. He had kept up the hope though, of slight expectation, of a sudden message like miracles that happened in the epics and fairy-tales or as shown in the movies. Every day, for the first few months he lived in the expectation of receiving the desired envelope, a touch, a message; even a plain paper from her. That would have sufficed, that would have put an end to the torture and torment; put to rest the tumultuous upheavals.

Those were however not to be. What he received in return were the odd letters he had started sending, all being redirected. Those put an end to all his hopes—even the faintest ones, which he had kept alive.

Till then, he had harboured hopes, illusions, and mirages, of the sudden appearance of an envelope bearing the seal of the Indian postal department on the postage stamp bearing the "beaming face" of the father of the nation, the smile blurred by the ink and the eyes not visible at all.

The blurred face on the stamp in a way summed up the state of the teachings of the great teacher. The best way to treat him and his memories as had become the order of the day was to pay lip service to his ideals. The annual rituals of the birth and death anniversaries of the Mahatma were performed to perfection. Promises, vows, oaths were taken only to be forgotten later, like the New Year resolutions. People at the top competed with each other in eulogizing him and pat each other on the back for outdoing so.

The great Mahatma survived on postage stamps beaming as ever, and in the form of numerous statues where the birds rested and deposited the droppings from the top. The pitiable state.

The days he spent at the college remained dull till he came in close touch with a fellow called Asif.

The roly-poly Asif was no less an enigma to Gautam. His classmate and a character! When the fellow laughed, his whole body shook. He could make the whole lot laugh with him. When he was off—rarely if ever he was, the spirit of the whole lot could be down.

Asif the man, who came from the plains near the hills, was virtually a portrait presentation of all the varied tastes that were possible.

He could sing and play the sitar; was somewhat of a player, a sportsman belying his roly-poly self, and was a philosopher too.

To his friends, he was a virtuoso. He knew how to play the sitar and played it at night when he felt like playing and often it was left to his friends who had to implore him to stop 'mewing'.

He called himself a vocalist. Often, he sang for endless hours in not too musical notes—*Hindustani* classical music, and had to be often shouted down for bellowing at unearthly hours.

He called himself a jack of all trades and not interested to be the master of any one in particular.

He got on well with the females, particularly well, and was a glib-talker. "Indian females are fond of roly-poly physique. Plump features are what they desire,' he said, "They know, the more rotund a male is, the less chance of their molestation, from the otherwise sex-starved Indian males."

"Moreover, woman are the ones to be pampered, they want to be pampered and flattered. And no one else but a fat man can do it best." He was a living advertisement for obesity.

Quite a character!

Gautam appreciated his discourses, the "philosophic" and otherwise. The philosophic 'pouring' he could deliver with consummate ease and clarity.

Despite his "sermons", he was loved at the class and his absence was felt when he was not around.

What he achieved by his infectious smile and sparkle in the eyes, only a few could.

His philosophy a part, his love of Hindustani classical music impressed Gautam.

To let Asif talk was like letting an avalanche off a cliff, or letting the surge of floodwater.

"I come from a family of singers," he said, "A family of gifted Hindustani classical singers who had been practicing their art for over centuries. Actually, it is from the sedentary postures at performances for hours and hours together you know it, it is a *sadhna,* that the family members got the size-I mean the roly-poly physique. I am the one from that lineage."

Asif was the "storyteller" in full flow. He could effortlessly draw his lineage when situation suited him. He could even draw his lineage to the legendary Tansen who graced the court of Akbar the great, in the sixteenth century. He could describe how one of the descendants of the great musician had travelled east and east, further east to settle and start his own lineage of which

Asif was the humble representative. All very well said. No dates, no chronology, no location, no specifics were ever required or provided for substantiating such worthy lineage.

Gautam learnt from him the history of Indian classical music. Of *Gagghee Khuda Bux, Nathaan Pir Bux*—all the early musicians, the names the found were all similar.

Then the *gharanas*—the system of presenting the style and tradition patronized by the icons in distinctive style and control; the hallmark of Indian way of preserving tradition and content. He counted the number of gharanas and the names: Gwalior, Jaipur, Agra, Aatrauli, all location-specific, jumbled up in the monotonous chronology of events and facts.

He learnt the name of great classical singers of Hindustani music —the unending names of Khans, Alladiya, and Rajab Ali, Abdul Karim, Faiyyaz, all.

Then, as usual, the deification: all myths and legends associated with great musicians. Of raindrops falling from the sky in off—season when it was least expected to fall, while the *Raga Magh Malhar* was sung (by the legends). Stories of elephants freeing themselves from chains when the *Taan Haati Chingar* was sung; also made their appearances.

Those were interesting to hear. But more interesting episode was to learn that while the last *nawab* of Audh which was a princely state in nineteenth century India, was composing and busy singing his *khayal*, the British took over his kingdom. The young *nawab* composed under the pseudonym Akhtar Piya, the love of music had certainly stretched a bit too far. (He found some similarity with another legendary figure that also fiddled while his city burnt).

What influenced Gautam was that over the hundreds of years—the Indian classical music was the meeting ground of all that was sublime in the Indian psyche, the Indian cultural tradition, and the Indian mind. The meeting ground of varied cultural traditions where fusion, diffusion, and effusion had taken place. The growth and propagation of Indian classical music—dynamic, inspirational, symbolized the undercurrent of oneness—the unity in diversity repeated so often but very seldom adhered to.

What Asif did was to infuse, inspire and diffuse the love of Indian classical music in Gautam which till then had been worth no more than the monotonous renderings of the monosyllables. That for good music you have to have "clean heart and clear ears" was the pre-requisite Asif stressed often.

Another interest that he grew was to listen to *ghazals* and *nazmas*—the compositions of love poems of a different structural variety but with a very similar appeal. Asif had considerable expertise in that form as well. When he got any chance, often he sought them at the variety performances at the college or at private gatherings, he read from his own compositions.

Dressed in *choga, achkan*, cap and *sherwani* or *shawl* as the time and season that asked for, with a red rose in the left pocket of his sherwani, Asif usually presented him for such shows.

Despite his roly-poly self, he looked nice; more so when he started his musical tones—the rhythm he said give life and spirit to his ghazal and nazam.

The music he called *mausiqui,* and the musical tone, the *tarrannum*. The *mehfil* seemed a place to reflect upon and introspect. Often, he recited his poems dressed like a perfect *shayar* in a gathering, presenting to the delight of the crowd who actually did not understand much and felt even less. The only thing they knew was to make sounds in chorus and say *wah-wah* in appreciation and encouragement, as was the style and tradition.

While he bowed his head and accepted the acknowledgement, his palm half-folded in gratitude; he reciprocated the gestures from the audience with a *salaam* touching the forehead with half-folded right palm bent upwards, several times.

Quite a character! A treat to watch!

Gautam used to be the sole companion of Asif at such gatherings. His other friends had better engagement to spend their time. Though his musical tones were certainly not very pleasing, yet the compositions (which he claimed were his own) impressed Gautam.

Mostly at such gatherings like all other people sitting in the front rows Gautam too had to swing his head to and fro in a gesture of appreciation. The swings meant understanding and being in communion with the meaning and spirit of the composition. Those he had to do as public display of understanding. He was after all, the sole companion and therefore the friend of a *shayar*. He of course tried to get to the meanings later on.

That habit, which he acquired of swings, stood him in good stead at the concerts where he had to accompany Asif at the nightlong renderings of Hindustani classical music. Such regular swings helped him train his ears and mind to hear those never-ending renderings, which gradually made him a lover of classical music.

In some of the Asif's compositions, Gautam found touch of pathos, of some lost times, remembrances, betrayals, passions and compassion, which he felt, he could identify himself with.

Hoto par nahin , jaam dil par lagayaa hai
Sharab nahin hamna gham ko gale lagayaa hai
Nazar ata hai chehra tera jaam bhi kya cheez hai
Chupayae hai chehra tera maykhana nahin
Yeh to lage hai teri mehfil kushboo aayay

To yaad aayay teri mehfil jaam uthatha hoon
Tu hi tu dikhti hai kya kismat hai
Who hoto se nahin lagti hai
Jaam dil se aap zaroor lagaiyay
Sharab nahin, sakhi ka chehra jo nazar aayay
(I have kept the drink close to my heart
Not to my lips, the sorrows I have embraced
Not the liquor therein, as I look in to the cup,
I see your face and not the wine,
The drink has concealed mysteriously,
Your face in it! Though it is so.
It does not look like a pub,
The ambience here is of your presence
The fragrance reminds me of the same.
As I draw the cup, I find you all over,
I am destined, not to drink but only look at.
Well then, I draw the cup, close to the heart,
Not for the contents, but for your face that I see.)

The reflections went on. Some of Asif's compositions were ordinary and some were touching. One such composition that touched Gautam at the right place at the right time went something like:

Ek bar phir se chandni hone ko aavee
Zindangi ki ek aur sham hone ko aayee
Umr guzari hai hamne yadoon ke sayee mein
Har lamha umeed tha, unke visal mein
Tazurba badta gaya, umr bhadti gayee
Hamereey inteezar ki ghari, nikalti gayey
Eh mauka jab hai, sham-e-zindagi ka
Aab waqt mila hai, fikr-o-sukhan ka;
Kahte rahhgiro se hum, pad le zaror,
Nazrey daley pyar ke zindani, in harfo pe zaroor.

(It is a moonlit night again,
Another evening in life comes through,
The life is spent,
In the realm of reminiscences:
Every moment is spent,
In expectation of her union.
The experiences have grown, as I have grown older
The endless wait still continues.
This very juncture now,
In the evening of life,
I am lift with time unspent,
Time for thought and reflections.
To those who traverse
The path of love, I say
Mark my words; glance at my reflections;
Those 'captives in love'.)

The composition was in Urdu but the "touch" was universal. The rendering in musical tone made it even more sensitive.

How well written, Gautam thought. Those words spoken or rather summed up his saga. The "endless" wait continued... the eternal wait. It could spill over to even further...life, reincarnation, as and what was said in epics, mythologies, movies.

Time, they said was the greatest healer. No drugs, no medicine could heal as well as, the time. From the shocks in the snow to the shocks in the ruins—the balm had to come from the time and it seemed to be so.

Only when the pangs were felt a bit deep, deeper and a sense of dejection, loneliness came over, Gautam would turn himself on to the Indian classical music that provided the much-needed solace, the soothing touches of a different kind that moved him, enlivened him.

The episodic life of his he couldn't fathom. The more he thought of her, the wrong he had committed to the purest of the souls. He felt a deep sense of unforgivable sin, a deep sense of anguish rose and he couldn't bring upon himself to absolve himself of the consequences that could or rather befall her—emotional and mental.

He conjured the vision...of him moving to the chapel to locate her and then she having reposed in him all the best she had in her and the traumatic event that followed. He felt helpless. Absolutely. How could he bring upon himself to do that he couldn't explain to himself. Having been at a receiving end once he had done the nearly the same on her! The only one he loved, adored and eulogized! The sense of guilt was overwhelming.

An ordinary mortal lives by all contradictions and conundrums he surmised.

The much praised "*Piya Bin Nahin Awat Chayen*" by the master, Ustad Abdul Karim Khan, recorded nearly half a century earlier filled his heart with freshness and sublimity, the nasal emphasis enchanting even more.

Gautam became some kind of a connoisseur of Indian classical music. And yet like many of the lovers of Indian classical music, could never understand the difference between ragas and how each one of them differed from the other. He was of course infatuated by the renderings. The

Ragas—the scales that included various patterns in exact sequences in both ascending and descending format that were time—specific, formed the basis of further renderings.

He was very much of an amateur to even spell out the difference between the *gayaki* style of singing, belonging to different schools of music producing very particular musical tradition. Like more than half of the listeners of Indian classical music in the country, he was not much concerned with the finer points. Those were left to the critics and analysts. He allowed the actual music to overwhelm him.

In his love for Hindustani classical music, which he believed, was genuine, he hoped and still hoped that someday she might appear before him in a dreamy ambience, like the one created by the rendering of the ragas like *jhinhoti* and *inddravol.*

With such growing interest and ever-present opportunity to bask in the reflected glory, he hoped to be like someone who could walk into a concert and feel at home with the music, walk into a congregation and talk of literature; walk in to a gathering and read out shayari (poems). Of course, he would take care never to venture on to his own compositions. In fact, he tried to shape himself up as someone who had the attributes, the extracurricular ones to charm into the chatteretti, which he knew could be useful in proving a career in management which he hoped to join upon completion of his degree.

The management career was said to be the career of the future. Everyone seemed to be talking of such careers to be able to place people into positions of authority and power. In addition to the business enterprises that the management experts were supposed to be running, some of them were within the corridors of governance. There were talks that managers of boot-polish making and paint making concerns were supposed to have become the kingmakers and were running the country.

He viewed himself as one such guy who could do so in future. The *polishers* and *painters* became perfect role models for him. Infact not just for him, but for scores of young men and women.

It was however not music everywhere, not even around the college. Not everything in the vicinity was so sombre or serene.

There were comic touches all around. Very interesting characters resided around the campus.

There was one Mr. Mona who ran an air-conditioned restaurant, whose exorbitant prices on the items he charged made the cuisine he prepared taste absolutely bitter. He however offered student concessions on some of his items, which he knew were the choice of the student customers, who kept his restaurant packed at off-time and during off-seasons.

The name of his restaurant written on a huge board with special marking of the air-conditioned attracted more people out of curiosity then out of anything else. When and if at all the condition of the air was ever maintained, nobody knew. He often apologized for the sudden failure of the system to the customers, on very hot summer days when sweating was the common occurrence in the hot, sultry, humid atmosphere. He maintained strict code in his domain not allowing liquor to be served openly, true to the tradition and the law of the land. To his cronies and friends who often were the big-brothers of the college, he provided the facility under a different set of rules. Liquor was the common serve in his private chamber and at his restaurant at night, when the restaurant was supposedly closed, at least for the outsiders.

He provided comic relief in plenty. The best one was often when the fat, plump, bald owner of the restaurant took his time off from running his show. He took delight in coming down from the upper storey of the building and helping himself to *kachauri* at the open-air local shop right by the footpath that sold sweetmeats; such shops sold their products on the footpath itself meant for the pedestrians.

"Mr. owner-of-the-air-conditioned-restaurant," Gautam often teased him, "you are doing a great disservice to yourself and to the fraternity of all great restaurant owners. Someone like you helping himself to kauchauris at the wayside *open-air* shops could be a great news items for local dailies."

The balding man then felt awkward. He knew he could not be oblivious to the fact that he was *the* owner of an *air-conditioned* restaurant, certainly an exalted position.

To do anything below dignity was not desirable.

The stay at the college was nearing the end.

Gautam hoped to qualify as an engineer and then proceed for higher education in management if he got the chance at any leading institute of the country. He could also one day grow and reach the position and status of the polish and paint *makers*.

The stay at the city had opened the world to him. The experiences he gained were unique, thorough and subtle, good and bad. The realizations kept coming to him the more he saw of the world, of make-believe, of snobbery and pretension.

He was fortunate enough to secure admission to a good management institute in another city-another metropolis. Many like him had also opted for such course. Higher education in the land was subsidized.

Asif however was not interested. He wanted to go back to his native state as he said he wanted to return to his *own* land, his *own* place.

There he was supposed to lead the life of a government engineer, chewing nuts and betel leaf till in a couple of years his teeth would shine as black as coal like the variety, peat that was abundant in *his* region.

There he was to become a paymaster, paying each time to politicians of all parties mostly during elections, to those in power and also to those who were not in power as well. No chances were to be taken: no chances with the electorate: no guesswork. All channels were to be kept open and he had to learn to live to the whimsy and caprice of the political masters, for transfer and posting of government officials was an industry.

Government being the largest employer and the largest investor was the *sole* arbitrator of a man's fortune. In any and each provincial government, the fate of government officials was similar, the fortunes of the officials and the politicians were tied, sharing the spoils of power.

It was expected he would be prudent. He had to learn to be able to swim with the tide, allowing the government money to flow back to the individuals-both in governance and not so in governance, to share the spoils. His percentage as pay-off for awarding contracts and supervising the works, calculated to the exact mathematical figure would come through to him. The circuit had to be completed.

If things worked out all very well and it was expected to be so, he was most certainly to marry a girl of his parents' choice. All his love making, the love songs in ghazals and nazms were to be buried and the consummation of the marriage was to take place on the appointed night. He was then to father children bi- and tri-annually while his waistline was to increase, the trousers becoming more and more loose, while her sagging breasts and bare protruding navel were to tell her part of the story.

Gradually he was supposed to grow more and more rotund and balloon like, pot-bellied, his cherubic face developing double chin in roughly double the time he spent at the college.

He was to thrive like the society that supported him. The culture beyond agriculture was the money- culture the one on which the system survived, money siphoned off from government projects, that supported the entire system. All got their due—the politicians, the power brokers, the contractors, the employees; the higher placed an individual was, the fatter the amount came his way.

Or if; if he was less prudent, tried to be upright, or showed any concern, he was sure to be singled out, cautioned, warned and an endless saga of victimization was to follow. Beginning with frequent transfers, being dumped in and at insignificant places and offices. There he would fare no better than a clerk signing files and writing notes, requesting the typists to get the letters typed (in any case they were not much expected to take note of somebody who didn't have *connections* and more importantly could neither help nor harm). If he could grease the palm of the politicians, the power brokers, the go-between, the middleman, all and sundry, he of course then didn't have to languish at such odd postings.

To live happily ever after, he had to be all things to all people, the great tradition of the great land. He had to keep everyone in good humour by currency notes, by awarding contracts, by inviting people to work at the government projects like those who were close to power. He had to look the other way while they enjoyed the *loot* of the government money—all at the taxpayer's expense.

The golden rule entailed that he kept good relation with the administration and the police who toed the line of their political masters. The bottom line for the two was the same—to mint money from all types of sources and *lawful* acts—off government distribution system, land deals, deals of government owned real estates, smuggling and drug business, liquor trade, flesh trade; all types of deals possible under the sun.

To survive and prosper in that kind of a setup, one had to acquire special skills. Many had gained such expertise that if anywhere in the universe, or in the other planets of the solar system the likes of such specialists were ever required, the society could send such people in thousands.

Gautam understood that the face of the society presented no better picture than that of his own. The approach to life and living was deplorable.

As Asif went to his *own* land, *own* place, Gautam went to another metropolis for higher education.

Both had to learn to live through the miseries like that of the society they had to live in.

The society after all seemed to be an inexplicable edition—a large sized reflection in an over- sized mirror where the images got distorted without presenting any clear form and shape. The evolution was complete. Like the society—the image in the mirror and of himself, *he had to be all things to all people*. That was the spirit that he was gradually becoming more and more accustomed to.

"To be all things to all people" was the spirit he had discovered. That was the spirit, the *mantra* of the society. That was the way most people in the country behaved and lived, the urbanite middle-class. To talk of something and do exactly the opposite!

The management education or MBA as they called it, was the dream degree from the institute, for the youth of country, to which Gautam had secured admission. He was happy; a good career seemed to lie ahead.

The nation however seemed to be in the grip of perpetual chaos, confusion and killings. In the northern state of Punjab, the terrorists delighted in killings, of innocent people at market places, gathering—quite a good number each day, by bomb blasts.

For those who decided to use the sophisticated guns, highways appeared to be a decent place. They stopped buses and cars, pulled down people of a particular community to shoot at point blank range. The government retaliated with even more killings, killing even innocents.

While ghastly killings continued in Punjab, the people in other parts of the country looked unconcerned, true to the tradition of the land.

There was only one bright aspect of the otherwise turmoil in Punjab. The killings or the news of the killings in censored form became part of the news telecast and broadcast, each day with specifics—at least the names of places were correct.

The news telecast and broadcast made the people of the country aware of the geography of the region.

An average Indian's knowledge (educated ones certainly) of geography was far worse than that of his history. In the vast land with huge population (nearly one fifth of humanity) with very little movement of people and even lesser inclination for knowing the people and the land, the nation in its entirety was almost left unknown to its own people.

The news broadcast over the air and the television educated the people of the country, made known to them the geography and the turmoil in the state of Punjab. The people were made aware of their own land.

All over the country, a particular sentiment, feeling prevailed which was not confined to any particular region, but spread over the entire nation. The resentment, the dislike, the hatred for the police—the visible sign of the strong arm of the state, was common. The police were thought to have become a law unto them.

The police in the country were seen as the most corrupt, most tyrannical and so most despised.

For any proud democratic set up, India had the highest number of reported custodial deaths in the world. There were instances where people were summoned to the police station or the police picked people; many of who never returned alive. People were said to survive the clutches of the criminals but not that of the police.

For any proud democratic set up the killings and deaths in routine police firings all over the country, was the highest in the world. Trigger-happy policeman resorted to firing mostly on unarmed people, agitators, strikers where *lathi*-charge and bursting tear gas shells would have worked.

For any proud democratic set up the number of people killed in encounters was the highest compared to that of other similar societies. In rural India, the police were the ultimate terrorizer and suppressor. All political parties supported them and their actions while in power and condemned them when not.

For any proud democratic set up, where the society was hopelessly divided, those who needed the protection most, were those belonging to the oppressed classes, the land-less labourers and the women. There were often allegations of women being gang-raped even inside police stations. Very few could walk into a police station to lodge complaints at the dead of night. They dare not do so even in broad daylight outside towns, in the rural areas.

Free India had seen atrocities committed by the police exceed those committed under the British in nature, number, form and degrees, if not exceed those.

Free India had seen crimes committed by the police equal those committed by the criminals.

Free India had seen people staying away from police more than they did so during the British regime.

Despite increasing education and awareness, the basic attitude against women (more so in some part of the country and in the rural areas) had not undergone much change.

No wonder, for any proud democratic set up India recorded the highest number of crimes committed against women.

With all killings, counter-killings, bomb blast, deaths in road accidents, deaths of hundreds of commuters annually in railway accident, killing and torture of women, violence and deaths everywhere; the general air was of gross unconcern. Politicians looked the other way; the perpetrators found cover; the people behaved in a fashion that resembled long herds of cattle in movement with the predators lying in wait.

The talks of human rights were laughed at. It was all western propaganda. The talks of human rights violation *meant* the ever-present 'foreign hand' out to *denigrate* the great land. Human rights were nothing special. It meant the right of some humans to live and the duty of others to get killed. No wonder, the value of human life was taken to be equal to that of poultry.

Any talk of human rights and the violations were taken to be the trespasses in forbidden territory. Any one questioning the human rights record was supposed to be questioning the *sovereignty* of the nation, the *dignity* of the nation.

The sovereignty, the dignity of the nation was never thought to be injured with illiteracy, poverty and corruption ruling the society!

The land of great religion, great spirituality, and great consciousness was the land of *great indifference.*

Forty years after independence in 1987 there was a new turmoil. With the strife in Punjab continuously on, a new menace had added bizarre elements. That was the crisis in the neighbouring island country of Sri Lanka —the Tamil problem. The destiny (of the nations) of the region was surely intertwined in a complex process.

The killings, the ghastly pictures of rows and rows of young boys and girls killed, each bearing a cyanide capsule around the neck was carried by the television, to be viewed by the people.

Like it did for events in India, the television introduced the nation of Sri Lanka to the Indians. The names of places became quite familiar to the Indian viewers.

Television enhanced the knowledge of the average Indians and made them even more immune to violence and killings. The television carried the films on wild-life, the flock of cattle, the herd of zebra or deer walking along the grass-lands brought down by the cheetahs, lions and leopards while the rest of the world looked and moved on. That sensation had spread amongst people as well as they grew more and more immune and unconcerned with the killings.

When the Sri Lankan problem was at the height of its debilitating influence that cast its spell on India, the mother of all tragedies began.

The wily president of Sri Lanka sought India's help. The Indians responded. The treaty amidst all confusion, contradictions, chaos and opposition was signed. India was to send her army there with the tag of Indian peace keeping force (IPKF in short) to do the dirty work for the islanders, trying hard to keep their honour and dignity intact. They did so while recording the highest casualties in the recent times, as it turned out to be so, later.

The treaty was signed.

The young Prime Minister of India went out to inspect the guard of honour at the airport before flying back home.

He was attacked from behind by a young soldier of the Lankan force who was one of the contingents that formed the platoon, when the prime minister walked past.

The sixth sense helped the young prime minister (all the

prime ministers were known to have more than five sense) move aside and save himself.

The tragedy of course lay elsewhere.

Baba had retired and settled at the 240 50/ N&920 51/E town, with Ma in the one and half a room of a house that he had built. There he spent time watching world events on television—quite an achievement for someone like him; no matter if the television set were a black and white and a portable one.

The old man was enraged. He watched in dismay the attack on the young prime minister of the country as the prime minister was hit on the shoulders from behind; he had moved his head away just at the time of the impact of the butt of the rifle, (the news telecast showed the details).

The old man was furious. Suddenly, the patriot in him rose, nearly after five decades, the zeal that had one made him torch the symbol of the British Gautam more than four decades ago, came back.

That time though with different result.

More than four decades later, he was physically weak, worn down by failures, of career, of dreams, of seeing the vision of a nation being torn apart to shreds (every freedom fighter's lament —a cliché).

He talked to his wife till past midnight about the dastardly act; the anger, the rage was evident which of course took its toll rapidly. By the early hours of morning, he suffered a stroke.

Ma was alone in the one and a half room dwelling to take care of him. She somehow managed to call her neighbours to put him at the hospital attached to the medical college where Uma was the final year student of medicine.

Uma was not the silent smiling self of earlier years anymore. She had attained the average height with a sharp nose and an even sharper feel. Her silence had given way to even more sombre poposition—all the hallmarks of a future doctor in the making. She wore glasses right above her sharp nose to have a better vision: sharp and proving, which a doctor ought to have.

She stood by her father's bed.

Gautam was called at the instant and he was fortunate enough to receive the massage. The first train he could board, he almost jumped in. He knew deep down inside, the trouble he was heading for. All he wanted was to be able to see his father alive, if not actually kicking. He was in turmoil himself.

The journey back home didn't look like an ending. All the while Gautam ruminated. The thoughts, the feelings, the reminiscences of the man who had fathered him kept coming in avalanches. Of the man, the stubborn, the upright, the righteous man who called a spade a spade. The man whom his friends and acquaintances said never for once lied in his life, a man who seemed to belong to an altogether different world.

He was the man who upheld his self-styled code of morality throughout his life. For a middle-class family that survived on values or at least tried to cling to (for nothing else remained to cling)—values acquired through tradition: the great land exemplified in its survival from time immemorial; he was a fine exponent.

When Gautam rushed to the bedside of his father, he saw the sorry sight. Bottles hung from nearly every possible place that surrounded his bed with tubes and pipes in and out of his body. It was a sight of perfect helplessness for a man who had lived a Spartan life with fullest confidence in himself and in no one else. He had contempt and sneer at all pretensions which even remotely seemed to be injurious to his self, and the values he had—moral, social and of all types possible.

When he opened his eyes for the brief time possible, he could not say or mean anything. His eyes were like the ones lost, lost in the world of his *own*. Only when for once he nodded at the mention of his son's name being told, Gautam moved closer to his father. The old man's eyes appeared to be in search for him.

Gautam drew his face closer to the face of his father. The closest *possible* he had done *so* in his life, so far. For the first time in his life, he felt he had been in the closest proximity to his father.

The man in tubes mumbled something. It was an effort to speak to his son. Gautam felt he heard something—a kind of a sermon, he had not heard in for years. He felt his father was trying to say something in Bengali, something like lead a righteous life.

The sermon on the bed—the last sermon perhaps.

Gautam felt the man had stretched himself a bit too far to be able to "see" and "talk" to his son —for the last time perhaps.

The *time* it looked was round the corner.

The condition worsened. The kidneys were on the verge of failure, the doctors said. In the remotest corner of the country, dialysis was not available. Everybody, it seemed, waited for the inevitable to happen.

The condition deteriorated further.

Finally…

He died. The man had freed himself.

The young Prime Minister had however survived that attempt on his life.

Gautam felt lost, again.

The man whom he had adored, admired, respected and honoured but very seldom loved, at least demonstratively so, was gone. He had always maintained a 'honourable' distance from the man.

The more he though, the lonelier Gautam felt, the more isolated, the more depressed. The first poem he had written had brought in the watershed in the relation. The last sermon, it looked was the parting gift from the man, as the man knew the time was up as he bid adieu to his son.

So, the end came to the once fiery freedom fighter, the incorrigible idealist, and the incorruptible man who feared none and true to the great indifference of the society he lived in, was stoic to personal gains and losses, miseries and sorrows.

The state of the nation had often agitated him. He felt that there were no attempts made to democratize the people—the spirit actually was never allowed to develop in the land. Democracy to him was not just another principle but as was the tradition of land, another religion.

He surmised that the way every religion had the compartmentalized sections of forms, rituals and spirit—all separate and at the same time intertwined, democracy too had its own variations of the same.

The institutions were the forms; the exercises like elections were the rituals, the constitution—the scripture, the democratic values—the spirit. The man concluded that the basic values of democracy had not evolved in spirit in the land, as had the forms and rituals like any other religion in the land. That he felt was because of the fact that, it was the land of great servility.

"Nearly five thousand years or more of monarchical regimes, feudal set up has made the people servile. Servility has gone into our genes. It is these acquired characteristics of servility that has stopped the process of evolution of democratic spirit in the country." Those were the blunt assertions of the self-styled analyst, who believed in Darwinian principles as a student of science.

To Gautam, his father was his hero. The more he saw the world, the more he came across people, the way of their life, the living, the life style, and the dehumanized snobs. Everything and everybody had a price-tag notion. The more he saw, the more he adored his father, the man who could resist temptations—or rather was indifferent to temptations. So, to Gautam his *Baba* was the hero, like the snow-clad peaks, the cathedral all-reflecting, glistening, shinning.

But, never a role model.

Because one *had to* love a role model. He understood that as all heroes didn't become role models, all role models could never become heroes. Also, the role models had to be emulate-*able*.

Gautam knew he could not emulate his father ever and he didn't *want* to, either. The world had changed beyond the old man's ideas. Where the old-time folks who had nineteenth century prejudices simply didn't fit in, he had to live and prosper. The modern-day realities demanded that models responded to twentieth century truths and not the nineteenth century abstractions, nor the fifth century morality codes.

His role models were those who made quick bucks in the shortest time possible, the high-flying businessman, especially those who were the proverbial rags to riches story, a combination of currency notes and abundance of common sense; the self-made man. Also, those who made their way up the echelons of power through and by any means.

The events in Gautam's life were so significant and some ominously eventful.

Tshiring—the wonder-girl, who had kindled the strange feeling of some kind, love for a girl for the first time, one different from the feeling he had later; was long gone.

Mary—who in his teenage years was the epitome of love and concern and feelings, all the tender graces of human heart was gone as well; though he hoped against all odds that she might appear before him when the miracle happened.

He was one who had ruined the best and most lovely relationship that could have ever happened to anyone. Mere remorse was not enough not even any sense of guilt that appeared to be cosmetic. He was desperate to find her and if possible, do his part of the atonement, not just seek forgiveness but do that what was the call of the time to reestablish the relation he had.

And then, the man who symbolized all that was true, righteous, morally tenable, fair and judicious —all the seemingly lofty ideals in and of human life; was no more. He had like the others before him become *history*. He was gone with all the realities and facts he manifested. What were left were the ruminations, reminiscences and remembrances.

The realization of loneliness, the feel of it appeared to become more acute if one were at crossroads. To him, the death of his father was one such. The man had ceased to be a day-to-day impact for long when he had moved to the convent but the influence nevertheless had continued.

Sometimes, the mere physical presence caused impact. The mere thoughts, the feeling that someone who cared was alive propped up the feel of satisfaction, relief or caution or a number of such other abstractions.

Of course, for Gautam no such hangovers had remained, then on.

The obsequies over, the Vedic rites of the *shraddha—obsequesis (death rituals),* where, as the son he had to perform the ritual at the end of the intense period of mourning, quite an elaborate and strenuous ritual, he felt relieved and *lonely*.

He was then *free* to *do* what he liked and lead the life as he *wished*.

Gautam went back to the management institute where he

had to complete the remaining portion of the course to obtain his management degree—the passport to a high-flying career.

There were sea changes in the attitudes of man and the society, at least in perceptions. Those of course percolated down from the confines of theorists to common man. The first lessons of economic liberalization were being learnt, though not executed.

The world was changing too. The soviet president was hell bent on presiding over the demise of the nation and the Americans helped him—after all the soviets were doing exactly what the Americans had always wished to do; the break-up of the Soviets. The Americans were ecstatic; *their* works were surprisingly being done by the Soviets themselves.

In the changing world, new thoughts were emerging in the land of the communists. New ideas and new convictions erupted there. New terminology was required to define new parameters in each case. One Bengali humourist proposed an idea to describe the ever-expanding horizons of the ideology. To replace the ever-increasing and ever-expanding realms like Marxism-Leninism-Stalinism-Maoism-Hochiminhism-Krushchevism-Breznevism, he found a simple algebraic substitute. Marxism —Leninism—*Xism*, where *X* was the variable that could mean any later addition!

He was the same man who had differentiated communists from the capitalists as those who "drove the capitalists out of their *own* houses to live *in* them; who praised their leaders while alive and hanged the skeleton by the neck till…after death".

To become refugee had become the destiny of the Bengalis. For a change, quite a good number took their *last refuge* in communism.

In the great land of the communism of the Bengali variety of escapism, unique in nature, great *revolutions* were taking place.

The engineering college drop-out and once-upon-a time—friend of Gautam in the land of communists found new ways and avenues of seeking fortune for *own* self, and no more for *greater* cause.

The transition of the young man was complete. He headed a business concern himself. While his father talked endlessly of the ideology, of the *Sarbahara.*

The business concern that Ranjan (the prodigal son of the veteran communist) headed and thrived on in the gradually opening Indian market. The company specialized in exports and imports, the cliched term forever.

He had started his entrepreneurial adventure bagging government contracts that came easily. He had high connections, helped by the ever-ready officials who desperately tried to get close. Critics said, his father had a lot to do in the sudden change in the son's fortune. Therefore, he had almost a *free run* up to the point of his global launch.

There he had to pause for some time, his indigenous ways needed a revamp for him to go global. But fortune smiled on him again; with the overseas connections that had developed mostly through his father.

His father was the top functionary of the party. The old man often went abroad to better ties with foreign companies who wanted to invest within the land. The votaries of scientific socialism sought investments from imperialists and capitalists. The ties were certainly bettered; more for the son than for the land for which the revolutionary father went abroad.

The son prospered. By leaps and bounds. The father as well. The father gained politically, the son financially.

The father got prominent coverage in the state-run television. The septuagenarian veteran looked like a hawk within the frame of the television. Surprisingly, he did the perfect opposite of what he said when it came to matters of his own, that of his son.

More strikingly, the old Marxists all over the world looked almost the same, in the deterrent state and in the others. That was the wonderful benediction of nature, which needed thorough probe, a truly *scientific* one.

It was the great wonder of the world—probably the eighth wonder of the modern world, of the modern civilization, that the exponents of *scientific* socialism at some stage looked alike.

All over the world, the old communists looked very similar, especially the septuagenarians. All over the world even if they belonged to the different nationalities or different races or different *faiths*. Their features seemed to assume distinct contours, facial distortions and special Martian attributes.

What the communists failed in their youth to do came out to be very true in their old age, before their death (if they had one, for communists were never said to die, they were known to *fade away*).

Gautam learnt to live through the strife and changes like people everywhere in the land, through the contradictions and confusion and chaos all through in day-to-day life, at workplace, at the marketplace, in the family. Like millions of his countryman who led a life of mere existence, desperately trying to keep their body and soul together, he learnt to live through his moorings and trappings, strife and stresses.

The land moved on with the ritual obeisance being paid to the leaders of yesteryears. The giants were made to assume colossal proportions by systematic and gradual deification over decades.

The days of rituals, celebrating the birth and death anniversaries of political leaders were something to watch: a treat to the eyes.

People standing in long queues, moving in front of the portraits, in long files, hands folded, flowers in them, head bent, singing in chorus when it suited them, praying to the lord to free themselves from manhood, as one notable individual commented; *castration* was on.

That was precisely on; the psychological one certainly, so that manhood collectively could be thrust on the leaders who were long gone. That way the giants could be made to look even bigger, so that they gradually passed on to realms beyond reach, attaining almost the state of divinity. Then the myths and legends could be spun around them, like the divine halo glowing.

The psychological sadism was on. People—especially those who mattered, surrendered their manhood, castrating themselves and enjoying the delight in reciprocation of having had to see others also castrate themselves, likewise.

There were of course, very other earthy reasons for that kind of behaviour.

It freed the men, who mattered—the political ones, particularly from any *pangs or stings of conscience.*

They could indulge full-time in their art of nation building (that included money-making, satisfying their physical urges, power game, all at the cost of the commoner). They had certainly given up all their honour, their dignity, their self-respect, if they had those left in them: the last iota of personal morality and their manhood. They had in fact *offered* all those to the great souls—the icons who had been made the repository of all lofty ideals and human values. That made the men who mattered, free from any sting of conscience, and inhibition, any moral prejudice, any debilitating concern for the nation or the society, any foolish and stupid ideal of patriotism. It freed them to act.

They could exercise their free-will to advance their own and sectarian interests which they identified with that of the land.

Amidst all the glorious realizations, Gautam completed his management education. He was now all set to embark on a career that would launch his rise, fortunes. He was sure to rise to a level where he knew he would be immune to all the shocks and disturbances like someone at the top of a skyscraper, where only the sky was visible and not anything down below.

To be successful in his future endeavour, he had to be as ruthless as possible. He had to keep away from the infections of any germs of any moral or human values. Any form of compassion had to be kept away. The value of self-interest was to be the only value to be valued in life.

Enjoyment was to be the core issue henceforth. The level of promiscuity was already very high. With new horizons opening up, newer avenues, modern thinking replacing the older values, sex was no longer taboo. The colourful lives lead by some of the politician and people in high and exalted places were the examples. With the chance to wield power came the opportunities for enjoyment, at the taxpayers' expense. It was common knowledge that those who swore by moral codes during the day; dropped their undergarments after dusk.

It was after all, the land of *Kamasutra*, the eroticism in full display from time to time.

It was the land of great promiscuity. For man, license had been granted from time immemorial, for women it was grudgingly granted with all levels of taboo. In the land of promiscuity, lechers came in all shapes and sizes. They didn't have to sport any particular feature—either physical or emotional. They didn't need any special kind of dress—no sartorial extravaganza was necessary. They came in very ordinary and commonplace settings. At offices, colleges, apartments, trains (buses didn't allow the freedom and the aeroplanes didn't allow the time and freedom for that), railway stations, police stations, political circles, social circles, everywhere even at hospitals. To them, the world nay the universe was to be found in the cleavages and cervixes. They demanded the performances as returns for their favours. Often, they demanded those in advance, in cases of advance *pay-offs,* most of the time they didn't return the favours. They had the advantage of living in a society, which didn't talk about the private lives and report even less. They could go absolutely 'scot-free'. It was the society that ostracized the victims more than the perpetrators.

The lechers carried on their exploits in all strata, at all level in all circles—not just political, but in social, administrative even in religious circles as well.

Of course, the values had been changing. It had become the turn of the women folk to get their pound of flesh. Wife swapping was as good as husband swapping. The act by mutual consent saw the women *choosing* their bedfellows.

The path of promiscuity was a two-way traffic. The evolution was on. "Kept and concubines" were the privilege of the rich. For the middle class, occasional forays were the usual route. It was then the turn of the people to explore new horizons. Going to bed with … was the answer.

In the age of churning and endless turmoil both social and political and of course in the business world the contradictions were evident. Gone were the moral obligations, the trappings and moorings of the lofty ideals, the pragmatic were the best role one looked for. One had to free oneself of all *ancient* values and imbibe the new and newer ones.

To be exact the conundrum had finally exposed the hollowness of national psyche it seemed.

Gautam too wanted to lead the life he had seen of late. He didn't have the obligation to swear by the moral code anymore. He could enjoy his life then. The change of values—the metamorphosis the society had undergone was the welcome change from his point of view. Everything was available in the *free-market.* The only point was the kind of premium, the value and the cost. Any desired fantasy was available for a price. The churning of the society's psyche was on and he relished the same. He had of course to keep himself safe from any kind of infections; condoms were the answer. AIDS already seemed to threaten the world and the sex had to be practiced safely.

He was unsure though despite being in the flow of times to be pragmatic. Whether he belonged there- in the new and newer brand of occidental values. Realization finally descended upon him to go on with the tide to rise up the ladder, if he had to, to be successful in the new world- so distant from his, the one in the forlorn mountains and the rural settings of the nation. He had to take a call and he did that with confidence.

Gautam was happy. Finally, he was to be in the mainstream, the upwardly mobile class, sneering at the dust, dirt and garbage all around him. He lived condemning the politicians for all evils and yet hobnobbing with them when it mattered, habitually being shocked at the violence and troubles and yet he ought not have any reservations against the use of same, if the need arose.

The best place to socialise with women of all ages, he knew, was the get-togethers and the parties where he best of lavish ostentation was presented. There knew, situations arose where the pack he kept came very handy—the pack of condoms, to live up to the situations. He knew like most of his colleagues, the need for that and the chances of situations arising, often quite accidentally.

The chatterati to which he *belonged* enjoyed good food, good drinks, exotic setting, and good sex. Man and woman enjoyed each other. Man taking women to bed fit enough to be their daughters; women seducing man half their age, ready to present their *possessions* at the sight of cute faces and strong biceps.

He had none of the desired attributes and yet chances came his way at the few such parties he attended. He made most use of all those. Condoms that he kept with him came to good use. He was not ready to let anyone trample; infect the insignia of his manhood, the very symbol of his existence.

At the threshold of his bright career, he learnt a few other things.

He learnt that corruption was the single most important principle on which the whole edifice of the society survived. It had become the all-pervading spirit. More importantly, it had gained social and moral acceptance.

Corruption at all levels, in all forms and in all places. Compiled with the law and its provisions. Those who flouted and more importantly got away with their acts; earned all the admiration. They were the newest avatars. There were in fact quite a few personalities who earned highest regards for having made their way through lobbies and patronage despite all the stories of their financial irregularities, which the rumourmongers spread.

Corruption had become the spirit of the society. Right from the lowest and poorest to the highest level.

It was the single unifying chord of the nation!

The more one got involved in the dubious deals, the more *izzat* one had. The macho image grew with the rise in the quantum and nature of the involvement. People admired them. The new avatars were replacing the older ones.

And it was a phenomenon pervading the length and breadth of the land. Not just limited to the metropolitan or big cities alone. Even in the likes of 240 50/ N, 51/ E places, the craze was overwhelming. Admiration and adulation came their way who could make quick money in double quick time by all means possible, making use of *all possible channels*; political, social, official etc. To be able to make money and sustain it was the sole criterion.

Sustainability of any phenomenon was the justification for honours.

Suddenly, the elusive chord that bound the society was being discovered. The underlying bond of cohesion that was making itself visible.

Corruption was the new spirit of integration.

It was institutionalized. The rightful place that was long overdue was restored. And the people were *thrilled.*

The politicians and the bureaucrats rejoiced at the phenomenon. Their *dream* of the society was finally coming to shape. They had all along been putting the best years of their lives for the sake of the society and that was beginning to show results. Their efforts to make the inhabitants of the great society understand reality that grease was the greatest cause of happiness (of the palm variety) was coming true.

In the perpetually divided society of thousands of years, the search for the spirit of integration was found at last. *The elusive coherence, the tie, that united the society.*

Surprise of surprises, language, region, religion, community were no barriers, those factors which had so far kept the society divided failed to divide again against the new wave of integration.

At various cities in the governments run by the different political parties, transfer-postings of government officials were accorded the status of an industry, the distribution of government funds, the awards of government projects and contracts were the money-spinners. Those were the great sources of revenue for those who were in the government and even for those who were not actually in.

All in the name of socialism—that was enshrined in the scripture. All at the expense of the taxpayer's money! Half of the population was illiterate. More than half reeled under poverty, not being able to provide two square meals a day.

From the big to the small, the rich to the poor, the upper class to lower class, from the politicians to the bureaucrats, from the businessman to the clerks, corruption was the presiding deity.

The signal failure of all the lofty ideals of the great men in their very land in unifying the society from thousands of years was very evident. What the ideals could not achieve, the down to earth practical common sense had done.

Socialism had found different meaning here. It meant equitable distribution (for those who belonged to the class of governance) of spoils of power (that existed everywhere).

Corruption was the greatest unifying bond in the entire society. It was all pervading.

If corruption was the symbol of unity, socialism the mantra, something else…

Something else—the condoms, became the greatest leveller in the land.

From rich to poor, from urbanities to rural folks, from one corner of the land to the other, the message was the same 'use condoms.

For reasons altogether different, the condoms had brought the society on the same plane.

If the poor used the condoms as an effective method of birth control, the rich used it as a method of continuance for their promiscuity.

The problems of below the belt had ultimately united the people. The solutions for problems of different nature, for objective poles apart, with nearly the same results!

The first lessons, the basic principles of the 'equitable society' were being learnt.

With the condoms fast becoming an absolute necessity more for the rich and also for the poor who anyway had more problems than fears, the importance grew.

Condoms were fast becoming the requisite. For acquiring immunity from infections, from *relief* from any kind of sensation, of not just one kind but probably of all types.

No wonder, the land was the largest producer of condoms in the world. The exports were reported to be rising very fast.

Still, they said it was only the tip of the iceberg—the market, of course. The huge market they said remained untapped within the country.

In a society, where the population control was a farcical exercise, the condoms provided the answer. In addition, the deadly diseases like AIDS caused concern.

The missile shaped condom—tiny, miniscule, but of great potential. That was the *perfect deterrent.* Actually, the missile shaped condoms when *capped* (like ICBMs) in full *bloom* resembled the nukes in shape if not in size.

Perfect solution for deadly problems.

So, the process of "condom-isation" of the society was on.

To keep the sensation away; of all types and values.

To contain unwanted pouring and depositions.

To keep at bay all types of infections of morality.

To keep away any aftermath of the consequence of the great castrations.

To make the society more and more responsive to the call of the spirit of integration.

The great renaissance of the society that looked imminent, was the delight of all concerned.

The protection from unwanted births, deadly diseases and immunisation from all sensations and values, all.

Truly, the process of evolution never stopped.

From the spiritualisation of the society, through the colonialisation to the condom-isation, the society had seen much, even the "revolution-a-isation".

CHAPTER 14
Apocryphal Reference

Gautam had become some kind of a city-hopper, a metropolis-hopper as he liked to call himself. That gave him a feel of world communion, a global touch to all he did.

He joined the international enterprise of the great K.K., "Globecon" at the centre of the nation's industrial hub. The great K.K. in the business circle was the boss of the show. The acronym was highly acclaimed that the man loved. Like the business greats as shown in the Bollywood movies, the acronym accorded a state of immortality to him. The great K.K was aged about sixty-five. The great K.K—the multi-millionaire, the great exporter!

The great K.K. named Krishan Kumar was actually Krishan Kumar Puri. A refugee from the western part of the land, which later became Pakistan, he came during the partition where he survived attempts on his life. All his family members had either been killed by the zealots who slit their throats open, as was the practice; or had died following the slaughter because of shocks and privations later. He was the only survivor of his family at the aftermath of the catastrophe.

In the short span of less than thirty years he had first built a fandom of his own, then a kingdom and then an empire of a stature that matched with the best in the land vying for the slot of the largest exporter abroad. His was a great global exporting concern that exported products from garments to condoms to even scented *basmati* rice. All in one, tucked in one, sucked up in one.

With the air of liberalisation going strong, it affected the industry. The air of liberalisation was actually the spirit in which one had to bare oneself—to liberate from all kinds of constraints and restraints. That certainly, he did exceedingly well, with official liberalisation or none of the official sort. He was a man of strong urges like the man of very strong physique that he was. In his characteristic Punjabi accent, he liberated himself from all compulsions; with his excellent health and physique he extricated himself from all kinds of codes for his urges.

In that way he was not unique. Like so many of his fellow businessman and entrepreneurs, some of whom were refugees like him, he developed and perfected that art.

Gautam was a young recruit in the Globecon as a junior management official. He knew junior or no junior, if he could show prowess as an employee and made himself worthwhile to the company, he could rise in the organisation. He had to make himself valuable to the great K.K. The great man was the boss of the show and no rule except his was to be followed. His writ ran large over the organisation.

Gautam entered the basmati rice division of the set-up. Within a short span of time he was moved to the condoms division and then elevated at the garments division. He knew he was on the rise. With so many others working at the concern for the great man, he knew he was one of the lots working there. He however was able to catch the attention of the great K.K. within the short span of one year through a whole lot of ways, with impressions from his works and his other extra-curricular activities. He acquired a position akin to something, like management assistant to the great man himself. That put him in an exalted status to have an insider's view of the working of a successful concern, and the life of a successful individual; also, the life-style and the mode of living of a successful family. He was happy. That was what he had been waiting for long to happen. Mr. Puri, the great K.K, had promoted him to that position with that opportunity to have that panoramic vision.

He was grateful to the great man and his wife, the pot-bellied woman with grey hair, who had taken a fancy for the young man. The aged woman was the traditional woman concerned more with her prayers and pujas, but her words carried weight with the great man.

The job of management assistant was very similar to that of the personal assistant but carried different connotations. He dealt matters of business importance, of financial and management values.

Mr. K.K—Krishan Kumar Puri was an institution. From being a small-time supplier at government departments he had risen to the position of an entrepreneur, an exporter of national status. That spoke volumes of his entrepreneurial skills, business acumen and confidence. He had all the qualities necessary to be successful in the land as a businessman, the attributes necessary to be successful in the sixties, seventies and through the eighties.

He could get his job done at any level he desired, and yet he preferred to get his work done at junior and middle levels. "A sword cannot do what a needle could do," he often said. At times, however and those were frequent, he got his job done from the highest office—the tremendous influence he had through the lobbyists seldom failed. He had connections at all levels everywhere and through them got his work done. Later, as the management assistant was to learn he had connections at even very high levels who figured on his pay-roll; or were showered with GOG (s) that meant gifts-of-gratitude. Those were the people, some of them well within the corridors of power and that extended everywhere.

He was very strong physically; at about sixty-five, he was thrice as strong as the young man, who was in the early twenties. With strong biceps and triceps, calf muscles, broad chest, tall stature, hardened face, he looked every inch a real toughie that could braze his way through.

With strong physique came strong urges. At sixty-five he could put the young man of twenty and something to shame on all accounts. With the maternal Mrs. Puri, her plump, balloon like rotund features prominent; keeping herself engrossed in the devotion to the lord—the flute playing *murlimanohar*; the great man found ample time, energy, and attention to satisfy his urges.

But he was very selective in the ways of doing so. He was very methodical in going about that. He had his pleasure resorts spread over the land and abroad as well. On his frequent trips to those places on business requirements he had his share of the satisfaction, of the urges. He took liking for the tall woman whose breasts didn't sag. He had strong dislike for anything plump. But he was very prudent in his choice of women. No one could ever seduce him with any general gifts of nature. He had special liking for the skinny variety that had shapely curves with exposed collar bones, especially while abroad. He had a few agencies working for him to spot such females who would suit his requirements. He believed that he gained the requisite doses of vitality from such kind of females. But he was careful to maintain anonymity and never took anyone twice. But those were less frequent exercises.

He took particular care so as not to get infected by anyone. He had his chosen women who care for him. Any other woman who shared his bed had to produce certificates of health. The reports of AIDS having spread to almost all corners of the world terrorized him. Particularly after the news of deaths and wide publicity of the casualties of Hollywood, he took even more care. Blood tests and authenticated certificates were necessary.

He even forced his women—the two, who were his constant companions over the years, to produce those. They felt a bit hurt by his probes, which they found to be insinuating and humiliating, a slur on their standings. They felt as if their virginity was being questioned. He however remained nonchalant as ever. He was as cautious, as prudent in the matters of sex as he was in the matters of business. The women—his women, stood the tests of the *agni-pariksha* grudgingly. They had very little option.

One of the two, who was his constant companion, was Anamika Sultana, the high society lady of all sorts, of whom the great man had become the sole arbitrator of matters below the belt, since nearly a dozen years. The well-proportioned, fleshy, passionate, of rounded bottom, high hips and big busts—Anamika took those tests and the circumstances leading to those, a bit deep in her heart. She was his partner when it came to tours within the country and in the neighbourhood, to as far as the places covered by the schedule flights of Indian Airlines. She was more than half his age and had the full flow of libido inside. Yet, she had resisted temptations on account of her commitment to him. She was sore but had to stand the test and withstood the feel of being let down. But as she knew, she came out unscathed. She however let her feelings known to him who however didn't give that any importance.

The other—Ramela Fernandez was the one who accompanied him on his foreign tours sometimes. She didn't travel along with him but left either before or after his departure. She was tall, lanky; slim- hipped, with rounded but not plump breasts. She knew such tests might come her way and had perhaps shared her time with other people as well when she was not doing so with the *great man*. But she was more careful as she was always ready with her *precautions*. She was unfazed but kept up that air of astonishment and bewilderment in her eyes and approach to him. He however took very little notice of the prostration; it was very difficult to impress him with such kind of emotional looks and gestures.

They both wanted to ask for *his* certificate, but could not do so. He gave them the impression that they might be the carriers of the positivity (HIV +) that offended the big-busted

Anamika who saw the talk of positivity as an attack on her womanhood. Both the women had their reservations and resentments and wanted him to produce his certificate of negativity but could not say it openly. That desire remained inside.

Anamika—big busted and high hipped—was born in a city—slum in the area of the famous "Dh" where she was known as Roshanara. With *kholis* all around she was the star attraction as her assets grew and she displayed them. She had her formal education for some time till her patience gave way. With politicians of all levels flocking around at the well spread out locality, she could come in close touch and contact with many of them. Those enterprising politicians took their chances of moving closer within the distance of her assets. Within an amazingly short span of time she was transformed into, rather metamorphosed into the hi-fi and captivating, Anamika the pretty. Her new name meant she was as loveable, as tender as the ring finger. With the new name, almost simultaneously if not preceding the naming episode, was her baptism—the baptism by fire in spirit and by fluids in form. With her body gaining precise curves at exact places, she was the documentary evidence of a politician's delight. From a non-descript locality she was taken to the most exalted setting catering to the needs of high placed people. The transformation to Anamika from the Roshanara was complete through the "My fair lady" like sequences. Only that the objectives were different. Everyone marvelled at her excellence. She could speak *pharratedaar* English, good Hindi, some Urdu and to please high placed solicitors like the great man who spoke their mother tongue at the very private moments of personal high; some Punjabi as well. She knew perfectly well from her wide range of experience that when men were in the high even if he were someone like the serious K.K. or any of the salivating bureaucrats, at the most delicate moments of *deliverance*, one turned to native dialects! She knew everything for she had to make the best use or her assets to cater to the need of the most desiring individuals. Like the age-old proverb, make hay while the sun shines, she had done and accumulated what was expected of her. She milked them when she wanted and they did so when they wished. With her knowledge of Urdu, which she claimed was her mother tongue; she picked up broken phrases from the works of the great poets. In addition, she composed verses herself. That endeared her to the half of the semi-literate politicians who thought she were some kind of a poetical genius; beauty and brains together with a sensitive heart deep inside the over sensitive breasts. She enjoyed while they did as well. Soon, she started walking through the corridors of power and through the contact—loving, contact-having politicians got introduced to Bollywood. There she had her share of rather many of her bed-throbbing exercises with guys who mattered. At the end of those elaborate experiences, she landed up at some roles, some way up the role of the extras and juniors, like those of the sister of the hero or the *bhabi* of the heroine. She had no pretensions, much hesitation to show her assets and possessions on the screen, or bare everything, but the crude view of censors came in the way. Then came the gradual flops, one by one, those at Bollywood had known and experienced. She of course learnt gradually, that only the beauty and the looks or adventurism, didn't suffice. Some kind of acting was also necessary on the screen; not the day-to-day kind of the thing she perfected.

She decided to withdraw from the *bazaar*. She turned more and more rootward. The slum she came from needed development and the inhabitants there needed help from the oppressors. She took cudgels on their behalf. With her erstwhile link-ups she tried to redress those.

She needed then a stable, sustaining and mature relationship, which she cherished most. Then one fine day, the great K.K. ran into her. Her personality and her looks impressed him. From her mid-thirties she was his. He was certainly not hers! Having found the man she had desired, she settled down. She catered to his needs, the needs of a man, the needs of a mature and a stable man.

She accompanied him on his tours within the land and on the areas in the neighbourhood where the scheduled Indian Airlines flight took them.

But the very unfaithful act of his hurt her. The tests, which she said were to *determine positivism,* (HIV +) were humiliating. To her those were indications of his growing negativism towards her.

So, Anamika reconciled herself to receive his passionate bouts of affection while bearing the assaults on her *fidelity* grudgingly.

With Ramela however, it was all different. She was young, younger to Anamika and free of such self-inflicting ideas. Tall, lanky with no visible bulges, one had to look to search for her assets. With her collarbones visible and shortened hair, she was the perfect woman of the eighties. She worked as a model in some films, the nondescript advertisement films. She waited for the big-breaks that she knew would come her way. Despite her very ordinary works, she had dreams of high qualitative offers coming her way. During the time when she worked for such advertisement films and shared her private moments with her boyfriends and the *filmwallahs*, she met K.K. In fact, at an advertisement film shooting for his products, she liked his stature and connections. She knew she had found the right match. The kind she had not very exactly experienced before. She had acquaintances with some of the directors and had approached them for breaks but the only experience she had was nothing beyond that on bed. She desperately wanted those breaks and knew that only high connections could pave the way.

With him she had her first experience of going abroad which was as good as the breaks she desired. Those foreign sojourns became more and more frequent for her as he took some kind of a liking for her. The experience she gained was the likes of the live-in variety as was frequent and commonplace abroad. When she however landed back in the country after her stays abroad, she felt she were a whore, which in any case she believed she was not. On those occasions she encountered some emotional problems, as she knew waiting for breaks in his arms disfigured her.

In her late twenties, she looked exquisite. She had been with K.K. for nearly four years. The break was yet to come through. She had not given up hopes certainly. With good food, good sex and good cash, she was not dissatisfied at all. Yet, she aspired for the breaks. With a couple of months in a year in foreign tours, spaced at intervals throughout the year with K.K., was not too bad after all.

For her, the AIDS test was not very surprising. She knew it might come someday. She knew high-placed solicitors talked of such kind of certification. She was a bit taken aback when K.K. asked for it. She was concerned not much by any emotional prejudice but by surprise. She knew he had undercover surveillance for her, to know her whereabouts. Yet, she had learnt how to dodge them and solicit people she wanted. She was surprised by his requirement, as she feared he had come to know of her deeds. To her immediate relief were his words of comfort when he said that, those tests were routine in nature. Henceforth, he said such tests were to take place regularly and nothing more. She stood the tests. To her satisfaction she passed as well.

They choose safe practices while they performed together, while they were together. The safe practices that could keep them safe from any and every intrusion! She had been doing so. But she knew those mattered little.

She wanted success and if for that, the capping had to be done away with, she would happily risk that but only when she was convinced that such a risk was worth taking. Or else, trying to practice safe methods she knew, she could end up nowhere, from bed to bed, with of course all the experiences of foreign stays and tours, fat bank balance, jewelleries and assets—the actual varieties. But without the much desired big-break that could launch her into the career as a supermodel.

She harboured those illusions and kept them very alive as she practiced safe methods with the safer man, K.K. and the likes and dislikes of him. She dreamt that her time was sure to come someday.

She dreamt herself in the role of the super models that were her idols. Those women she hoped to emulate someday, with her gorgeous looks, almost six feet tall stature, skinny body, exposed collarbones and slender, and shapely breasts.

Only that she was not sure if the super-models needed such high placed connections in their land as was required in her land. That she asked herself. She was hopeful that her K.K.

would one day recommend her name to some international fashion designer. That she would one-day sport such exquisite wears, walk down the aisle with people cheering her assets more than the fashion-wear. She would swing her hips in the dream steps of a majestic catwalk. She had however kept her other channels open, those with when she had been practicing the safe methods for long. Those she did with aplomb, making fool of the undercover men who were placed to keep tabs on her movements and acts, those required for safeguarding the interests of a big businessman. She lived with those dreams while she practiced safe methods and went for regular routine tests.

True to the need and requirement of the prevailing conditions, the great man's son followed his father's footsteps.

Anil Kumar, the rising "A.K" in the business world, was the great man's son. The great son of a great man! He had his own kingdom to build. In the gradual blossoming of the corporate world under the new regime of liberalization, the A.K.s saw it as a god-sent opportunity to computerize the society. They wanted to go as far as they could. With the name of one Bill coming to the forefront much, much before the other bearing the same name, they found to their surprise, the market had grown beyond their wildest dreams. They had the backing of their parental capital and entrepreneurial expertise, which they put into very good use. A.K, as he was called, took his interest beyond that of his father in all matters on earth.

As an industrialist and businessman, growing beyond the confines of condoms and clothes was excitable enough. To add variety to the already existing spices all around, was the equal liking in extracurricular activities if not more; in addition to the curricular ones. He was educated abroad with business degrees from the universities of U.K. and degrees of computer technology in U.S.A. In addition to the formal education abroad, he had his informal education—mostly practical as well, there. He had acquired other tastes also.

No Indian woman suited his needs. In some cases, he shared his father's likes and dislikes. Like his father, he abhorred fat, plump, and rotund woman. He would most certainly have married one from abroad, one with exposed collarbones and very shapely breasts. But for the interests of the family business, he could not resist the temptations of a huge dowry that came with the marriage.

But he had a rule for his wife. His wife by whom he would have a couple of children, had to keep in very good shape for her husband's wishes than for herself. Any layer of sub-cutaneous tissue, which he touched from above, mid-way up the body when he had nothing else to touch, had a very deleterious effect on him. The cold touch made him jittery. To please him and satisfy once-in-a-while exercise she had to keep herself in the shape and form, he desired. Her advancing years beyond the mid-thirties had a very strong and serious effect on her.

The unwanted layers of fat below the skin and just below the breasts, on and around the waist made her grow round. To add to her discomfiture was her husband who often had a look at her and chided her. That made her even more cautious. However hard she tried, the initial and the first layers of fat, she couldn't remove from her body. She knew, and knew very well that those depositions that were from within worked as very strong deterrents for deposition from without, vis-à-vis her husband. A.K. had very little of interest in him for her and she had to fend for herself.

She thought of taking time off from attending her children to spend profitably in the company of like-minded and like-sentenced companions who in their delight of liberty and freedom found new recourses. Group adventures had the ingredients to make exercises very exciting with special males and females. Those forays, which were enchanting to the others, excited and incited her also. However, at the point of execution, the heavy-bottomed but chicken hearted A.K.'s wife fainted, more out of guilt than out of fright. The chauffeur of her Rolls Royce had to carry her in his arms, strong arms to her car. That act cemented his ties with her, and her ties with him. That proximity and closeness had an invigorating touch of fantasy firing within her. She had all within her grasp, she thought and believed so.

The man—strong and able-bodied, whom the growing star-businessman, A.K. had employed to guard and eye his wife, responded favourably. It was all confined almost within the family. No extra adventure of any kind was really necessary. What she did was not much beyond her own circle of reason. If A.K. could do at random almost anywhere in the world with almost anyone he desired, she too could exercise her discretion within the *range* and the *fold* of the family.

The business tycoon-in-the making A.K. (his friends pronounced the metaphor as if he were a raccoon of the Americas, probably in keeping with his education and business there) had other priorities. He was a tireless worker, sincere to the marrow; he was a master strategist. He knew in due course of time his father's empire would come his way but there his sisters also had their share. For the time, he decided to devote his time and energy to his own concern.

Those apart, he had tastes and likings similar to that of his father, not much differing in kind but in degrees. A.K. had a special liking for anything western. No local beauties sufficed his needs- mentally, emotionally and physically. Added to his special fondness for the colour of the skin and dislike for anything plump, was his special desire for shapely breasts. Not the very likes of local varieties which were rounded and spherical right from the root to the tip, but of the special-shaped, which he had to look for, even abroad. The likes of the elongated banana like variety that curved right midway through the length and curved at the tip roughly maintaining nearly the same if not totally the same plumpness excited him. He had several agencies that worked for him which searched for woman with that kind of perfected shape. The desire and the likes he had acquired during his long stay abroad sharpened his tastes. Those tastes had persisted.

During his sojourns back there, which he had often, almost staying there for nearly half the year, he relished his tastes. His acquaintances that had those attributes nearly twenty years back, here had developed distortions and he despised them. In addition to the special liking for the breasts, which was his prerogative, he was fond of bulges at right places. The bottom bulge was the one, which he liked equally. Lovely, shapely bottoms which he could pat when he liked and caress when not!

All those special qualities, all in one body were seldom found locally and hence his liking for the woman abroad.

While A.K. continued with his fantasies abroad, his wife found routine satisfaction in her chauffeur—the appointed watcher by her husband.

The children in their own way found their share of excitement with their friends—boyfriends and girlfriends. They were aware of their father's exploits and their mother's ambivalence. Like other teenagers they were physically strong and fiercely independent. They had their own lives to lead without any hangovers and prejudices; they carried on with their parties and get-togethers and adventures.

Those excited their senses and infuriated their passions. The new and newer experiences they shared almost every day and every-night enhanced their maturity and their personality build-up; those were the prerequisites for being successful.

The role of the Management Assistant entailed a lot of work, more than the usual ones related to business deals alone. At times Gautam had to cater to the not-so-business matters of strictest conjectures. And his was an exalted position. He was the centre of envy at the concern. He was the centre of suspicion for his colleagues and superiors.

His was in an all-time job. During office hours he had to attend his job, the business deals of K.K. and during the evening, the personal affairs of K.K. that the great man didn't like to place in someone else's hands. That brought the Management Assistant in close contact with the As and Rs. The Anamikas and the Ramelas! They were at first peeved to find a nondescript, not at all macho looking man in early twenties carrying his seal and stamp on his act, which even they had after so many days and night together failed to corner. However, prudent as they were, they very soon and pretty nicely understood, he was the man who could lead them somewhere, the place they desired. The Management Assistant too had his urges and felt the sensations. Only he knew he could not express his desire and run the risk of becoming a pawn in their hands; and put his job and survival in jeopardy.

The great man was a master builder in addition to being a master businessman and a master exporter. A master builder of huge sky scrapper like buildings in addition to being master builder (and destroyer) of human fortunes. How or why the great man came to trust him, Gautam could not understand. To help him at his deals, the great man chose the wimp and the shrimp of a man who had very little expertise. That made the young man circumspect. Perhaps, he believed the great man had taken a fancy for his clean-shaven, boyish looks that smacked of innocence and ignorance. Perhaps the great man believed that the young man had some sensation left and had not become totally immune. Little did he know that like all other management assistants anywhere else, the young man had also the pack always with him, ready, for any eventual use!

The Management Assistant waxed more and more like a perfect businessman when required, and waned when not. He was prudent enough not to demand for anything. He adopted a posture that resembled something like "I-don't-deny-if-things-come-my-way", almost as if reluctant to oblige the invitations and approaches from the beauties around him. That ploy he found to be highly successful as plenty of opportunities and chances came his way where he had to remain as stoic as possible. He was flooded with offers. He actually didn't say no to anyone as long they satisfied him and his needs. Only he was careful enough not to get too close to anyone in particular that could not have gone down well with other colleagues or could not have gone unnoticed by the great man himself.

He preferred to play the role of a gracious male ready to oblige a lady if she asked for it, and not like the salivating males who asked and got the rebuttal; and not made to look mad after the desire. That ploy worked as he found out after some initial experiments, that *gracious stoicism was the gateway to the interiors of a solicitous individual.* That philosophy he discovered to the chagrin of the solicitous ladies who were not quite able to know and understand him. The females who were used to being pampered and chased to be asked for the gift till they consented were taken a bit by surprise by the young man in the early twenties, who simply watched and observed them, but said nothing. No advance in any form from the young man; that was a bit unnatural for someone in that position. Those feelers which the adventurous woman expected from the young man didn't come and they were taken aback. They hated the *"leap-year"* like situations which seemed very imminent and that was intolerable. He saw them, eyed them, all their possessions and yet chose to keep silent, not going beyond the harmless gestures that put the enterprising females in dilemma.

That would have gone on forever, were it not for an enthusiastic young woman who in her mini-skirts and bare legs approached him with the neck line as low as mid-bust to which he was titillated beyond his own amazing level of self-imposed and tactical restraint. She spotted him, observed his looks and knew he was no different after all. She was a past—master in those acts. Obviously, she had betted her money to be able to bring him by the nose and she won her money handsomely. After demonstrations of initial reluctance, which were mere part of the strategy, he gave in but not before she had a long and frustrating series of unanswered and responded overtures, his way of enticing the likes of her that he seemed to perfect well, beyond all his contradictions. He was as usual very cautious. The safety measures and methods he resorted to were beyond any reasonable measure of doubt. He resorted to those even if those were unacceptable to the woman who took those with a pinch of salt.

That was the truce. *To get him to do was their priority, how he did was his.*

That particular episode virtually opened the floodgates; the series of such invitations fortified his individual fiefdom of authority and position, which the great man had bestowed upon him. The stoic posture helped him retain some kind of immunity. They knew him to be a tough man, not given to easy approaches and cajoling. But they knew very well that as the saying went—persistence pays he also was amenable to very suggestive and persuasive measures over a span of time. He continued with his outward show of smiling and restrained self though he was burning and dying of the desire deep inside. He enjoyed the epithet "a restrained but a considerate man" the most.

He was given to adulation, excitement and praise like any other management assistant anywhere else. He was on a bed-spree and he loved all those experiences and adulation from the women in their highs. Those made him feel almost omnipotent; the stature, which even the great man, would have cherished.

He knew those who could not approach the great man, and actually very few could, vied for him. He was aware of the pitfalls. He had gradually learnt the ways of the business and leading a successful life.

He already had his share of enjoyment. He only wanted to make sure that he didn't fade into oblivion. Any slight mistake, any loss of the slightest of the equilibrium could spell disaster, of which he had to be careful.

The plan of launching his global enterprise was getting stronger every day. All he wanted was to learn as much as he could in association with the great man and the great enterprise.

Only that he had his share of enjoyment, excitement, highs all intertwined.

***

In the dream, Anamika grunts. Her grunts are as explosive as the firecrackers of Diwali and the burps of the *bhang*-takers of Holi. She grunts as she places herself in a cozy posture after the act. The contours of the water melons—shaped, sized, rounded but not plump; are held in a tetrahedral form squeezing his head in between. His eyes are closed. The caretaker Saleema appears across the screen, the middle-aged manageress of Anamika's household and tell her everything in ready—the food actually.

He mumbles something, the after effect of the drinks he had taken and of the depositions he had made.

"*Kya Anap-Shanap Bak Rahe Ho*!" she tells him condescendingly.

"Nothing at all," he replied. For him this is a new experience, for her this is a typical one.

She settles in to tousle his hair—a touch of calamity he knows if he were not careful. She breaks from her high and comes to terms with reality.

"*Dekho Na*!" She complains. "K.K. promised me to launch me in his films, in the films that he finances, but that is not as yet coming through."

"But in what role?" he asked as he feels her waistline.

"You silly!" she rebukes him," Do you thing I am past the age of becoming a heroine? I am quite sound in shape and form. If the past forty women can dance around with the guys in mid-thirties, why can't I?"

He nods. "That's right," he says. "If you can take someone in early twenties on your groin and make him see the *world*, you can certainly do a film, or rather everything."

She pinches his cheeks as she fondles him. She is the woman of the hour. There is no denying the fact. Then comes the long-awaited wish which both are expecting?

"Why don't you see if I get a chance in the C's films. I know K.K. is supposed to finance those."

He feigns ignorance. She looks with surprise and suspicion in her eyes.

"*Bachoo*", she says, "For the last twenty years I have shared my bed with lot many great people. I have seen them all, all their assets—bare, everything. You are but too small a fry. Don't try to fool me." He protests and swears. She looks at him with even more suspicion in her eyes.

His innocent look pacifies her. With a pause, she tells him, "Promise me, you are going to help me in my efforts to be a heroine."

He promises vows; he knows that the Urvashis and the Menakas are not to be tampered with and their feelings not at all to be taken lightly. That usually brings disaster. He resorts to plain facts.

"Look, I deal strictly with business matters. The filmy matter is somewhat outside my domain. I have heard him speak to Mr. C. But I have not as yet been asked by him to deal with Mr. C on his behalf. If the situations demands, I can surely do something for you, I believe."

To that she looks satisfied as she breaks into her smile, she presses her tetrahedral assets, more tightly against his head. He is besmirched.

Then he frees himself from the 'pressing concerns' as he tells her, "I can surely do something, I hope. But before that you have to take his permission so that if need arose, I could plead your cause."

Safe pronouncements from all angles, he wisely surmises. To that she replies with even more pressing concern, "Ok, Ok baby. Now, for that favour, why not take another dip?" She doesn't wait for an answer from him. She is on her act again.

He just watches her. She is the perfect one. Capable of switching over from one high to another! With if not greater passion, then at least with the same level of excitement. The treat over, she is her jovial self again. He is no better than a corpse. "*Bekar Ka Aadmi*!" she pinches him again. "*Itni jaldi sab kuch ho jaata hai?*" She smiles at him.

"Never mind! I am here to learn the intricacies of the art. The finer points, the deeper points."

She caresses him. He is reassured. He knows he has delved too deep, much deeper than he should have done. Something disastrous lies in wait for him if C's film does not come through, he knows. But for the moment, his perspiration and her exasperation bear the same smell and same contours.

He is confident of his catches. He knows it is all, because of the great realization that he had experienced some time back. Playing the stoic role helps as no other approach helps. Playing that kind of role, decidedly helps to attain the position of coveted importance from there, no demand need be put but they come on; the chance lies in the prudence of accepting or declining the offer.

Another fine approach he has learnt gradually is the non-dominating, playing the sub-dominant role that he has so nicely perfected. That sub-dominant role he knows has put him in a very good spot in relation to women. He is putting that acquired knowledge to test. That he learnt from his encounter with Ramela, the slim-hipped abroad-sharing woman of the great K.K.

The slim-hipped but not plain-chested Ramela, with round orange shaped delights (no other comparison he could find as she came from Nagpur), had taught him a lesson or two on that account. The encounter occurred quite suddenly and unexpectedly. Before he could actually relish, it was over. The encounter occurred at the most unreeling hour during the lunch break at his chamber—the chamber of the Management Assistant where she had walked in when no one else was present. She had mercifully no hang-ups or hangovers to push or prolong the likes of the sentimental blurbs, of Anamika. She was a down to earth woman with the burning passion of making it to the top, to be a super model like the Crawfords and Campbells. She only needed a break.

Mere experiences abroad with K.K. were not enough. She wanted the real global launch to which he showed interest, but dodged the issue. In desperation she tried her hands on other people like the management assistant, whom she believed could help her make her way in the world of cut-throat competition.

She made herself comfortable in his chamber. The *wimp and shrimp* of a man seemed to be the guy who could find for her the initial catches in the world of globalization.

"Hey man," she addressed him.

"Hello!' He relied as he concentrated his attention on the screen of the personal computer while his fingers played on the keyboard. She drew close as she almost touched the keyboard with her oranges there by giving him the chance to finger them as well. He *stood the test with titillation everywhere* but remained *act-less* all the while. Finally, she had to give in.

"Don't you have any passion?" She blurted out in anguish, moved by the sheer uncaring attitude he had shown. He looked at her and smiled. That infuriated her. She had not known males to look so condescendingly to her on being invited, not at all! Her looks conveyed the feeling that she was not used to the preposterous ways of rejection. Here the young man seemed to have a disdainful view of her. But in her heart of hearts she knew, no male was ever known to decline offers from a female, that too from a beauty with possessions of precise magnitude and contours. In rage she caught hold of him in an act of frenzy in the broad daylight (visible outside the chamber), which was more than dimly visible inside. She had her last laugh. He resisted the onslaught with no particular force and allowed her the privilege of doing everything. That made her even more bitchy and enraged.

At the end of the ordeal he was satisfied, tremendously. His desire that he had inside him for long was satisfied. Also, the idea, the philosophy he had was triumphant.

The sub-dominant role was indeed rewarding.

But he was careful and prudent as ever. Even in that moment of imminent ecstasy, he never forgot the saviour he had with him; the pack of latex-made-*deterrent.*

What followed were the usual tete-a-tete tales of her career, between rings of smoke and sips of foreign liquor and his assurances that he would look into her affairs. She left satisfied. He was happy.

Playing the sub-dominant role came naturally to him, commensurate with his position, stoic approach and his burning desire. Caution was the name of the game. For him the laid-back approach was the best choice.

It is time to go back to Anamika and the management assistant holding each other's assets. The ordeals over both have a cozy and relaxed posture.

She says in her characteristic sentimental way that varies between her superbly coded understatements and plain facts "*Dekho*! K.K. sahib is a man of such great qualities himself. May be, he is a bit busy and goes abroad often. I wished he took me there as well, but then he has other priorities. Anyway, he has promised me to take me sometime later."

She satisfied herself about that. But she knows and the management assistant as well that those assurances mean nothing at all.

The great man had particularly great taste for everything round. He disliked anything plump and fat, but had a fancy for anything round, perfectly round. No compromise on that account was acceptable. What he settled for was the round, high-hipped and rounded waistline in the country. Abroad, his tastes were different. He favoured the slim-hipped varieties of the likes of Ramela. Anamika's chances were very slim.

Saleema calls again, as the food is ready. The Aroma of the *mughlai* dish spreads the message. The aroma of the *biryani* and *kababs* responds with the characteristic applause for the great man, his prowess, his contacts, and his exploits.

"Look, no!" she says, "K.K. has so much of clout. He is the financier of all the films the great C makes. Yet, he cannot do that- the recommendation of my name. That is the sad part." She continues her mouthful of chewing off the plate before her.

"He is the financier of all the election campaign of S. They have a first name relation; I mean they call each other by the first name." He nods. He knows it. What however interests him is that the likes of Anamika, who bed the leaders do acquire the gift of political astuteness—the intricacies of all the permutations and combinations. He wants her to say more and more. She obliges. The rubbing of her assets with the like of S has sharpened her political thinking.

"There was election the year before last to the house of…the members had to be bought and K.K. had to garner support for the candidature of one of the cronies of S. K.K. rang up everyone and promised his pay-off. All from here! Through the phones of my apartment." These assertions give her a pleasure of having been a party to all that had happened. The witness to all the compromises and arrangements. She was the witness, the only witness to the compromises. She had known all compromises of all kinds that she had so gleefully perfected over the years.

She smiles at him and he smiles back. Her compromises were as good if not better or worse than that done by S. She thinks herself to be some kind of a kingmaker's consort, keeping the man of the hour in top from. That gives her immense pleasure of having played the role of a modern day Cleopatra. The *whore* in her suddenly gives way to a more important figure that could decide the fate and fortunes of the rulers. She feels the role suits her. The role of a modern day avatar!

She smiles at him again and he responds. The pleasure that she had just bestowed on him where he played the sub-dominant role, make both happy. All the moments where she is made to feel the importance of having been the decider of the course of events satisfies her. The ego naturally. That she has bestowed her favours on the young man makes her look magnanimous.

That is her way of going one up on the great man K.K. for his *deplorable* tests of positively, the bloody *fidelity* tests. The young management assistant understands that.

She had her share of the pie, of good food and of good sex, of good circles. She had her share in deciding the fate and fortune of the likes of people coming to her pleading their cases. Those were certainly very pleasing.

Only the last desire remains, to captivate the world through the celluloid.

She has hopes, but those tests from nowhere have ruined her disposition.

***

The Management Assistant made his way through. The lessons of sub-dominant postures helped him get entry into the very private moments of the family. Encounters with the sisters- the daughters of the great K.K. came his way.

The tall, heavy-bottomed, strong, with protruding bulges was Reeta—the eldest daughter of the great man. She lived mostly abroad where she was said to have some kind of a husband they said, in the middle-east from where he controlled an empire. She travelled to India often and in the channel shade that covered her eyes, she looked as discreet as possible. She alternated between the Turnbull and Asser white shirts and the Saville Row suits coupled with the Cartier Panthere watches and Mont Blanc Pen, to match the bulge of the breasts. That was awesome. If he were running an empire somewhere in the Middle East, she was running hers. That squared matters up; though no one was ever reported to have seen him, every one saw her.

She was a globetrotter, travelling all over the world, for the cause of her empire, from Greenland to Iceland, and from Scheyelles to Sweden. She was a very strong woman. She had very strong fascinations and fantasies. From the old malts like spring bank to Choiba cigar, she drenched herself in Guice fragrance. She travelled alone. Between dining at the Aubergine in London and the Balthazar's in New York, she picked her man as well. Her strong tastes went along with her very strong discretion. As a careerwoman, who travelled alone, single handedly taking on the world on her own terms, she needed time to relax. The relaxation was to be on her terms and choice, at the places of her design and with man of her choice, with the exact physical and mental proportions; the standards she fixed. She almost always changed the requisites to add spice to the taste, variety to the routine. She employed experts to choose and pick up people—men of exact tastes, possessions and passions to her precise desires. Between choosing her furniture from Porada in Italy for her fortress like residence in London and employing architects to design her staircases in Honolulu, she spent her holidays cruising down the Nile; or spending some days at the remotest island of the Atlantic, with men of her choice.

She didn't have the exact desire to run or drive her 91 X S4X Austin or her BMW within the country. She chose often her other cars—like the Toyota Land Cruiser, for roads in the country were much *country*-like.

That of course sufficed her other needs. She had her urges to cater. On short cruises to India where her chosen man couldn't be carried along, she resorted to the *desi* varieties. But she was very discreet and even the management assistant took no notice. Till something, that happened one-day. When he was actually cornered by her almost to the point of no return.

She rather ordered to get into the car and he obeyed dutifully. Then at the place and time of her choice, she put the back seat of the car to the best possible use. The back-seat culture along with the imported cars had travelled to India. But to the totally bewildered Management Assistant, it was more of a shock than being a pleasant surprise. She had maintained her discretion. She didn't want to walk with the shrimp of a man to any resort and do that. For someone like the fellow, the back - seat of the car was the best place, rather the only place. Luckily, he thought the shocked wimp of a man, that he carried his pack with him. He carried it every time, even at his office because he knew that the dictum eternal vigilance is the price of freedom applied everywhere. He knew his chances might come anywhere, anytime which even would have to be consummated on tables, lift-boxes and unused staircases; he was therefore prepared for any eventuality. On that particular occasion the pack came as the only reprieve. The pack he carried saved him, that day.

She was in the mood for a quickie. And quickies were quickies. No time or attention for niceties or plays, both before and after! She ordered him and he was not actually used to such gestures. He was used to invitations and some aggressive intentions when he played the sub-dominant role. But on the back-seat he had to shockingly obey her orders. She seemed to be in a hurry on that occasion, as if she had a very important matter to attend and needed that specially. As he was ordered to perform, he felt his manhood was being crushed under the car. As she shoved his head with scant respect for his olfactory senses and his visual abilities, he was almost dumb-founded. It appeared she had some kind of an itch that needed very urgent attention. His wish of the male priority was thrown to the winds.

He had a view, a very strong view that he held, despite his stoic postures and sub-dominant gestures. If it were the invitation of a lady to go along, then it was the prerogative of the man to ask for something of a favour. The reciprocation had to be in that act but pertaining to the performance. He wished and expected to be *capped.* He didn't want to do all himself. That was the symbol of the male ego being kept-up, for him. He wanted that and had his way always. But in the backseat episode that was totally disregarded as she showed no respect and was totally indifferent to the male ego. He couldn't even ask for the favour. He had to do all by himself.

He felt he had lost his manhood!

The episode was over but the memories and the scars remained. The shocking experiences left some immediate marks in the form of scars; the dry skin peeled off to remind him of the injuries her nails had caused at some places. That made him scared of her. Any more thought of such outings with her frightened him.

His episodic life had new and newer events for sure. Every moment of the episodic events he thought of her—the one he longed for—Mary who never appeared to pass into oblivion. No matter how much he tried the memories would rush back especially after such episodes and he felt a dwarf of himself—a self-abnegating sort of a personality who had done nothing right. However true to the test of the times he and the society plummeted through the apparent resurrection though short lived were evident.

The mid-thirties woman, Rita, had terrorized him with her ways of taking on the world, the world of business, all the male dominated bastion, even the back-seat domain. He began to have some serious thoughts on his stoic posture and sub-dominant role as being the perfect antidote to aggressive adventuresome overtures. He got some kind of a relief and reprieve however when he had his share of the experiences with the youngest member of the family.

The younger daughter of the great man who didn't brush aside his male ego, nor treat his self-respect with contempt, nor mistreat the insignia of manhood! The earlier shocking incident had some kind of an effect on him making him wary of woman for whom he had taken a fancy. He was not sure how they would react under such similar situations where they would call the shots. His manhood had taken a beating.

But the younger daughter of K.K restored his dignity and manhood to some extent. The younger daughter Neeta—who called herself Aneeta to add global acceptance and touch to her name in the world of globalisation and liberalisation—brought about the restoration. She was the truly likeable character in the family.

With her education abroad, she had knowledge of everything academic and not so academic. She had no hang-ups either. She had new boyfriends each time she travelled to the country and proceeded to some deserted forts—the *havelis* in places like Kings than to spend her holidays. She had her designer dresses and yet, could opt for *lehenga choli* or jean-tops as and when she liked. She was flexible. She could swing between sips of Gold and Blue label whisky and her own barrel from Scotland. Between smokes of cigars rolled on the thighs of her chosen men (she ordered for those special kinds) and the desi varieties, she had an amazing range of resilience.

She preferred a Lamborghini!

Amazingly, she felt not a bit below her dignity to take people to holiday resorts and havelis when she liked. She had an astonishing range of choices between the tall, broad-chested, well-built models of Greek sculpture, like stature to the five feet tall wimps and shrimps, whom she picked up with ease. She was the real transport to ecstasy.

After a few months with her, the Management Assistant found her to be the woman of his dreams and desires—gentle, kind and accommodating. He was surprised beyond his wildest range of expectations when she told him that she was happy to be in the company of a knowledgeable man like him! He did not know how to react. He was not sure if that were a compliment. She reiterated what she had to say, all the while looking very meaningfully at him. Then he realized something was on the way. He believed, something of the kind, he wished, might come through.

And by God, it did come! More than once, on two separate occasions. She was the ultimate woman!

She picked him up and made it off to a holiday resort. He didn't know if that role he played was the one to be played again. He decided not to give much of a thought. He even flattered to deceive, for a moment though, to think himself as the man who satisfied her. Such was the "bliss of the bless" that she produced. The non-dominant, passive, stoic, the wimp and the shrimp of the man was elevated to the level of happiness personified as she made him feel like a man. No bruises anywhere, no ultimate scars anywhere!

And she did the unbelievable thing. She capped him. That reassured him. That feeling which had taken a battering for the worst by the early encounter with her sister was soothed to perfection. The relish was wonderful. She took care for his feelings, his senses, and his concern for the safety of the insignia of his manhood. She was happy it seemed to him, as he liked to believe it more and more; that she was happy to be with him. He was ecstatic. His ego and manhood were restored. The exposure was very satisfying. She thrilled him. He missed her when she left with her boyfriend. But by then the blissful continence had given way to a complacent feel.

The man at the threshold of his career learnt bit by bit the story behind the successful man and his successful family. He learnt about their life and their style of living. From very close quarters the young man learnt the mode of living and the runaway success that emanated from leading that kind of a life. Only, he was not sure if leading such kind of a life brought about success or if success brought about that kind of life-style. But he was certain, and very much certain that success and that kind of life were inseparable. It was then, when his own dreams began to take shape gradually.

The dream of being able to reach that kind of success and there- by lead such kind of life, excited him. He dreamt of himself being clad in Armani jackets and Versace suits, ready to chair his own company, smoking Choiba cigars, with a Waterman to sign his papers, getting off from his Mercedes with his ping golf set. He dreamt of strolling on the 16th hole, rubbing shoulders with the political top brass. Those gave him tremendous pleasure, even more than the momentary illusions of "heavenly pleasure", which he experienced from time to time. He dreamt of cruising off to exotic locales, like spending his holidays nearly three hundred miles off the coast of Greece, in a lonely island with the woman of his choice, supposed to have designer breasts and perfect novelty down below. In the dreams for sure, the shrimp had become a giant. He could certainly afford to do that. In the dreams at least, he was master of all what he did, master of what he surveyed. He knew that the dream could only be transformed to reality if he decided to follow the footsteps of the great man. That was his goal.

The world, the young man learnt, had undergone genealogical changes. Already the fashion revolution was upon the people of the land. Hitherto lesser-known or even non-descript fashion designers who excelled in presenting females as scantily as possible on raunchy rumps, had become or were on the path to become corporate brand-builders. The cleavage exposure and bra bashing were becoming the order of the day. Sex and sensuality, so strong in the nation's psyche but not displayed, were being liberated from constraints and bondage. He marvelled.

The priorities had undergone sea change as well. People excelled in spending lavishly, putting on trendier clothes, and finally liberating themselves from any restraint of any kind. Amazingly, even the food habits were all set to change. Soups and green salads had replaced *aachars. Naans* for *rotis,* wine for water, one cuisine for a few, one gravy dish for many: cataclysmic changes had indeed set in.

Gautam knew he could make his way to the top. Success lay strewn all over. He had only to pick the right course.

The track he knew had to be the right one. The prerequisite was to keep one away from any real sensation. The terror of the deadly disease had kept him away from the 'real' sensation, anyway. The symbol of immunity had almost made the society immune to all kinds of feelings. The scaled down versions of the look-alike of nukes were the real deterrents, the only saviours, and the perfect antidotes. He had made his choice with some space to cater for the allowances, like the wish to be capped, or playing the sub-dominant role. He had to castrate himself, in addition, to make him further relieved from any 'manhood' syndrome. The insignia—the only physical symbol that stood alone—had to be saved from any infection of any kind.

He made efforts to that end. The chances of his being a top-rate exporter were bright. He had to gain expertise in finance and management. With the global opportunities opening up with the ever-widening horizon of liberalisation he felt his chances were excellent. He could export almost everything—flowers to the west, machinery to Africa; from being a 'middleman' brokering arms deal to dealing foreign exchange in a clandestine manner, his range of choice was enormous.

Even as an exporter he could take advantage of the incentives by under-and over-pricing the invoice as when required. Even within the land, he could fool the financial institutions and dabble in the share markets to build up his fortune, with the outside help from conniving officials.

If, however, he didn't succeed the way he liked, he could choose another innovative profession, the most recent one. He could become a guru. The craze of a section of people to get the desired had made them seek alternative ways. Black magic and casting charms or even plain counselling with a bit of *yoga* could change his fortune. He, like many, could become a globetrotting guru, earning in millions—the supporting flocks thronging him ever, their numbers ever rising.

He had to be in the mainstream, the upwardly mobile class for whom that ostentation was a part of life. No matter what came by, he had to see that his interests were saved. That was the need of the hour.

The reorientation of the mindset made him happy. The urge, the inspirations he so badly needed, came from within. The reverberations of such lofty ideals seemed to be echoed back from the society.

At the crucial juncture of his life when he was all set for his global adventure, after he had overcome his trappings and moorings, came the great battle.

It was almost like the great battle, the Armageddon—the eternal saga of clash between the good and the evil, the bad and the good, the benefices and the malefic in the land of virtues, of values, of human heart and mind, of attitude, of everything.

When he had placed himself in the mainstream to accept:

(*1*) *The multiple standards,*

(2) Addition of new dimension to democratic norms,

(3) Solidification of feudalistic perceptions,

(4) Relegation of actual issues to oblivion;

There was the topsy-turvy, when populism was the spirit. *And corruption was the jewel in the crown: Dynastic succession was institutionalised, in the democratic set up!*

Truly, *exotics never ceased to occur in the land.*

Several decades after the real Mahatma, the expectation of a new *saviour* coming surfaced, at the far end of the eighties. The world was preparing to leap into the new millennium, ready for last moment adjustments to be done in the last decade.

And then came *he*!

He, who was the Singh of the weepy variety and people called him so, sometime later, when the sting of the Singh that he caused to the nation in the nineties of the last century became perceptible; he faded into oblivion but not before had lowered the nation into bickerings of caste and endless feuding thereafter! He truly was the "New Mahatma" of the lowest order possible!

He was the new "Mahatma", the self-styled pretender of course, who single-handedly took up the crusade. He road in style, cap on his head, the cap made from the skin of *karakul* deer (the mother had to be killed in the fifth month of pregnancy for the foetus to be skinned to make the costliest and most comfortable cap in the world!); wide-eyed and bespectacled with the *panoramic* vision for the land!

The people had looked to the new avatar with hopes and expectation, which were to be dashed soon.

The pretender came with his cronies—the rustics, the brats, the jokers, the melodrama masters, and all clowns in their own right. Those who understood statecraft less, economy lesser and the spirit of the land the least, found themselves jockeying for power.

The circus was complete with the modern-day Mahatma, playing the snake-charmer's tunes of sectarian politics engrossed in the debilitating dung-hue of self-destruction!

Yet, the nation didn't plummet to any new 'low'. The tremendous resilience, the spirit of survival stood the land in good stead.

For the young hopeful, the land was stated to be a caged tiger, ready to leap as a dream economy of the next century. Despite all the visible signs of the largest middle-class and the largest poverty - stricken mass living together, side by side, dreams continued.

Exotics? Perhaps yes.

After all, it was the land of great hopes and great expectations.

CHAPTER 15

The Apocalyptic Expectations

In the setting of the nation that seemed all prepared to enter the last decade of the millennium, where through the tumultuous upheavals in the land, the nation prepared for the onset of the twenty-first century, the young man prepared himself as well.

He had to take the initiative. In the last decade of the century, he decided to launch his own enterprise. He needed at least ten years to consolidate his position. He hoped to build a fiefdom if not an empire as K.K had done, by the turn of the century. He believed that by mid-thirties he could become a man who had to be taken into account. He was, after all, a very calculative young man, nearly everyone opined.

What he needed was to perfect the art of big business. In the land where the art of the impossible was perfected, he knew that he could master the art of the possible, however difficult those might be.

In the land where dynastic succession was perfected, where rituals preceded the spirit to perfection, where the castration was perfected, where the exotics perfected the art of peaceful co-existence of the largest middle-class and the largest poverty stricken mass living side-by-side; he was confident to be able to perfect himself and his concern.

He believed he could do it. Only that he had to follow some golden rules, his variation of the *Paanch Sheel*—the five-fold path:

(1). To be all things to all people. Keep everyone in good humour.

(2). To be supremely indifferent to any cause that even remotely identified itself to any emotive issue.

(3). To be able to circumvent the laws and get away, while being as generous as possible, posing to be a zealous supporter of law and law's decisions.

(4). To keep all channels and contacts open with all political parties.

(5). To keep oneself immune to any sensations and safe from any infections.

Having formulated his own principles, he was sure of his success. He had to mould himself according to the need and demand of the hour.

Having decided so, he wanted to go back to his old place for the last time, to severe the ties with the 240 50/ N, 920 51/ E like places, which could only retard the progress of a man, especially for someone who was hopeful of sky-rocketing to success.

For the last time, he wanted to take the train journey, which could take him to the desolate place, through nearly three-dozen railway tunnels. Henceforth, he knew; flying would be the only means of transportation for him in the future.

In the hustle-bustle of the old railway station, the one that was the gateway to the north- eastern corner of the country, he seemed to be drowned in the madding crowds around him. Smell of everything, from that of garbage to that of hot tea in the strange admixture of occurrences, made him distinctly uncomfortable.

Suddenly, he felt a heavy hand on his shoulders. "Hey man! Eternal lover!" the voice was familiar. The giggling self from not-too-distant a past seemed very close.

Gautam turned around and saw him. It was Ronnnie—Ronald Lego, now very fat and wide, his huge frame was no better or worse than that of a sumo wrestler.

"Ronnie!" Gautam cried out." I can't believe it is you! It's wonderful meeting you after so many years!"

"Yeah!" Ronnie answered. "I am here for my tour, bound for the metropolis."

It was a heartwarming embrace for the two old friends.

They had time; plenty of it, to talk to each other—about life, saga of nearly eight years that had elapsed in between.

"Hey man!" Ronnie said, "What about Mary? How and where is she at present? What news have you got about her?"

"Er.... no...no." Gautam murmured. "No news".

"Talk straight man." Ronald hardened his voice. "Don't you know at all, anything about her? Didn't you have any contact with her at all? Ever?"

"Well...yes...and no." Gautam gathered himself. He had to cobble up some kind of an explanation to answer Ronald.

"We had contact with each other for the first couple of years, but somehow it snapped, you know; after all the distance plays its part. Nearly a thousand miles of separation and becoming twice as much as that! That's quite a bit. Somehow, it didn't work out." Gautam knew, he didn't have the courage to look into Ronald's eyes, as he spoke with his head lowered.

"I thought so. I do not quite get you, man!" Ronnie said. "I am getting all the more confused. You are right, possibly so. May be, the distance plays its part."

Gautam had nothing to say to that.

"So, you have absolutely no knowledge of her. Yeah? I am surprised. I am shocked to hear that." Ronald paused for a moment and then went on.

"To me once, both of you meant love personified; the symbols of love. Probably I was mistaken. I was a fool then, and may be still I am. Teenage love is fleeting, they say. How true it is! You have proved that. You are no exception. " He looked a mix of surprise, anguish, shock and a lot other things put together.

"Well, you know; I went to the city for my education and she went to an obscure village to teach at a school run by the church, up in the hills. We had contact, but gradually we lost it…since then, I have no news of her…you know how it goes." Gautam gathered composure to be able to narrate something he had never thought of narrating to anyone ever.

"I am shocked. Well, to speak the truth, not shocked in the real sense of the term. I have become immune to every shock, every catastrophe. I have had to bear lot many of those, in the last eight years myself." Ronald stopped for breath and then continued again. "Yet, this was the last thing I could have ever imagined. Both of you parting ways! I still can't believe it."

Gautam was quiet. He had hardly anything to reply.

"Poor Mary!" Ronald sighed, "Poor creature. I don't know why and how could the lord make her so soft. She had to go through such sufferings. Sometimes, when I think of her and her plight, my faith in the lord gets shaken. Anyway, I never was a great believer in his rule!"

Gautam looked pale. "Did you ever meet her after she went to the hills? Where? When? What was wrong with her? Why?" Gautam was anxious to know everything.

Ronald looked deep into his eyes; raised the cup to his lips—the cup of tea, sipped half the contents of the cup in one gulp, put the cup back on the plate with a noise and cleared his throat. The whole exercise was disgusting to Gautam.

"Why do you look so disturbed? So perturbed? Anyway, she doesn't matter to you anymore. Does she?" Ronald looked at Gautam.

"Please, Ronnie. Please don't be that harsh. You know I loved her once." Gautam almost implored.

"Yeah…loved her once. Very well said, my dear boy. The fact is you are no better than a scoundrel." Ronald was even harsher.

"The best and the most gracious amongst the girls loved you. She was madly in love with you. You were also, I believe in love with her." He coughed a few times to clear his throat.

"It must have been your stay in the city that has changed you and your views. You are after all, someone from the plains. May be the guys at the college were right. That guys who were fiercely opposed to your love. I was a fool to have believed you once. Of course, I remain a fool to this very day." He talked as if he had nothing else to say. He was talking to himself more than talking to Gautam; who was rather lost in her thoughts and not actually listening to Ronald.

Gautam was silent. Absolutely silent. Lost in the world of hers. He came back to speak in a very soft voice to Ronald as if he were speaking from a lost world.

"Ronnie, please do not take me otherwise. I tried to get in touch with her, as best as possible. But I never got any information. Please tell me what had befallen her. You do not sound at all encouraging, I am afraid. You sound ominous."

"Hmm…yes. I do not sound very encouraging. My voice sounds ominous?" Ronald answered from his lost world in a distant land.

"If Gautam, you had come to her aid, I am sure she would not have met such a fate. Poor creature!" Gautam was about to interrupt him when Ronald raised his hand and asked Gautam to stop.

"She was a teacher at a school run by the church in a desolate place up the hills. You know that, it seems. Why and how you couldn't get in touch with her is something, I don't know and I can't understand. How could you, least of all people, a man for whom I had respect, a man whom I thought loved his beloved dearly, ditch her? Shame. Anyway, you cannot hold anyone else but yourself responsible for the tragedy that befell her." Ronald continued his story.

"I had an inkling though. I didn't have brains in proportion to my physique; but I had something else that others did not. I could watch the eyes and look for love. Man, it was this fool (he pointed his finger towards his chest), the one sitting with you and talking, who had one sultry evening said something. Do you remember? I hope you do. I had told you that I had seen love in her eyes far more intense than what I *had seen in your eyes.* That was true as events have proved so.

"The conclusion I had drawn was correct. I thought if a woman loved more, the love sustained. If a man loved more, it failed. In your case it seemed to have been the same old story, but in a roundabout way. The woman loved more and the love failed; the man ditched and deserted her. " The big fellow almost broke the tea cup with the bang that hit the table, off his fists. He was inconsolable for his conclusion had suddenly gone wrong, the one, which he knew and believed to be a universal truth!

"You, you are responsible for what she had to suffer!" Ronald said, in the same grave voice that seemed to be the forerunner of something perilous to follow.

"Ronnie, please! Please don't be so cruel. Tell me...is... she...alive?" Gautam caught hold of Ronald's hands, with both his hands.

"I don't know. I don't know for sure," Ronald said slowly as he slowly removed Gautam's hands.

Ronald's words were almost calamitous to Gautam. After so many years she had come back with such a force that seemed to blow away everything else.

"I don't believe she would have lived any longer. If anyone-as chaste, as pure, as innocent had to face events of such disastrous consequences, one could not have lived any longer. The ways of God are so difficult to understand. I have lost faith whatever little I had, in his ways." Ronald was unambiguous.

Gautam could not look into Ronald's eyes any more. He didn't have the courage to do so. He kept quiet. He knew Ronald was moving to the climax, which he knew was certainly something catastrophic. He didn't want to press the issue any harder.

"She, as I was told, was very devoted to the education and care of the young students of the school. Students, mostly orphaned children and those picked by the church, who lived within the school premises. In the care of the church they lived, like as she did some fifteen years back. She loved the children. And the children, they loved her more than anyone else. She was very dedicated to the service of the church as well. The social service she rendered at the near-by villages, mostly on her own initiative, made her absolutely endearing to the people around. The people there said, when she fondled young children—the infants, mostly orphans and destitute, she looked as if she were the Mother in flesh and blood, with all smiles and care for them. She, they said, never cared for even her bare necessities. Often, she forgot to take her meals. The people at the village, around the school, those at the church loved her." Ronald made himself comfortable in the chair.

"But then, strange are the ways of god. Nearly six years ago, just at the stroke of Christmas, when the school was on the threshold of being closed for vacation, they said arrived a Satan, in the form of a man. The caretaker of the school and the church, was the only man in fact, who saw him.

The old caretaker said the devil was of a middle height, and darker complexion—someone from the plains, it was evident."

"He came to the place and surprisingly, Mary greeted him with joy. The ecstasy, the brilliance in her eyes which the old man said, had not been noticed before." Ronald paused for a moment and then started again.

"How and why, Mary got acquainted with the fellow remains a mystery to me till today and for that matter, to anybody and everybody else. The people of the village told me, when I went looking for her later, that the man had bloodshot eyes, big moustache and a dirty beard, that he smelt of liquor, a perfect devil; which I believe were all fanciful stories. The old caretaker was the only man who saw the fellow, it was in the misty cold evening and he didn't take much notice.

"The next morning the fellow was gone, before the old man could take a closer look. He was gone, with her, of course. It was clear, the fellow was very well known to her, and could have been to her liking. I believe, and it is actually my own assumption that the guy must have been someone working in the church—the big church at the town, where lot many plains-people worked or attended. Anyway, Mary told the old man before she left the next morning that she was off, for holidays; with that devil, full of joy, full of glee…

"When I met the old man later, he was full of remorse. He was cursing himself for letting the devil go when the fellow came back. The fellow had come back again to the place looking for her, within four or five days again on a foggy evening. The old man had plans to catch and tie the fellow with a rope. But before he could do so and ask for help, the fellow was gone in a flash.

If he had caught the fellow as he had planned, that would have been the end of all mischief."

Ronald rued the chance the old man had lost. He sighed as if he had the mortification of watching the chance slip away!

Gautam looked pale as he listened to the narration.

"And then…" Gautam could not help saying.

"And then," Ronald replied," When she returned from the vacation, nearly a month later, they said she was a changed woman, devastated and broken. No one ever saw her smile again. All the grace and charm were gone. She had black shades beneath her eyes and was pale faced. She was a lost soul. Lost and totally lost, in herself and her thoughts. Brooding all the time, even in the class. She would spend hours in the chapel, kneel before the lord, weep and pray. She was altogether a different woman, a poor soul."

Ronald sighed, took a deep breath.

Gautam listened, his eyes motionless; he held his breath as Ronald narrated the events.

"She spoke very little, they said. Not even to the young children—the orphans, who were surprised by her sudden change of attitude towards them. She received no letters. The old caretaker told me, the only letters she used to receive earlier were long blue envelopes with stripes of colour across the flaps, usually twice a month. She refused to receive even those. She sent those back to the village post office, who it is said redirected those."

"Then, they found it out. The cause of all the strange behaviour that she had developed. The fact became clear gradually. It was and it became known to all, the people at the chapel, in the village. As the bulge developed, the body showed, I mean when her body showed all the signs…!" Ronald was stopped by Gautam through the narration.

"The bulge … The signs…" Gautam shouted at Ronald. "What do you mean?"

"I mean what I say." Ronald was very calm. "She was pregnant. I believe she didn't know that or was not sure of the developments, till others found it out for her. Only when the body showed signs, the outward ones, she became sure like all others. Then, all hell broke loose. It was the beginning. The mother of all calamities." Ronald stopped for breath again.

And Gautam, he was shell-shocked. He felt as if he were on the verge of the precipice again. About to fall into the crevasse, in the heaps of snow! The nightmares that haunted him some thirteen years back came overwhelming him again.

"The whole church was in a turmoil. The whole village where she had acquired the reputation of a selfless soul in the service of the needy was stunned. She was questioned; she was grilled. There were some who called her a whore, a woman who had defiled herself before god and the church and had brought into disrepute all of the lord's teachings."

Ronald's narration was in the mould of an epic catastrophe!

"The Reverend offered her a way out. She could seek transfer from the place, he said. In fact, she had to leave the place. If she didn't, she would have been thrown out, anyway. Others said, the sympathizers certainly, that she could get an abortion. The local midwife in the village could perform that, or the best way was to get it done at the town by a qualified doctor. For days, she kept mum. The best possible solution, the well-wishers wanted had been suggested. That certainly would have been much better, made matters much easier.

"But the foolish girl that she was, she would have none of that. All the insults, all the humiliation, all the slang and the slur; she took those in her own stride. She would reveal neither the name nor the identity of the bastard, of the fellow who did that.

"More importantly, in the surprise of surprises, she didn't even seem to know the best way for her. She didn't even want to remove the devil's *gift*, the one that was growing inside her. She kept quiet and suffered silently through all the humiliation, the insults, all the mental torture to which she was subjected.

"Then one day, she vanished, they said. Vanished, before the people got to know much about her wishes. Someone, possibly a villager saw her in the very early hours of the morning, walking down the road, past the chapel, the bus stop, then out of the village, all alone till she went out of sight. Probably, she took one of the stray vehicles that took her to the town, might have been one of the loaded trucks, those that carried logs from the forests to the town."

Ronald finished the narration and asked for another cup of tea. Gautam listened to Ronald, with his heart in his mouth, literally. He held his head with both his hands while his elbows rested on the table.

The dreams, or the nightmares, those that he had in his adolescence, of falling off from great heights, like off the top of the cliffs, snowclad ones, the cathedral; all came back with renewed vigour to him, even as he sat fully awake. He didn't have to go to sleep for those nightmares to come and haunt him.

"I came to know of all those when I visited the place in search of her. I had gone there to find her, to know more about, after I heard a lot about her. You know well, how fast the gossip travels in small places. I actually went there after I had seen her once."

"Seen her? What do you mean?" Gautam was curious.

"Yes. I saw her. I saw her at the town where I live, at the bus stop at the marketplace. I thought she saw me as well and wanted to get away, hide herself. But I saw her all right. That was before I had heard or learnt anything at all of the episodes. I went to her to talk. She was not alone though. In her arms, I saw a child."

"A child?" Gautam screamed at Ronald. People at the teashop looked around at them.

"Yes. A child! I saw the child. I talked to her. In fact, it was the first time I had seen her in almost about three years. I was delighted. She looked frail. Very frail! Gone was her smile. Even her dimples were worn out. She didn't look at all happy to see me. I felt she was trying to avoid my queries and me. I asked her if the child was hers. She replied in the affirmative. I asked her when she had got married and when did she have the child. I congratulated her on her attaining motherhood. She said her husband lived in the plains and that the child was about six months old. Then she hurriedly took her seat in the bus that was to leave the town. Her behaviour seemed so strange, so unlike her, the Mary I had known. I guessed, not everything was all right with her." Ronald paused.

Gautam listened, surprised and astonished.

"Later, I learnt. A friend of mine from the church told me of a girl, a teacher at the school run by the church in the interiors, called Mary who had gone astray and had brought disgrace and dishonour to the order. I nearly broke the bones of the guy. Obviously, he didn't know her and had heard about her from someone else. I was curious. I wanted to know everything in details. The episodes that I had come to know in bits and parts, I wanted to settle for the truth. The uncharitable rumours about her moved me. I could not believe my ears. Never could I have imagined such things from her."

"I decided to go to her workplace to know the facts. When I reached her workplace, the chapel at the village, she was not there. In fact, I was told that she had left a year before. What I learnt from there, I have already told you. I knew she could never have been the one, people were calling her. That the bastard had made a fool of her was clear. Her innocence was what the fellow had made a mockery of."

"When I came back from her workplace, I tried to get in touch with some guys from her native village. I learnt gradually, all the details, bit by bit, in pieces, from different sources and I collected all the information."

Ronald made himself comfortable for another round of narration.

"After she left her workplace, it is said that she went to her native village. There she stayed on; till the time she gave birth to the baby. She was, I am afraid, not able to receive the medical attention at all. The nearest town had the medical facilities of the kind necessary but the villages had practically none of the kind. That she survived with her baby was nothing short of a miracle, given the sufferings she had to endure. I believe, she must have developed some kind of complications then on.

"There was further trouble for her at the village. The rumour had spread at the village also. Some of the ruffians, the young men wanted her. They pretended to be her suitors. To them, she was still charming, beautiful, and lovely. The bloody hounds! She kept them at bay till the time she could do so. Then, at the opportune moment, she fled the village, with her baby. If you were to hear her sufferings in details, you could feel the same torments, I am sure. But then, you behaved in a fashion no better than a scoundrel, Gautam!

"I hold you responsible for her plight which could have been avoided, had you taken care of her. How on earth could you stay away and not keep contact, when you were ready to die, for her once?"

Ronald fell silent. Gautam was silent, too. He felt dizzy. He felt he couldn't stand any more on his legs. He felt like falling down. Never before, did he feel, so helpless, so utterly helpless.

"The bloody bastard!" Ronald's remarks brought Gautam back amidst the conversation. "The bastard seemed to be one, known to her and known very well. She was the last person I knew, to move out with anyone unfamiliar. If I could ever, ever land my hand on that fellow, I for sure, would have taught him something." Ronald fumed.

"The bastard, I promise you man, I would have killed him and then gone to jail with not the slightest of remorse or repentance in my mind and in my heart for having done so." Ronald laid his hands on the table top and reflected.

"Strange are the ways of God. If she had come to me, or had I known of the episode and then met her, I would have gladly accepted her. To me, she was nothing short of being divine. But the bastard, how on earth could he do that to her and then ditch her. The poor foolish girl! How could she believe the bloody bastard?"

"Did you get to know anything of her, later?" Gautam gathered some courage to put the question through.

"Nothing much. Only that one day she escaped from her village. With the infant! She managed to get a job I learnt, in a far off place. It appeared she deliberately did so, to avoid the people, the place, and the preying eyes, away from the gossip and humiliating gestures. She took up a job at a government school in the eastern part of the state, where the known and familiar faces wouldn't be around to mock at her. Though I am not sure where she lives now—the last time I heard about her was two years ago. I learnt, it was away from her native place, far away from her earlier work-place. I also learnt from someone that she was not keeping good health. Others said, she had developed complications. Something was terribly wrong with her, something wrong there." Ronald pointed the index finger of his right hand towards his head and indicated.

"Something was terribly wrong with her. She wasn't at all well…" Ronald kept repeating to himself.

"Could you please tell me where to look for her?" Gautam asked Ronald, still unable to meet the eyes of his old friend.

"Look for her? I don't think, there is anything left now to look for at all." Ronald couldn't help saying. "Anyway, it is better late than never. I am not sure though, where to. I was told her half-sister works at the government hospital at the district headquarter town of Tezu, I am not absolutely sure though. If you desire, you could get specifics at her native village, I suppose."

Ronald had spoken of Mary, of Mary and Gautam all along. He didn't want to speak about himself. There was no happy news either. He had very little to speak about himself. He worked as a clerk at a government office. His parents had died. His brothers didn't have much in common with him. He had two marriages; one after another and both the wives had died. The only child he had by the first wife had died of malaria.

Ronald was thinking of a third marriage between his daily doses of booze. He had very little else to do.

He heard and learnt about Gautam from Gautam himself. The information of the career, life and life-style, with eyes wide open. The mention of the global enterprise made him wonder. He promised to visit Gautam at the city if and only if the best quality whisky was made available to him.

The rest of what he spoke meant very little to Gautam. His views of how the world had changed were irrelevant. Gautam was a bit surprised that despite his personal losses and bereavements that he had to bear, he was more concerned of others. Quite a character!

For Gautam, life was eventful, more ominously though. Full of changes and variations! It appeared it changed faster for him than for the rest of the world. So, Ronnie's remarks that world had changed meant little to him.

In his life that was in only the mid-twenties, the episodic occurrences were an integral part, those that came with more than their fair share of impact with wanton regularity.

The episode, the meeting of the 'old-friends' at the railway station was one such occurrence. It was the prelude to the climax.

Suddenly, he was full of grief and remorse. He wanted to cry, cry aloud, no matter if people were around. Yet, the newfound, new-discovered fatherhood, at least the feel of it, made him happy.

He wanted to cry and rejoice, at the same moment.

The sense of loss, the plight of the woman he once loved, the sufferings that she had to undergo tormented him. And then the news of his fatherhood, the paternal affection for the child he had not seen, but decidedly *of* him, all made him experience strange feelings—of joy, of fear, of happiness, of sorrow, of ecstasy, and of trauma!

He seemed to be a different man altogether.

He sat there, at the station, not knowing what to do next. The sense of loss was overwhelming. The news however, the news of the child brought anxiety with happiness, concern with pleasure. He sat and watched as each train passed by. He sat, not knowing what to do next.

Ronald had taken leave and gone off, on to his tour. Gautam knew he had to think over the matter and arrive at a decision.

He thought at the first instance to put aside, set aside the news of his fatherhood, of which he knew. He was not sure if Mary would have revealed it. Was the child really his? Was Mary still alone? Did she still harbour any hope of him coming back? Was she in the state of abject collapse as was stated?

But then, no one could answer the questions that came up. If he wanted answers, he had to explore himself.

He wanted to go to the region that he had left years ago. To the hills, to find out about his family.

The launch of the global enterprise could wait.

His *wife* and *son* were more important to him.

The call of the conscience was clear. Actually, for the first time, he heard the call.

To go into the search for her and her child and *his*, too!

He was then, flooded with emotions of all kinds, of all tenderness, of all sublime feelings of newly discovered fatherhood, of love, of compassion, of all the heartfelt love for the little one.

Was the child all right? And the mother, as well?

Was Mary ready to confer fatherhood on to him? Was she ready to forgive him? After all, it was the woman who attributed, conferred fatherhood on man, from ages.

But if she refused to do that? What could he do then?

He felt the pinch. He was off-balance. He could only close his eyes, hold his head with his hands and try to gather himself.

He had to leave for the search.

***

The ordeal began for Gautam. He simply didn't know where to start. He had collected the name and location of her native village, of her father, and of her half-sister. He was unsure of the response from any of them.

It was the child whose thoughts completely overshadowed him, overwhelmed him. More than the thoughts of her! It was the child all the way, as he kept thinking. Between the two, for the first time there was a new entity. The child, the third entity!

Among the three, it was the child that demanded and received, attention and concern, more than she did!

He left the idea of proceeding to his 240 50/ N, 920 51/ E place and decided to go and look for his family. The family, he had no idea of having started. That which was the result of an accident, perilous, sudden and abrupt—with a calamitous sequel to the blissful dreams of a happy beginning. He had virtually given up hope of her long ago, and pushed her almost to the oblivion. He had a bright career to cater to, which lay in wait for him. One such stray incident happening some half a dozen years ago should not have mattered at all.

That one blood-smeared-all-over evening could have such consequence of eventful propositions, such painful propensities, he had not taken into account, even in his calculative mind.

He had seen those things happening in the movies and read about those in the works of fiction, where melodrama was the main ingredient. He had least imagined that such events could occur in his life.

So far, his life of twenty and some years had certainly been an eventful one.

Having changed his course, he made towards the hills. The child, the thoughts of the child whom he had not seen, kept coming to him; the child of his and her flesh and blood. The reminiscences, her thoughts kept coming to him as well.

During those romantic days, when dreams were as good as facts and facts could be dreamt of, when love was in the air, Mary had her high. She used to speak of a family, sometimes of a family her own.

Later, when they met during the fateful vacation for Christmas, she was more forthright and he, more assertive.

In the ruins, where they visited and when they met with the glow in their eyes, before the catastrophe, they had a dream.

While he lay headlong on the ground with rows and rows of rocks, statues and images, ruins spread all over; where the grass was the perfect cushion to support them, with the strange ambience, the aura of bygone times surrounding them; resting his head on her lap and she ran her fingers through his hair. He got a full view of her breasts and she kissed him on his forehead.

She was in her own world. Lost. In her dreams!

She was talking to herself.

"If I have my son, I will name him Mark." She said as she looked in the distance, with a sort of a blank look.

"And if the child is a daughter, then?" Gautam had asked getting interested in her run of imaginations.

"Then I am going to name her Martha." She was still daydreaming.

"Thank God." Gautam had replied as Mary looked at him with inquisitive eyes, coming back to her 'senses' from her dreams.

"Well, thank God, again." Gautam had laughed. "It means you have plans to settle down and raise a family of your own."

Only then, did she realise what she had said. She could only blush.

Gautam had knelt in the act of prayer, crossed himself and looked upward to the skies, to the heaven.

"Oh Lord! At last, you have given your *blessed* child a sound idea." Mary did raise her head. She was feeling shy, as if she has said something premature, and out of the world.

Gautam had kept on teasing her. " All along, I had thought that this lady would join the order, become a nun and leave me nowhere. Lord! I pray to thee. I thank thee for having blessed her with some kind of a future programme."

"What do you mean?" Mary had asked him.

She looked coy. Or did he feel the urge that made her look coy?

"Well, very simple. Very plain! For raising a family, I believe you need someone's help for sure." He had kept on teasing her. I don't think this is going to be another immaculate conception. Right? You surely need someone. So, I stand a chance. Don't I?"

Mary was embarrassed, totally. She had covered her face with her hands. Gautam had left her undisturbed for a moment. Slowly, he had removed her hands and raised her chin. Her eyes were still closed.

"Mary, I love you," Gautam had said very softly, as if he were whispering in her ears." You are the one, I dream of."

"Do you want to know what name I have in my mind for my son, I mean our son?" He wanted the conversation to go on.

Mary had opened her eyes slowly, and cast a side way glance.

"I will call him Rahul, That, is the finest name I can think of. There is some similarity, Gautam's son—Rahul. Anyway, you could call him Mark. That would be your choice. For me though, he shall always be Rahul."

The chain of thoughts was broken as the bus in which the new-discovered father travelled in search of his son and the mother, came to a screeching halt. He found himself at the place, at the threshold of search for Mary and her son.

Where to look for them, he didn't know.

He decided to begin his search from her native village. He had collected the name and location of her village from Ronnie, and he set out to reach her village.

A day of bus ride in the interiors and then after a night halt at an inn with bed bugs and mosquitoes making a merry of him; he walked for nearly eight hours to reach her village, Mary's village, as a complete stranger.

He soon found her native home. It was on a raised platform, as good as a *machan*, as was the practice. A big room with bamboo walls, the whole structure resting on bamboo poles. The hogs and the fowls reared, lived beneath.

There was her father, lying on the bamboo floor, coughing. He was not very old, but the torture he had inflicted on himself showed the signs. He was bent with bowed back, emaciated, and smelt of country liquor. All around was a nauseating smell, strong enough to make the stomach regurgitate all its contents! In the otherwise very clean surroundings of the forest, the young man's handkerchief found its best use.

The man looked at him with dull, swollen eyes and then asked him in a language, a mix of local dialects and spoken languages.

"Who are you? What do you want? Why have you come here?"

"I am from the church, in the town," Gautam answered. He had no better reply. That he thought, would ease up the conversation." I have come here to enquire about your daughter, Mary. In fact, I have been sent by the church." That looked the only way to save the situation.

"Oh Mary! The wretched girl." The man coughed. "Why does the church enquire now? They were not kind to her. What do they want now?"

Gautam had to resort to another round of lies.

"Well, the church has realised the mistake. I have been sent by the Reverend to fetch her. They want her to join the work place again."

"But she is gone," he said. " She left the place for good.

"But where to?" Gautam was anxious to know.

The man looked at him. "The girl—my daughter—she was so good. How could she fall into the trap, I don't know. She gave birth to the child, here. There were so many nice young men, rich and well-to-do in the village. They were her suitors. But she would not agree. I wanted her to marry one of them. But the stupid girl wouldn't listen. It is because of her that I am in such a poor state. She left suddenly and left me nowhere. She didn't tell me that she was leaving, or else I would not have let her do so. I would have rather tied her to the bamboo pole and forced her to marry one of her suitors." The old man was bitter.

"But then, she had a job and worked somewhere. Didn't she help you?" Gautam wanted to engage him in conversation.

"Yes. But that was more for her sister, her half-sister, Martha. The girl too left me without any hesitation. As soon as Mary sent a message, Martha also went away to her, simply went away. Now, even for my daily want of liquor, I have to buy. Earlier Martha used to prepare that for me. The girls are selfish and I pray to god that they suffer the same way, that they have made me suffer."

The caustic father, drenched in country liquor, appeared to be the most abominable creature on earth.

"Don't they send any money to you?" Gautam wanted to know.

"Martha left me nearly three years ago. I am alone here, since then. Mary used to send me some amount every month through the local post-office till about six months back. Since then, I am left with no regular amount of money being sent. Whatever I had saved are nearly all gone."

"You are her friend, Mary's friend. Aren't you? " The man suddenly asked "Could you help me?"

Gautam knew what the old man meant. He searched his pockets for the currency notes and whatever he had; he handed over those to the man. The man was delighted. He asked

Gautam to stay. Gautam declined to prolong his stay in the debilitating surrounding.

Gautam felt relieved. He had helped the man. The man after all, whether he liked the man or not; however much he despised the fellow, was her father, his *father-in-law.*

Truly, *relations die hard! More so in this land!*

"The child she had, could you let me know anything more of him?" Gautam asked the man.

"When she left, the child was nearly two years old. Not as fair as she was, the child was darker in complexion. The child of a plainsman! I hated the child, the cause of all her troubles and my ruins. But she loved the child." The man needed no incentives to talk. He carried on.

"She called him Mark. Not for a single moment did she ever leave the child alone. She carried him on her back in the folds of the cloth that every mother ties to her back. She received a letter one-day and the next day she was gone with the child. Later, I learnt it was the offer of a job. I had almost arranged her marriage with the headman's youngest son. She was to be his third wife, the most beautiful and educated of them all. That would have made me a relation of the village headman. That would have placed me in a comfortable position, without much worry for my food and liquor. But she didn't allow me that comfort for the rest of my life. God will never forgive her for that treatment to me, her father. I wish she suffers the same way that I am suffering."

Gautam had already lost patience with the fellow. He had no desire left to prolong the conversation.

"Could you tell me where had she gone?" Gautam asked him.

"Mary sent me money from the town across the mad river, on the other side of it, in the Lohit district, the town of Tezu, When Martha went away, I learnt she was there. For the last six months, I have no news of her whereabouts. Martha, she said got a job in the hospital there, you know where they treat patients and distribute medicines, free of cost. If anyone could take me there, I would have gone. Could you take me there?"

Gautam felt sorry for the man, for the first time. The feel of helplessness with no one to take care could make even the strongest man decimate. That man however, was worn out and wretched.

He assured the man of doing something and left.

He had only one goal. To get to her. To know about her and their son. To see if they were well. Things didn't however seem to be so. He had some kind of a strange feeling that everything was not very well. He had decided to go in search, for them. Nothing could stop him, not his carrier, his global launch, not anything in the world.

His entire life, his mission, was to be the atonement, the expiation of sort if need arose; to bring his family from and out of humiliation; and restore dignity, from obscurity to proper recognition. He felt the new discovered fatherhood and new-acquired family consciousness had made a man out of him, in an altogether different context, much different from the one he led in the city. In the air-conditioned office surrounded by personal computers, talking to the entrepreneurs abroad, manhood meant being successful everywhere, even while picking up right women. The manhood had different meanings in different settings.

Gautam tried to restructure the facts. The family, Mary and her son—Mark, were quite well till a year ago, at least alive. There was no news of Mary to her father for the past six months. That was the cause of concern. Whether they were still at the place—Tezu—old man said was the question. Anyway, inquiries at the hospital, the school, the church or even a chance encounter with an old acquaintance might happen, which could be of immense help.

He could think of no other way, no other scheme of things.

He set out for the sleepy town of Tezu, more plain-like than being hill-like. Far across the mad river Digaru that was no more than a stream in the driest of the months, was the town. The river that was harmless during winter when people could walk across, assumed tremendous fury during the monsoons. With strong current, when no boat could ferry across, the only recourse was the ride on elephant back, no joyride certainly. Even, the elephants sometimes were afraid to walk across the river in full flow during the rainy season. The trained pachyderms, with human loads on their backs often tested the strength of the current in the river with their front legs in the river water for some minutes, and then proceeded to walk across. If they found it was impossible, they retraced their steps back, with their customary calls of anger and resignation. There were reported loss of lives sometimes back when people unaccustomed to rides on elephants, slipped from the back of the pachyderm on to the water below, sometime a single fellow in trying to gain grasp—the grasp for survival, pulled down people, from among the fellow passengers. Those who went down, met their inevitable gory death, their skulls smashed against boulders, their bodies carried over long distances by the fury of the river current.

For Gautam though, no such episode was in store. It was the winter season, the early part of the calendar year. It was when the mad river was no better than being a dry stream when people could walk across. The river was on its way to change its course, which usually it did after some years, as it flowed past the sleepy town. The change of course of the river was getting faster and people said that by the next few monsoons it could completely change its course and flow through the sleepy town.

The mad river Digaru, from the hills, of the lower reaches of the Himalayas was all set to change its course.

The change of course appeared to be exactly like that of someone else's life that seemed to be on the edge of a precipice, on the threshold of a sudden change, on the brink of a change, hopefully not for disaster.

The watershed was visible, literally.

In the sleepy town,Tezu, the people seemed to know each other. If not very well or particularly well, then by name or surnames, or by the offices where they worked or at least by their *specialties.*

It was therefore, not much difficult to search or trace anybody. The only precaution one needed to take was not being over inquisitive, when people could be unwilling to share information. Only casual approach was the better option and he decided to try that. He concluded that the hospital and the school were the two important and most likeable of all places to seek information and the shops close to those, form where information could be collected. He had to be careful enough not to show any excessive interest that could raise eyebrows.

He got to know something about her at the school.

Yes, they said. There was a lady teacher, an Adi woman; Mary Pertin was her name. She had a kid—a son whose features were not fully tribal-like (by tribal features, they meant Mongoloid ones) and that she was at the school for a short period. She was transferred to a place about eighty kilometres away, some four thousand feet higher up, in the hills.

To know more about her, they said, the best person was her sister, Martha who worked as a nurse at the government hospital. That was a minefield of information for him. When he learnt that, he was off to meet her.

Martha was a bit shorter than Mary was. A bit more round, plump but carrying the same facial features, the Mongoloid faces didn't always look all similar. She was attending a patient, clearing the pus and putting on the sterilized bandage cloth when Gautam went in to meet her. For a moment, he thought Mary was standing in front of him till he realized that there was someone else looking at him.

She looked at him, the stranger, and the displeasure was very evident.

"You want to meet me? Talk to me? What for?" she asked. " I don't know you. I can't see what we have to talk about?"

"Well, Ms Martha. I have something to talk to you. You don't know me but I know you." Gautam paused. "I gather you are the sister of Mary Pertin. As a matter of coincidence, Mary and I, we studied at the same college in the plains more than a decade ago. We were classmates."

"If we have to talk, you will have to wait till my duty is over." she replied nonchalantly.

Gautam waited for her. Every minute seemed like a decade spent in anxiety, of impending calamity, in expectation, of anguish. When she was free from her duty, Gautam could talk to her sitting opposite her in the tea-shop nearby. The looks of an aggrieved man, he could hardly conceal. His unshaven face and dirty hair made him look more like a brute, brat and a brigand than a weary traveller.

"You said you knew her. But I never heard about you from her," she started.

"Well, we were very good friends. We were classmates. She was such a nice girl." Gautam replied.

"Yes, she was a very nice girl. And a foolish one, too. Or else why should…anyway, Mr. Gautam, Mary is no more. She is dead." Martha stood up, ready to leave.

"Dead!" Gautam cried out. "What do you mean? Please, Martha. Please don't be so harsh. Why don't you tell me everything? I have come all the way to look for her."

"But why should I tell you? Someone from the plains wronged her, a non-tribal one. You are one of them. Why should I tell you?" She was stubborn.

"Please, Martha." Gautam appealed, almost implored. "We were very good friends at the school and the college. We attended the same church. And she sang so beautifully."

That cooled Martha down. She sat down, motionless, gathering herself.

"Mary is d-e-a-d. Poor Mary."

He found it difficult to control himself.

"She was a foolish girl. Poor creature," lamented Martha. "She came here to escape the clutches of the goons who tried to molest her, on more than one occasion. They felt if she had been *done in*, they could do it again and again." Martha opened up.

"She came here with the infant when he was about a year old. Yet, bringing up the child as an unwed mother was not a very happy situation. So, she choose to move away from the place and go higher up where the acquaintances and inquisitive faces would be fewer. Till she was here, she harboured a faint hope, an illusion of that scoundrel turning up for her and the child," she told those in response to what he said about her, about what he had heard about her, from her father in her native village. He made himself presentable to Martha, or else he knew information could not be obtained.

Martha continued.

"Even when the possibility of the scoundrel ever returning seemed remote and the chance seemed nearly over, she decided to leave the place which I believe was not at all good for her health. She had developed abnormalities. The change of place could not have helped her. The sufferings she had to endure were far too much to absorb. The troubles, the humiliation, the treachery all had their affects. She had brought me here and I got a job in this hospital. She moved with the child, up in the higher reaches of the hills about eighty kilometres from here. There her condition deteriorated. The abnormalities, the mental ones became more pronounced. One of her colleagues took the troubles of informing me one day that she was in a very bad shape. I rushed to the place immediately. Truly, I found her in dire straits. Her health was failing and failing rapidly. She had thinned almost to her bones. The loneliness there seemed to have affected her even more, for the worse. She often sat alone, gloomy and marooned, not talking. Not talking to anyone. Not even to the child, taking care of him and of her. The child was nearly abandoned, while living with his mother. He had to fend for himself. It was the same child who had been her only solace and she could never ever leave him alone, even for a moment. She had to bear the entire trauma and humiliation for his sake and yet then, she seemed to have abandoned him. She was gradually going out of her senses, losing her balance." Martha finished her long but painful narration, and went on.

"I thought it best to take her back to this place, the district headquarters, for better care and better medical attention, care for both the mother and the child, with the hope that her health and condition would improve. But that was not to be. She would not even look at the child—her son, at all. Never did she care for him anymore."

"The infliction was severe. Not at the physical level though: but at the mental and emotional levels. Even her spirit seemed shattered. Poor soul! In fact, I had to take care of the child and for me it was absolutely difficult. Anyway, I had not much love left for the child, the *devil's* child. I knew, she had very little chance of improving." Martha paused for breath.

Gautam looked at Martha. He could barely control the upsurge of emotions. The pangs of guilt, of desertion, of abandoning his family seemed severe. The pain was immense.

He looked at Martha with expectant eyes.

"The child was the problem," Martha continued. "I thought the best way was to place the child at an orphanage. She didn't object to it. In fact, she had lost her mental balance to judge. She responded to the idea with blank stare. However, there was nothing of the sort—I mean orphanages, in the whole area. One day, someone told me of a home of a different kind set up by a gentleman some miles away from the town, that took care of the children, on a very modest scale.

"That home, the sort of orphanage, had just been set up and benevolent gentlemen—an elderly gentleman of the local *Mishmi* tribe by a retired medical practitioner by he name Dr. Chai. He had set up one at a place near the Parasurama Kunda, nearly twenty kilometers away, the place that the Hindus adore. Where thousands descend at the mid-January festival to have purifying baths at the river Lohit. What do people get from those baths I do not know. Mr Chai had set up his orphanage at that location.

"I went there to inquire. Though the facilities were very modest, yet, the sincerity and devotion of the gentleman was unquestionable. His love for the children was overwhelming. Some formalities were necessary. I got a form, which they gave me for placing the child in their care. I intended to place the child there in case of an eventuality."

Martha continued her narration unfolding the details bit by bit.

"More surprises were in store. While filling up the form, she asked the name of her son to be recorded as Rahul and not Mark, which was the name of the child. To me that appeared surprising! I thought something had gone terribly wrong with her. She had after all developed mental abnormalities, which were worsening. I tried to correct the name but she would have none of that. I didn't know what she had in her deranged mind.

"Before her condition worsened further, I decided to place the child at the home. It was not a very happy occasion to take the child away and leave him there. That for sure was a touching scene. But again, she was terribly calm. One last look at the child where it seemed all the maternal care and love and affection in the world was in the look; then it was all over. She didn't look at him again. The child was too perplexed and confused to understand much. He was overawed by the situation. For nearly a year and a half he had developed a sort of fear of her, getting used to the uncaring ways and treatment form his mother with no demonstration of love. But that event was a bit too much for the child to bear. He knew something not very happy lay in store for him—for a four-year old child, grown precocious by the events, that was intelligible to him.

"Yet, I cannot think of the scene again. As I led away the child, she refused to turn and look back again at him. The child called out at her and she didn't respond. She was abnormal; she had lost her mental balance. Even I found it difficult to take on the situation. Tears were in my eyes but surprisingly not in hers. I took the child and left him in the care of the elderly gentleman who had set up the home. The child knew, he had found a new home where he could get love and care as well."

Gautam allowed Martha to go on. He didn't interrupt her. He had lost any strength to do so. He allowed Martha to empty her heavy heart.

"The next day, she was calm and quiet as ever, grave and serious. She made me promise that if someone came, ever looking for her and the child, I should lead him to the child. She, it appeared, still had hopes of the scoundrel returning. She handed over to me a bunch, a packet of some sort and asked me to hand that over to the child when he grew up. No one else but her son alone was to open it."

"Little did I know, what was in store for her and for me. Only when I returned from my schedule, I had the night shift, the next morning, I found on that fateful day that tragedy had struck. She had taken an overdose of pills, those that I had brought for her medication. It was too late by then. She had taken those, probably by the evening. In spite of the medical attention of what was possible at that stage, she didn't survive. The church was informed; I had to arrange for the funeral. The next Sunday she was interred unsung, unwept, and almost unattended except for me and those who performed the service."

Martha wiped her tears. And Gautam? He found fluid flowing from his eyes and nose. One handkerchief was not enough. His voice was choked. He had to get up, wash his face, and clear his throat thrice, before he could speak.

"Martha," he said very softly to her." Could you please take me to her grave? I would like to pay her my respects, at her last resting place."

Martha nodded.

Some two miles to the west, was the church. In the backyard lay the graves, some not cared, nor attended. There was grass growing all around. Among the tall grass, few mounds could

be seen with wooden cross on each one of those. Each cross signified a grave. Stray cattle moved freely. To a bamboo peg struck in the ground was tethered a calf while the mother cow tended and licked her calf. Goats helped themselves to the tall, long, delicious fodder.

Through the grass, Martha led Gautam to a mound where lay the remains, the mortal remains of his ladylove. On the concrete block at one side of the mound (Martha paid for that, only a few graves had concrete blocks) with a cross above it was engraved:

'ANGEL MARY PERTIN (1965-1990)'

His beloved, the Lord's chaste and devoted daughter lay in blissful continence, of eternal sleep, never to be disturbed again. With her dreams, of her family, of her son, of her desires and very simple aspirations, she lay there, resting. Rest forever.

Gautam had nothing to say, utter or cry. It was all over. He stood there in front of her and then knelt down and kissed the grave as Martha stood beside him. He looked up to Martha and asked, "Supposing the man who wronged her were to return one day to look for her and her son, what would you do?"

Martha couldn't conceal her anger even in the somber ambience.

"The scoundrel!" she said, "I would just simply ask him what had this purest soul done to him that he should have avenged her that way."

"Then, do what you please, Martha." Gautam was cool and calm as never before. Martha startled; she was confused and looked at him for an explanation.

"Do what you want, Martha. Avenge your sister's death. In the name of the Lord, the offender, the sinner is before you." Gautam couldn't control his tears from coming off.

Martha with tears in her eyes looked in disbelief. She was shocked, struck by the plainest of the words that came from the man kneeling before the grave, in front of her.

It took her quite a while to recover from the shock, the unexpected occurrence when she least hoped for anything of the kind. The man before her, in front of her, was the man who had wronged her sister, the man of whom she had heard so much, whom she hated, who was responsible for the plight of her sister. He was now in front of her, deep in grief and remorse. She was speechless. She had no answer, being overtaken by the events. She didn't know how or what to respond or react to. She was not sure how to respond to the man kneeling beside her sister's grave, with anger or hatred or sorrow.

"Martha." Gautam said as he tried to clear to lump in his throat. "I am the offender. But I can assure you what had happened nearly six years ago, was an accident. Later, just after that I tried to get in touch with her. I went back to the chapel—I mean her workplace, but she was not there. I couldn't go to your native village, as I had no information. All the letters I wrote to her came back to me. Those were not received. So, I gave up writing. I lost touch with her, then on. I never thought that the situation could have become so grave, so serious, so bad for her; or that she was a mother. Had I known all that, I would certainly have done what I could. Now that she is no more, I do not know how to atone. How should I repent? Whom to ask for forgiveness?"

Martha, her face almost totally devoid of expression, of neither anger nor happiness not any other emotion, looked at him.

"Please, Martha." Gautam said in a broken voice. "Could you please lead me to where my son, I mean our son is?"

Martha nodded. Then she spoke as if she were speaking to herself.

"The poor soul, the purest one. Mary had gone to her old school in the plains where she had studied once to meet the Mother Superior after the incident, who was the only person who could have comforted her, provided her the solace. But by them, the mother had left. Or else, or else she would not have been so humiliated, so cursed.

"She came back to village, broken. I was too young to notice that, then. But she looked gloomy and pale and spoke very little. It was only after about five months that she came back to the village from her workplace with her bulge that we got to know everything. But she would not reveal the name of the father of the baby. We thought anyone amongst her acquaintances—lot many were her suitors, had done that."

Martha looked at Gautam. Her looks were of forgiving disposition. He understood that.

"After the baby was born, the troubles started," Martha went on. "The troubles were from all sides. She didn't have proper medical attention. She was already in a state of shock and trauma.

"Her health was not very good either. That she survived and her baby too, was because of god's grace upon her. The local mid-wife took care of the childbirth in the village. She never regained her health after that.

"Then started the ordeal of bringing up the child in the village. She had very little money. When the child was about six months old, she took him tied to her back to the near-by town and I accompanied her. There she applied for a job as a teacher at a primary school. The application has to be processed through the office at the town. I had to promise her that I would never reveal the information to anyone, back at the village.

"Already, the people at the village had begun to take notice of her. There were a few young men; the village headman's son was one who proposed to her. She tactfully kept them at bay. She had to. They were all ruffians, boozers, and could do harm.

"She confided everything in me, except the name and identity of the father of her baby, never ever. Not the name of the man who wronged her, I mean your name." Martha looked at him and lowered her eyes.

"When she got her job offer, the offer came through a letter through the village post office, we kept it a secret. My father, you probably know was no better than those brutes. Had he known anything of the sort, her escape would have been extremely difficult.

"Then, one morning she left with her child. The baby was nearly a year old, then. She left without any belongings as it could have raised eyebrows. Only I knew where she was off to. Later, I had to pretend that I did not know anything at all, to my father and to the village folk.

"When she came here to work at this place, I believe she began searching for you. That was nearly two years ago. So far as I gather, she wrote to your address, but got no reply. She had brought me here and I got a job as a nurse at the government hospital," Martha concluded.

"If she had written to me, why did I not get those letters, then? If that was two or three years back, then I must have left the college. My god!" Gautam exclaimed. Martha kept quiet.

"Now that you are here. I know you will look for the child, now. He is at the home of Dr Chai. I saw him nearly three months later, after her death. I can assure you, the child looks very similar to you, especially the nose, I mean. Both of you have similar nose." Martha tried hard to smile at him. For Gautam, that was the only solace he could find amidst sadness all around.

"The child is very cute and cuddlesome. We called him Mark. At the Home, he is called Rahul. He responds to both the names," Martha said.

"I don't know whether you would go back to the city or not. If that were so, I mean if you go back to the city, I wish you took him along. Only then I know; her soul could rest in peace.

I myself would be satisfied as well. If, however you choose to leave him here, I would certainly have nothing to say. Anyway, the expectations were over long ago.

"I only wish her soul rests in peace. The plight of the child for the present is all right. The future is however uncertain. Mary's soul, wherever it might be, I believe, I know can only be relieved if her son has a proper upbringing, the rightful one in his father's care. Of course, the choice is yours."

Martha said as they walked out of the church and the graveyard, as they crossed the bamboo fencing that marked the surrounding.

For Gautam, she was part of history. History by herself! To him, then, the only beacon light was the child, their son at the Home. He wanted to see his son. He was dying to see his son. Only if the could fly, he would have done that without wasting a second.

The son, Mark for her and Rahul for rest of the world.

She had done her duty. Probably, she knew he might come one day looking for her and not find her; the only solace left then was sure to be the son. The secret, which only they knew, and no one else! Or why or earth did she name him Rahul for the world?

To him, the child was:

MARK/RAHUL.

The child, their son, was the manifestation of the great expectations of the apocalypse.

The apocalyptic expectations!

CHAPTER 16

The Charmed Bliss

Having made his credentials clear, he was ready to meet his son. Martha had to ask for leave the next day to accompany Gautam to meet the child, who was at the Home of the benevolent gentleman who had taken up the onerous task of rearing the children.

That was again a contrast. Some leave their children who are left to fend for themselves; and yet, there are some that pick-up children form garbage dumps to give a fresh lease of life to the very young.

They set out on their mission. No scheduled conveyance was available. It was because of the off-season when no regular vehicle was available to take people to the *kund*, the holy place. The off-season continued for about ten months of the year, usually. It was only during the season of just about two months in January and February that regular conveyance was available. That transported people from the town to the obscure place, up in the hills where the river Lohit swerved to enter the plains to rush on and then move with great velocity to meet the sacred Tsangpo flowing from Tibet and river Dibang to form the might Brahmaputra, in the plains.

More than thirty miles away from the sleepy town, through the thick monsoon forests, thinned only by the human exploitation, on either side of the road that appeared like a huge serpent, coiling and uncoiling itself, lay the place.

The road was metalled for most portions. The vehicle they took was a small one. It was hired at quite a high price. There was no other alternative. Moreover, it had to be 'reserved'.

The owner of the vehicle, who was also the driver, took them to be pilgrims or interested tourists, whom he felt were the 'prize catches' of the day. The vehicle needed a few pushes before the start. The driver was at the steering wheel. Gautam and the boy who worked as the assistant of the driver had to push the vehicle—the worn-out jeep, a few yards, so that it could gain the start.

Finally, it obliged with puffs of grey smoke thrown all over the face of the two pushers. Only then could Martha and Gautam get in to the jeep and the boy sat at the rear. The driver had them agree to the condition that he could pick-up stray passengers, if any, he could find on the way. They agreed. They had to. That was the only conveyance they could get.

For Gautam, no matter what conditions came by, he was dying to get to the place.

The vehicle puffed and ranted as it pushed up along the road that led to the place, more than thirty miles from the sleepy town, winding up the road. The cooler air of upper reaches enlivened their spirits.

From the road below, the traces of the river, Lohit to the people in the region was visible. The traces became gradually clear to present a view of bluish stretches against green backdrop. That gave him a new sensation.

It was a pilgrimage surely, though of a *different kind.*

As the jeep moved around the last hillock, the sound became audible. It was nothing short of a fantasy coming true, coming alive. The road changed, its gradient gradually becoming steep.

At the place where they stopped the vehicle, the owner-driver retired to the tea-shop where he had it appeared quite a few acquaintances.

The ambience was near perfect and enlivening. The touch was very soothing. The place he had often heard in the past was the Parasurama Kund that was almost divine in its location and setting.

Up the raised hillock was located the Home of Mr Chai that cared for the children, mostly the orphans. Steps made by spades and shovels, with bamboo poles and railings for support greeted them. They made their way up to the Home climbing those steps.

At a distance, the loved river flowed down below. Gautam looked at the surging water of the river Lohit that moved with great velocity to meet the Tsangpo and Disbang to form the mighty Brahmaputra of the Indian plains.

It was enthralling.

Martha led Gautam to the place up the steps, where the Home was located. The gentleman Mr. Tangleso Chai lived there, loving and caring for the little ones. Mr Chai's Home was located on the hillock overseeing the river that flowed below. From the top, the surging water could be seen dashing against the rocks; the roaring sound was audible from a great distance, of gushing, dashing water. The view from the top was no less enchanting.

Mr Chai called the place as 'KRISHNA HOME'. There were a few young children in his care. Mostly, the infants were cared for. Children from the age below one year to that of five years were present. And elderly woman looked after them; there were a couple of relatively younger woman who assisted her.

The gentleman greeted them at his office—a small room with corrugated iron- sheet roofing and walls plastered on bamboo walling. The bespectacled man with smile on his lips appeared to be the repository of all the tender values, tender graces of human heart. For him his world revolved around the children. Their up-keep, their education, their medical attention, was all he talked about.

"For me, they are all Krishna(s)," he said to Martha. The love for children, the veneration for their being the manifestation of divinity existed in all societies, all faiths, from very early times."

"To me, they are all the likes of *Bal Gopal* (infant Krishna) and infant Jesus." He talked to Martha. She was acquainted with him and his Home. Gautam listened with anxiety visible on his face. His heart beat fast as he was hardly able to control himself.

Martha introduced Gautam to Mr Chai as a gentleman from the city—the metropolis, on a chance visit to the place, who was interested to visit his Home. Mr Chai thanked Gautam for the interest.

The gentleman took Gautam on a round of his Home. He and those who knew about the Home picked up lost and abandoned infants. The infants, some a few months old were lying on their little cradle-beds, with little quilts, blankets over them. Small oily sheets acted as bedsheets so that those could be cleaned.

The infants lay in rows, attended by the caretaker women. Mr Chai walked past each one, asking if they were in good shape, fondled them and the children, the infants smiled back at him. It was a sight to watch.

But Gautam was getting inpatient, all the while.

After the round was over, it took nearly an hour, they returned to the office. Every minute he spent was in agony.

Then, Martha said, "Mr Chai, could we look for Rahul. The gentleman would like to see him." She indicated to Gautam.

Mr Chai called for the boy. He was among the group of young children of his age playing outside, in the backyard.

Every second seemed like a decade spent for Gautam. He could almost hear his own heartbeat. He could barely control his anxiety.

Then the child appeared at the doorway. The expression of surprise, fear and inquisitiveness was evident of his face. His little eyes tried to gauge, feel the situation; trying to figure out the strange uncertainty in the air.

And Gautam? He was almost paralyzed by the pleasant shock; he could hardly control the upsurge of emotions. He wanted to jump and hug and kiss the child, take him in his arms. The child, his son and hers, Mary's, of real flesh and blood!

The child was his. It could not have been anyone else's. He had the Mongoloid features of Mary but the nose and ears were all *his*. Particularly, the nose! That was *his,* without any doubt. The blob, the rounded tip of his nose, the raised nose with the special globular tip was exactly on his son. That particular trait which was his specialty, in fact it was their family characteristic— genetic, hereditary specialty!

At the spur of the moment, suddenly, Gautam found his own hand going up to his own nose to feel the rounded, globular tip. It was some kind of an involuntary spontaneous action. He suddenly realised that he was looking for evidence, for proof, of the child being his son, on himself. Perhaps, substantiating claims of fatherhood as if he were searching for his identity, as the father of the child, his son, on himself!

The child could not have been anybody else's. It was his child, his son, and their son, his and her.

The nose, slightly bent upward, curved upward in the middle, long and raised, broad at the base, with tip, round and globular was the mark of his family. His father used to call that a 'family specialty'; everything had to be special, even the not-so-beautiful nose had to be eulogized, and the old man did that to perfection.

The nose, on the child's face was beginning to take the not-so-lovely curve; as if someone had cut it off from Gautam's photograph when he was in his fifth year and planted it on the child's face some twenty years later.

Amazing. No more proof of parenthood, fatherhood was really necessary. That was the nature's paternity test—bonafede, verified, tested, and substantiated. No more evidence needed.

The child looked at him—the only perfect and complete stranger in the room, with innocence and anxiety in the eyes and face.

With his voice nearly choked, broken, Gautam called the child to him.

"Come here," he said. "Come to me." The child approached and stood near him, in front of him, maintaining a distance. With trembling hands, he touched the child softly, drew him close, tousled his hair gently and closed his own eyes.

He wanted to cry, kiss his son and hug him but could not do so. No public demonstration was warranted.

He closed his eyes and in the heart of his hearts he remembered her, Mary; as he saw her smiling face. He said, "Forgive me Mary, this time I am not letting him down. Our son has found *his* father."

For Gautam, the hesitant embrace of the child was the ultimate bliss. Was it then the kingdom of God in heaven transplanted down on earth? Surely, that was. For Gautam, nothing else could have been that. That was the actual, the perfect kingdom of God.

"What is..." Gautam tried to clear the lump in his throat." What is your name?" he asked the child.

"Mark...Rahul," replied the child, still in embrace, within the folds of his father's arms. The child was surprised by the reaction, amazed at the sudden fondle, the tussle of the hair and the caressing of his face. That was the best the young father could do under the circumstances. Embrace, caress and fondle, restraining him from being any more demonstrative.

The catharsis was on.

"Are you doing fine here?" The father asked. The child nodded. Hesitant! The child was trying to fathom the depths of the sudden demonstration of love and care from the stranger. In many months of his short life, he had not encountered such strong show of love. He tried to compare the sudden burst of love and care with that he had nearly forgotten, that he used to receive from his mom.

For the young father, that was the bliss of the lifetime. Never before, had he experienced such feeling of happiness and satisfaction. He decided not to prolong the scene any longer. He was not sure of his reactions. The gifts—of all the chocolates and biscuits—he left at the office for the children there.

They, Gautam and Martha, took leave from Mr Chai after seeking permission from the gentleman that Gautam would soon return to the site, at the place where the river Lohit formed the pool and then flowed on.

They came out of the Home and looked below. Down below amidst the mist and fog flowed the river, with surging water dashing against the rocks and boulders of the river Lohit. The sound was music to his ears.

The surging water formed some kind of a pool what was better known as a kund, the Brahma kund aka the divine pool. In the period from the around mid-January every year, all over the land, the harvest festival under different names was celebrated—the practice followed over centuries.

Like as in other places, *Makar Sankranti* was celebrated as well. Thousands of devotees and worshippers followed the ancient Indian custom of taking holy dips in the pool to wash off their sins. The came from different parts of the land, far and wide. It was over though, by almost three months. What ahead was the Bengali New Year's Day.

As Gautam and Martha travelled back to the sleepy town, Gautam formed a different plan. He wished to stay at the place for some time to get acquainted with his son before he could request Mr Chai to allow him to adopt his own son.

On the way, the surging water of the river looked more endearing.

Nearly one hundred miles away from the legendary Mansarover Lake in Tibet lies the Tarchok glacier—the source of the river Tsangpo. The river flows through the almost entire length of Tibet along its southern territory before suddenly and abruptly making a U-turn to enter India through the hills and mountains of the Himalayan region of the north east, down to the plains. As it prepares to enter the plains, two more tributaries, the Dibang and the Lohit join to form the mighty Brahmaputra.

The river Lohit originating from the hills forms the pool, the divine pool, the kund for the Hindus to have dips at the place.

The myths abound in the ancient scriptures. How the Gods used to come, descend from the heaven (they numbered in millions) to have dips there, for ablutions. The pool had gained divinity thus. Hence the divine pool was the centre of pilgrimage for devotees and worshippers.

The mythical legends about the great times when gods visited earth soon gave way to more earthy human existence. Of kings, emperors, sages, saints, common man, warriors and fighters, who spread across the land to set up human habitation in the vast territory.

Aeons later, in still mythical times of ancient India, the name of a violent mendicant—a sage, who was more warrior-like than being saint-like, is met with.

He was the sage Parasuram*a*, born in the priestly class, to parents Jamadagni and Renuka, leading their conjugal life as ascetics in the forests. The couple had five sons—the youngest one being the sage *Parasurama.*

Legend had it that a royal couple that was supposedly on some kind of a pleasure trip visited the forest where the family lived. The king Chitrarath and his queen were deep in the act of love-making in the forests, oblivious to the fact that they were being watched.

It was none other than the holy ascetic Renuka—the mother of five sons, who happened to watch the act and enjoy the scene. That aroused her (any live performance was sure to do that) and she fantasized herself in the position of the queen.

That was all. The father of the sons, the old sage Jamadagni was an accomplished sage of a very high order. He was an *antaryami(omniscient)*, one who could know and read other people's minds. The passion in his wife's eyes was evident to the sage. In a flash, he knew what had happened.

That was all. No adultery even if it were a momentary deviation, even if it were only mental and emotional, only a fantasy and nothing physical; could be tolerated.

The spark of passion, the uncontrollable lust, the momentary flicker of unmanageable urge of getting physical with someone else, enraged the sage. That was the moral transgression of the highest order! Chastity, loyalty, fidelity, everything gone! The episode was enough to disturb the moral code of conduct.

That has to be punished. The sage was enraged beyond control. Nothing short of capital punishment was appropriate, in the court of law where he was the sole arbitrator, being the lord and the master and the judge, only one who could sentence his people.

He issued the death sentence.

To execute the sentence, he asked his sons to do so in "the letter and the spirit", one by one. All the four sons who were older refused to carry out the order. They were ordered to leave the house instead.

Disobedience was not to be tolerated.

Then came the turn of the youngest son.

The young hermit pleaded with his father to forgive his mother. Those had no effect and enraged the father even more. The father ordered him to carry out the execution. The obedient son obliged. With his axe that became his insignia, he performed the act. The father was happy. Very happy for the matricide - the obedient son!

"Now ask for a boon, as you have pleased me. That shall be granted," said the proud father.

"If that be so, I pray to you to bring back to life my poor mother and that she leads her life normally, thereafter," the dutiful son implored.

"That shall be granted," said the sage. It was granted. She came back to life. The couple lived happily thereafter.

The father was pleased. He was happy that at least one of his sons was obedient and loyal to him. Loyalty, obedience and even obeisance to individuals were the hallmarks of the society in the land even in the mythical times. He was doubly happy that his wife had regained her life. The punishment was after all for her *karma* and nothing else.

So much so far the descriptions in the *Puranas*. The folklore recorded the later events.

All was not well for the young ascetic; his karma didn't leave him. His act was unpardonable. The young matricide had to bear the punishment. The axe with which he took care of his mother stuck to his hand. Penance, meditation, atonement, everything he did but those were not to much avail. The axe could not be removed. It stuck as before, to his hand. To wash off his sins, he wondered all over taking dips in the holy rivers all through the land, but no relief was in sight.

Till, one day, an angel asked the ascetic to take dips at the divine pool—the Brahma Kund.

The ascetic travelled, traversed the land, in the mountains till he arrived at the spot where was located the 'divine pool'.

There, he prayed to God and took his dips, the holy dips at the Brahma Kund, the divine pool. Lo and behold! There he got relief form his torment. His axe came off from his hands.

The axe was freed but the ascetic could not free himself from the axe. He, the legend said took up his axe to free the mother earth from the rule of the despots. The kingly class, not once or twice, but twenty one times! Quite an achievement!

The Brahma Kund acquired new name and significance from the sage of mythical times. The pool came to be called the Parasurama Kund, meaning the pool of Parasurama.

In mid-January, especially on the Makar Sankranti day, thousands gather at the spot to have holy dips in the river, at the pool to wash off their sins. The auspicious period spread over nearly a fortnight attracted devotees, worshippers, tramps and vagabonds alike, at the place.

How and why Mr Chai set up his home at such a place was never clear to Gautam. Probably he wanted to lesson the sins of others at the holy place.

Gautam decided to come back to the place, the day after, to live there for a while, to familiarize himself with his son before he could take him back; to care for him, to give him a life of hope and aspiration.

The very next day, Gautam went to the place, in the vicinity of the divine pool. He lodged at the inn nearby, which for most part of year lay empty. The keeper was delighted to have an inmate, who strangely enough choose to stay there for some time, even during the off season.

The indigenous people of the hill tribes, the *mishmis*, living in the forests, from ages guarded the holy place of the Hindus.

Perhaps, that was the phenomenon of ossification of better understanding.

For Gautam, the setting was exquisite. There, stop the hillock facing the skies, with the river Lohit flowing down below, shrouded in mist and fog, he had met his son - the child in his fifth year, who had to be given the love and care.

At the Home, Mr Chai was reflective.

"In the serene setting," he said, "I wanted to set up a home for children. That was my wish for years. But that it would be some kind of an orphanage, I hadn't thought of.

"Every year for the past fifteen winters, I kept coming here. Not much for the holy dips though. Rather to watch people who took dips to cleanse them. To meet people from different parts of land. Mostly, the spiritual ones, the holy men who came here in groups. Talking to them was surely experience gained. Sharing their thoughts were lessons of sorts. I loved coming here."

Strange, Gautam thought. What strange dreams people have! The man had a dream of setting up a home for the children. That was the mission in the man's life. Or in the part of life that was left!

While, he had a dream, too. Of launching an enterprise, a business concern that would be global, and the returns running to millions.

The missions were separate, poles apart.

"On one such occasion, as I came here nearly three years ago," Mr Chai continued, "I came across a strange sight. I saw a corpse, of a woman, surrounded by her three children. She was a pilgrim. Probably she had come here to seek peace and solace. Due to extreme cold and fatigue she had died. She was extremely poor it seemed. Her two children were sitting around and the third; the infant was sucking the mother's breasts. It was a painful sight. The authorities here disposed off the body. No address was available and the young ones could not explain their location." Mr Chai paused for a moment as he cleaned his glasses and put them back.

"The problem was to take care of the young children. The plight of the children, especially the infant, troubled me. I thought it was a god sent opportunity for me to put into action what I had all along dreamt of. It was so sudden that I didn't even get any time to draw up my plans.

"I was a retired medical practitioner. My wife and children, I mean my two daughters were no more. They were the victims of a boat tragedy in my native village when the monsoon was in full fury, some years ago.

"I decided then and there, to make the Home, as you see. It had a very modest beginning. The three young children had to be taken care of. The elderly woman you have seen here helped me take care of the children. She has remained with me from the day one when I managed some iron sheets to serve as roof and got the walls plastered on bamboo walling, split and dressed.

"The children have since lived here. The eldest one, a girl, goes to the school with her brother at the primary school at the village nearby. The youngest, the infant, has grown up to be a cuddlesome baby.

"From that day, as the name of the home got known, people have come straight here with children, infants, babies in their arms. They have made it a perfect orphanage. This is my little world." The man smiled.

"But Sir, aren't you cash-strapped? Surely you need enough funds to meet the expenses." Gautam asked him.

"Yes, of course. But there are donations from people. Even the pilgrims, who come here, often donate. But there is this strange behaviour on the part of men and women in this land of ours." Mr Chai moved his hand over his bald head.

"People come here with children, young infants in their arms, from hospitals, pick abandoned children even from roadside, and bring them here. Well-to-do are not hesitant to donate money either. Yet, what surprises me is that these people are wary of adopting children. Even childless couples wait their lives in the hope of becoming parents, visiting holy shrines, praying, spending huge sums for medical treatment which often bear no results; and yet, they do not go for adoption.

"I tell them, what the young ones need are not just food, clothing and shelter. These are the necessities. What the children need in their lives is something different. The love and affection, which probably no money can provide! This is the strange feature of this land. The compassion, the feel is *restrictive*. People treasure their own blood, and the spirit of adoption has not caught on. The *accident* of birth has always been more important than the birth *itself*, here, from ages."

Mr Chai was philosophical.

"The problems are many. Providing schooling to them is a major cause of worry. The primary school, the government one at the nearby village caters to their needs for the present. Beyond that, when the children pass out of primary level, providing education would be a problem. Then comes the question of supporting the adolescents and adults for a life of their own." He paused for a moment.

"What torments me more than that is, how are the young ones to fare in this world after me. I am an old man, past my sixty-fifth year. I am of very sound health. But for how long can

I continue? Then, what happens to the set up? Are the young ones to be orphans again?"

Mr Chai reclined back on his chair and closed his eyes.

Gautam was silent. How missions do differ for individuals on earth? How torments differ in degrees as well as in kind.

Here was the benevolent man tormented by the mere thought of young children becoming homeless and love-less once again.

The children he had only reared and not fathered, were the prime cause of his existence!

In contrast, Gautam thought he was a man who had abandoned his own child. The new- found fatherhood was the source of delight. He had come here only to look for his son. The other children around, his son's playmates, the inmates of the home, he could only sympathize with but could do *little* about.

His thoughts revolved around his son, only.

The residents of Mr Chai's "Krishna Home" represented the miniature India, in diapers.

Babies had features of all varieties, right from the Mongoloid to the Dravidian to Aryan to the mixed types was visible, some in good health, some not so healthy. They understood one language, of love and affection.

Whenever he visited them and they smiled back with feeding bottles in their mouth, he felt happy and cheerful. Never before in his life, did he come across such a sight. Of rows of infants lying in cradle - beds being attended.

"Does the ambience of holy site influence people?" he wondered.

He could feel the cathartic changes in himself.

But his attention was centred around his son, "Mark-Rahul". The child was for him the only source of happiness.

For the young father, the bliss of fatherhood had come as a dawn, of a new life, with fresh air in plenty; the nightmares had given way to hope and the desire to provide a better life for his son.

When the child smiled, his son, he felt the happiness of the entire world was in his bosom.

The paternal concern, care, anxiety were new experiences for him. The child provided all the balm. For the first time in his life, even the sermons that he used to receive from his father came back to him, nearly fifteen years later. He remembered those, some very vividly. Surprisingly, those no longer appeared distasteful.

His life was an eventful one, very eventful.

Though not so ominous, he could say for sure, no longer, any more. The 'accident' in a cold wintry evening had resulted in some kind of bliss, sublime bliss, through peril to him.

His acquaintance with his son grew. The child was more familiar with him. Gone was the initial hesitation, the shyness. His son was more approachable.

"You got two names. Your mother called you Mark. Here your friends call you Rahul. What should I call you? Can I call you Rahul?" He asked his son.

The child listened with attention. That was a problem, a real problem. Two names. One could not have two separate names, so different.

"Do you love me?" The child asked him very softly.

"Oh yes!" Gautam replied. The tenderness with which the child spoke suddenly aroused his paternal love. He drew the child close and kissed him. "I love you very much."

"Then, call me Mark," said the child. "But why do you too want me to be called as Rahul?" the little boy's inquisitiveness had to be replied to.

"Well, long ago a small child, a little older than you perhaps, too found his father many hundreds of years ago in the hills not much far. He longed for his father's love and wished his father came to him. And finally, his father came to the child and the child was Rahul."

"Then, call me Mark, if you love me," said the child.

Gautam was taken aback. The bottomline was not much confusing though. If he loved his son, he had to call the child Mark.

"But why? Your friends here call you Rahul. I want to call you by that name," Gautam stated.

"Here I am known as Rahul. My friends at the home call me by that name. But..." he stopped.

"What?" Gautam was inquisitive.

"My mom used to call me Mark. Always! She loved me very much. But then she was ill, you know. Very ill." The child drew a sorry face.

Gautam got over the shock. "But the name..."

"My mother loved me very much. She called me, Mark. So, if you love me, you call me Mark as well, like as my mother did." The child made his mind clear.

"But the name, Rahul, it is as good. Isn't it?" Gautam tried to convince the child.

The child thought for a moment. Suddenly his eyes glowed. "You call me then, by both the names. But at different times."

"Different times? I don't understand." The father stated his inability.

"Very simple," The child replied. "When you love me, kiss me, caress me, you call me Mark. And when you don't do that, you may call me, Rahul."

That was it. That was the golden rule laid threadbare. When the father loved the child, he loved Mark. When he didn't the child was Rahul. That amazed the young father. Bewildered at the child resolving the problem. The child did that very simply and logically!

Everyone, even a child in the land, it seemed was initiated into peaceful reconciliation quite spontaneously. That was the wonder of wonders. The child indeed was "the father of the man."

How many more such revelations were in store for him, Gautam didn't know? *Wonders never ceased to happen.*

Gautam decided to tell his son, the prospects; the future prospects. That he wished to take the child with him, away from the place, had to be told.

"I have got something to talk to you," Gautam said one day. "Something important, Rahul." (He *did not love* his son then, so he had to call him Rahul). The child looked at him with concern.

"I have thought over everything." Gautam was thinking how and where to begin. "I believe you need a good house, good dresses, good toys to play with."

The child nodded, the eyes gaining the shine Gautam was looking for. "Those things you need. Need in plenty. But those things can't be provided here." Gautam was cautious to tread further. "What if we move to some other place I mean you and me, both together so that we could have all these in plenty." He pressed his eyeballs to impress upon his son.

But the child didn't seem much convinced of the idea.

"Why can't we live here with everything as you say, dresses and toys with my friends?"

"Well, that would have been very good for all of us. But then, you know I live at a distant place and I have to go; but I want to live with you. I mean, we must live together, there in the city with cars and aeroplanes flying high, zoo…m, zoo…m". Gautam had to show the flight of an aeroplane with his hand.

The child understood but looked worried.

"Then, I have to leave my friends here," he said looking very serious.

"I am afraid, yes. You will have to. But then new place, new friends, new house! Everything new is fine, isn't it?" Gautam was all set to impress upon his son.

"When we go together, live together, you and me with kisses and hugs; eating together, playing and studying, we can have a great time. You know what it is like. I can't live without you, Mark." Gautam appealed and that worked, as he kissed his son.

The child looked at him and nodded. He agreed to go along. Gautam felt he had conquered the world.

Having made his point, Gautam wanted to be more father-like to the child.

"Well, suppose, not just suppose, say when we—you and me live at a place far off, just you and me loving each other, what would you call me, then?"

The child was silent. He looked at Gautam.

"I wish you call me Baba," Gautam told his son.

"But what does that mean?"

"Baba means father."

"But why should I call you Baba? You are not my father."

"Well, that is true. But if you call me that, I will be very happy. I can become your father." Gautam could find no better reason.

"Can anyone become a father, if he is not?" The child put Gautam in a tight spot.

"Do you know anything about your father?" Gautam tried to shift the focus.

"Yes," The child smiled. "I know. He lives far off. He lives at a distant place far away, like you do. He lives in the city where there are tall, huge buildings, cars and people, all around."

"Really! That's very nice." Gautam comforted the child.

"You know, my father is a big man. He is rich. He has a big house in the city. He has cars, good dresses, everything." The eyes glowed again.

It was Gautam's turn to be amazed.

"But how do you know all about him?"

"I know everything." The child smiled and widened his eyes. "My mom told me all. My dad loved me very much."

"That is excellent. But have you met him?" Gautam asked.

"No, not exactly." The child went back into his shell.

"Mom told me, my dad would one day come to me, love me, kiss me and give me everything. But you know my mom is no more. So, my dad could not come. How was he to know me if my mom was not here?"

Gautam wanted to bang his own head against the nearest wall he could find. But there was no wall around, nearby.

Suddenly, the child asked, "Do you know where my mom is?" Gautam shook his head. He didn't have the courage to meet the eyes of the child.

" I know," The child replied. "Come along! I will show you."

Gautam followed his son in the star-lit evening to open space outside the home.

"There!" The child pointed out in the sky. "There she lives. Among the stars! The brightest one! Do you see? That's my mom."

Gautam gently caressed the head of his son. "How do you know she is there? She could not be far away from you."

"She is not far. She is the one living in the brightest star. From there, highup in the sky, she watches me, all night when I am asleep."

There was silence for a while. Then Gautam heard the voice, even softer one.

"She lives among the stars that twinkle every night. She is sure to show my dad the way up here. To tell him, I live here." It was almost is if the child spoke to himself.

For Gautam, it was another wonder, of a different kind.

"Do you know my dad?" The child asked.

"Well, no. I don't know him actually. But I am sure I can, rather we can find him. Together, someday, in the city." Gautam found a way out.

"That's fine." The eyes glowed again. "We could find him together."

"Sure. But for that you have to come with me. Together shall we live, play and eat. You have to grow big. As big as him! Big, rich with cars and houses." Temptation seemed to be the best ploy Gautam could think about. The child was happy.

"So, if we live in the city, you have to call me something and if you call me Baba, I shall be very happy." Gautam came back to the point.

The child looked at him and thought for a while.

"But then, what shall I call my father when we find him?" The child had compromised with the situation; the prospect of locating or to be able to locate his father was of utmost importance.

"Hmm…That's a problem. Gautam came back with a solution; the solution for names like his son had done before.'

"You call me Baba, and when you find your father, you call him Daddy!"

The child was happy, very happy. The worries were sorted out for him. He could then proceed with his Baba to search and locate his 'daddy'.

"When are we leaving?" The son asked the father.

"Very soon. But think, you have to leave all your friends here and saying good - bye takes a lot of time, isn't it?'

"Yes, but then, I have to grow big, big like him. That is more important, isn't it?" The child was more eager.

For the young father, the child had indeed grown big within so short a time.

"Yes. Only then can you find your dad." Gautam comforted him.

"Now, Mark. Please call me Baba," Gautam kissed his son.

After the initial hesitation, the child said, "B-A-B-A."

That was the moment of truth. The greatest moment in Gautam's life had arrived. He was filled with emotions. He was dying to hear that, Baba—the *address* of a lifetime.

He found it difficult to hold back his emotions. The stiff upper lip gave away. As he clasped his son to his chest, he allowed the drops to roll, of satisfaction and atonement.

What lay before him was to explain to Mr Chai, the desire of his heart. To ask Mr Chai, the permission to adopt his son! He was confident that Mr Chai would grant him the permission to adopt his son. He was sure that Mr Chai would allow that. Then he had to move to the sleepy town to meet Martha and tell her of his decision and he was sure, she would be very happy, too.

Next what remained were the legal formalities to be completed. For that he had to arrange the requisites for a trouble free hand over.

He wanted to take the child to 240 50/ N, 920 51/E places where the child had to be acquainted with his lineage, to be made familiar to the society where everybody seemed related to everybody else.

But before that he had to go back to the church, to the backyard where the bamboo fence protected the place where people lay in eternal sleep. There in a nondescript stretch of earth she lay as well. He had to go there and thank her for the wonderful gift she had left for him, ask for her forgiveness and promise her that her son would be taken care of.

Gautam talked about the matter to Mr Chai.

"Sir, I have something to ask for," he said one day, " I believe I can be of some help. If you allow me, I would like to adopt one of the children here."

Mr Chai looked a bit surprised. "As a matter of fact, I encourage adoption." Mr Chai replied. "I believe the best place for a child is the family. That spirit is yet to evolve in this land. But your desire surprises me. A child can only be happy in a family with parents and children."

He took out his glasses and looked at Gautam.

"But you are young. As you have stated, you are still single. Do you think you could provide what the child needs, all love and care and attention? I mean, do you think you could be a good father?" The old man asked.

"Sir, I believe I can do that. Over these days, I have been preparing myself for the same. It is not just out of compassion. It is out of love and affection, that I speak," Gautam answered. He knew, deep inside it was not all altruism.

"Even if that were true and I believe that it is so, I still have my apprehensions," said Mr Chai. "You are young. Sometime in near future, you are sure to get married and raise your own family. Could you still take care of the child, then? I don't want to disappoint you but, I resent sending someone, a child in particular, from one orphanage to another."

For Gautam, that was another moment of stress, very personal. No way he could tell that the child was his own. That was impossible. More importantly, how could he convince the gentleman in front of him, that he was dead serious, that the desire was not the outcome of any fleeting compassion?

"Mr Chai," Gautam said. "I can't assure you just by my words alone. Mere words can't convince anyone. The conviction has to come from within, I know. For the moment, I can only tell you, Sir, please, I implore, please give me a chance to prove myself."

Mr Chai looked at him. For a moment Gautam thought he was again on the edge of a precipice. The looks from the deep-set eyes observed him. As if the gentleman searched for truth inside Gautam's heart. As if he could clearly view the inside, of the father-in-waiting!

The moment of scrutiny, screening over, the old man said.

"All right. But you have to arrange for the legal formalities. In addition, as a special case you have to assure me in writing that the child you adopt shall never be mistreated anytime in future."

Gautam heaved a sigh of relief.

He thanked Mr Chai for his benevolence, for the confidence Mr Chai had for Gautam.

"Well, then," Mr Chai asked, "Whom would you like to adopt?"

"Sir, I could and would like to adopt, if possible more than one child. But since that is not possible, if you allow me, I would like to adopt, Rahul." He knew once again that he was not stating facts, true to the tradition.

"If you so desire, it shall be done." The old man said. "But we shall have to seek the boy's approval as a formality."

He sent for Rahul.

Once again Gautam felt his heart beating fast.

As Rahul was ushered in, Gautam felt the beats.

"Rahul," Mr Chai said." This gentleman loves you very much. He wants to have a new house, new dresses, and new friends for you at a new place in the city. Do you like to go with him? He could be your *new father*." The old man touched the child's head and face.

For a moment the son was silent as the father felt his own heart beats. Then, to his relief, the child raised the head and nodded. The nod of approval!

"Yes," the child said very softly.

There was no holding back. In a spontaneous action, Gautam pulled his son to his chest and breathed his lungs out.

Everything had to be done without any further delay.

Gautam went back to the sleepy town and informed Martha, who seemed to be more than just being pleased. Then he went to the church with her, to the backyard, where the bamboo fence marked the extent of the graveyard.

The bunch of flowers that he took, he kept at her grave and knelt before the grave.

"Mary," he said. "Forgive me for all what I had done. But I can assure you that your son, our son would not be left uncared for. No more shall he be an orphan. I promise and this time, it won't be broken."

The parting tears he could not control. The silent tears from him that time.

He turned and saw Martha wiping her tears: her share of the moment.

Gautam was impatient and almost restless. The child calling him Baba was what he wanted to hear, more and more. The newfound, the new-realised fatherhood made the joy more intense every moment.

He didn't like to waste any time. He had a fear that all might he upset by any other sudden tragic spur of occurrence. He was *wary* of all events.

His son, Mark-Rahul, the new vision of a new generation, millions like him carrying the hopes of the land into the next century, the next millennium.

With the 'deterrent state' still menacingly gnawing and gnashing at the land, with even powerful actual 'nukes' and missiles fitted within its territory directed towards India, posed as a real demon. The *demon* that had insinuated the people on the right side of the Himalayas with innuendoes; threatened with more terrible missiles, at bases like Da Qaidam, Xaio Qaidam, and Delingha, ready to strike at a short notice. Some more sites with higher pay-load and more efficient delivery systems with more precisely strikable missiles being developed; were on the anvil, for more peril.

The nations that comprised of one-fifth of humanity were supposedly gnashing at each other!

The young father wondered if in the new century, the new millennium, the scenario would change: or if a friendly dragon would replace the demonic state? Or if the next generation of Indians, even in the next millennium would have to live under the threat of actual nukes and missiles?

Like the threats from across, the infections from within needed concern: rather more concern. The new sets of values, which the land had seen in the first fifty years of her *latest* existence, were the internal nukes. In the next fifty years with the new generation gaining adulthood, the likes of Mark-Rahul, the concern that the young father harboured was, if and what immunity was required for *insulation*.

He had *every right* to be wary of events.

The formalities had to be done. For that, Martha needed a holiday. In a couple of days, it was Easter.

On the D-day, the Easter Sunday, Martha accompanied Gautam to the Krishna Home of Mr Chai up the hillock overlooking the surging water of river Lohit, near the divine pool—the Brahma Kund/the Parasurama Kund.

The formalities were over in less than an hour, the laws of the land satisfied. Gautam and Rahul came out of the Home, the father and the son, the son clutching the hand of the father, on the Easter Sunday.

And Martha followed them.

Gautam felt the satisfaction of the lifetime. He was a father after all, more so *legally*. He had a job cut out before him. To rear the child, to bring him up, so that his son could have a decent life! He could strive for providing a better life as much as he could. But the actual nukes and missiles were beyond his domain. If the age-old peaceful co-existence could be replaced by actual 'demonic deterrence' in the form of actual nukes and missiles for the two oldest civilizations in continuity, the decency was certainly out of question. In addition, the adversaries within, who rejoiced at the relegation of the land into a cesspool, an abyss, where self before everything was the bottom line, would never allow the decent life to take shape.

Martha had to go back to the sleepy town for the Easter celebrations.

But for the father and the son, Gautam and Rahul, they had no such obligations. They were completely and truly, free. They had nothing else to attend to, only themselves— the father and the son.

Down below the river Lohit gushed down from the hills, to the plains. The Brahma Kund/ the Parasurama Kund, with circling water currents within, was ready as ever, from time immemorial to wash off sins—ethical, moral and social of the humans.

The celebrations of Makar Sankranti were long over. The hordes of devotees, worshippers, the holy men, the tramps, the vagabonds, all had left. Even those who didn't have anything to do had left as well. The place was almost deserted.

Those left were the ones, who had to stay there, the stray individuals who worked at the inn and people who lived around. They had no desire or wish of 'washing their sins off'. They carried on with their routine baths at the pool.

As he watched people taking baths, he felt the urge, the desire to go down on the mid-April day to have a bath at the divine pool.

Overcome as he was, by the succession of event—he needed a bath to relieve himself of fatigue and exertion.

He wanted the bath. Martha had not much time left. She wanted to leave for the sleepy town, early. She wanted him to have the bath, with no loss of time. He asked Martha to take care of the child, as he walked briskly down the stony steps to the pool, to have bath in the cold water.

He wanted to sing and recite again. But he was afraid. His first composition was the harbinger of disaster. His second series of compositions had actually led to one. He didn't want to do the third.

The fatalism of the land had overtaken the rationalist, the self-styled protagonist of scientific temper.

As he walked down the stony steps, the events—the flash back of events of his life, in his not-so-long but eventful life came back to him.

In the cool soothing ambience, he could smell Rosa Macrophylla, larger than anyone's palm, of the face in eternal sleep clutching the beads—the dried rose in it, the stone curved image of the Lord in meditation, the eyes in deep meditation, the sermons from a righteous man, the wonderful profile of smiling lips in the fresco, the smell of tea leaves, the blood-smeared cross, the destroyer God in tandava dance, the ragas—*indravol* and *jhinjhoti*, the concrete block at the mound; all came back in quick succession!

The reels of real life were set in motion—backward.

The fear of a third calamity stopped him from any further composition; he was unable to mumble anything to himself. He was hypnotized by the events, His mind mesmerized by the succession; he found it difficult to pour his heart, out of fear.

Gautam took his dips at the pool, in the cold water. He felt all his anxiety, stress, tiredness and exhaustion, gone. Soon, the chill overcame him. The perfect chill of the cold water!

He understood, how and why the people—the holy men, the devotees, the pilgrims, why all of them chanted hymns, or recited or sang, as they took their dips in cold water.

To overcome the instant chill! To distract attention from the physical condition to which the body was subjected. If the attention, the mind, the thoughts could be removed; it felt less.

For him, he could not help recite what he had heard long before from his father, the Vedic hymns.

The only solace was, it was not *his* composition, not anything *his*.

His teeth clattering in tandem, his body shivering, his limbs trembling - all out of chill and cold getting down to his bones, he recovered himself. He stood tall and retraced his steps up the stony path. He looked for his little self, his son. The child and his aunt were atop the hillock, overlooking the pool, like two tiny specks against the horizon, waiting for him to come up to them.

Not very far from the place, some hundreds of miles away, in a tiny Himalayan kingdom, several hundred years ago, a prince tormented by sufferings and miseries of life had set on the path, the path he did not know but was determined to traverse the path of salvation.

Yet, he was firm. In the dead of night, he chose to leave. He wanted to kiss his son—the infant was asleep, the prince wanted to plant the parting kiss. He moved towards his son. The young mother was asleep, too, his wife. She held the infant tight, with her arms around, least the infant roll out of the bed and injure himself. The prince stopped. He could not have kissed his son without awaking the mother. That would have been the end of the mission, even before it had begun. So, he chose, with a heavy heart to have the last look at the sleeping child and the mother with her arms around him—the protection the infant needed. Out he came then, in the dead of night, shaved his head, gave up his attire, all the paraphernalia of regal identity, and without looking back vanished into the forest for a truly greater cause—the salvation of mankind. He was past his twenty-fourth year, then.

At the far end of another age, in the last decade of the twentieth century was another man— a very ordinary mortal, in the search of his own, very personal, 'kingdom of god'.

He went up the stony path, in broad daylight, on the fateful Easter Sunday.

The resurrection of his manhood, his new-found fatherhood was in sight. All in the vicinity of the divine pool —the ambience of hope and aspiration transpiring through.

The surging water of river Lohit in the divine pool rushed and made circles, down below. The foams, the bubbles, each series, formed and then lost was the story through the ages, being repeated over and over again.

It was the land that had sheltered the persecuted and the refugees all religions and all nations on earth. Right from the earliest Zoroastrians to the early Jews who came when their temple was burnt by the Romans, to the early Christians in the first century to the followers of Islam who came and made the land their home.

Was it then, the land of exotics?

For Gautam, those philosophical discourses were not of much importance. For him, the symbol of love and care, his son, his descendant was in front, ahead of him. He had a 'mission' in his life to accomplish.

His *redemptive resurrection* to manhood was nearly over.

Gautam went up the steps, the stony steps, to embrace his son, to lead him into the world. The atonement over, he was to respond to the call of his new-found fatherhood, past his twenty- fourth year.

For him, the kingdom of God on earth, was within his grasp. As he went up, he saw against the horizon, the smiling face of the mother with the infant in her arms, the smiles surmised all the human values possible.

Was it then, a delusion or illusion?

Gautam didn't know. He had no answer.

For him, something earthier, more mundane, more heart throbbing was before him. His son! The child—his son, was standing almost on his little toes to locate his father.

Gautam approached the child and his aunt. The child had all the smiles in the world to greet him.

For the young father, the new-found fatherhood was a revelation. It has other connotations also. That of his redemption! The redemption in store for him; from the saga of the big red rose—the Rosa Macrophylla, the saga of the cross, smeared with blood.

Was the child a Hindu, or a Christian, or one blessed by the Buddha?

Was the child a tribal or a plainsman, a Bengali?

Those were of no importance and of no consequence, either.

The final redemption was one Gautam thanked his destiny for.

Gautam opened his arms wide and from the top, the child nearly jumped on to his arms, while Martha watched.

Deluge?

Illusion? Or delusion?

Those mattered little.

He held the child very tight in his arms and then slowly put him on the ground and held the child's hand into his.

The father and the son then walked as Martha watched.

The father was leading the son into the world.

The world of charmed existence
where every one desired an
Ounce of Joy.

Glossary

1. Gompa – A Buddhist temple
2. Dungchen, Dung kar, Gyaling – Tibetan musical instruments
3. Dramyn, and Piwang – Tibetan wind musical instruments
4. Cho nga or Loknga – Tibetan percussion musical instruments
5. Tsorgen – Village Headman of the Monpas
6. Monpa – Tribe living in North East India
7. Lumpa – Buddhist deity
8. Avalokiteswara – A form of Buddha
9. Dhyani Boddhisattawa – Buddha's incarnations in past lives
10. Chuba – A long sheepskin coat made of thick wool worn by Tibetans
11. Tamading – A mythical horse, God of Tibetans
12. Ta and Hang – Hose and blessings
13. Jamaibabu – Husband of one's elder sister
14. Bhadralok – Bengali Gentlemanly class
15. Sala – younger brother of one's wife, used as a slang
16. Aamerika – U.S.A.

17. Rakshashas – Demons in Indian Mythology
18. Dushman – Enemy
19. Khokshashas – Demons in Indian Mythology
20. Bhagwad Gita – The Hindu scripture
21. Quran – The Islamic holy Book
22. Bengali – People who speak Bangla, a language of Indian subcontinent
23. Sadhu – A Mendicant in Hinduism
24. Zamindars – Landlords in feudal India
25. Rajas – Kings
26. Pujas – Ritual worship
27. Annas – Food made from rice
28. Brahmin – Hindu priestly class
29. Sarvahara – The Have-nots
30. Mantra – The scriptural intonations
31. Amra Phani Khaiya Ek Sange Thakmu – Shall stick together on even plain water(colloquially spoken)
32. Yogic – The union of soul, mind, and body through Yoga
33. Saraswati – The Hindu Goddess of learning
34. Sakya thupa – The lord of Shakya tribe, meaning Lord Buddha
35. Sakya muni – The sage from the Sakya clan, meaning Lord Buddha
36. Kheys – A man of noble blood
37. Monyul Khyimozong – Happy valley of the Monpas

38. Ganden Namgye Lhatse – The heavenly abode with an enduring presence
39. Mala – Garland
40. Dada – Elder brother in Bengali
41. Mujhe Bachao – Save me
42. Manushi Buddha – A form of Lord Buddha
43. Swabalambi – Self reliant
44. Sahib – Lord, a reverential address
45. Rasogolla – A traditional Bengali sweet drenched in syrup
46. Kharram – A traditional footwear of Hindus made up of wood
47. Tata bye bye – A parting gesture, shown by waving hands
48. English-o-fying — Anglicizing (colloquial slang)
49. Adi – Tribe living in North East India
50. Diwali – A Hindu festival, also called the 'Festival of lights'
51. Holi – A Hindu festival, also called the 'Festival of colours'
52. Meghdottam – Cloud-messenger
53. Durbar – The court of kings, rulers
54. Bidis – Traditional smoking tobacco
55. Bandhs – Strikes, mostly agitational
56. Hartals – The act of closing shops or suspending work, especially in political protest.
57. Avtaars – Incarnations
58. Kothas – The dwelling of nautch girls/women, also a brothel

59. Choli-ghagra – A traditional Indian dress
60. Mithuna – A sexual posture
61. Glaaley – A tribal dress of women worn around the waist
62. Tandava – The war posture of Lord Shiva
63. Chowkidar – The gatekeeper
64. Hindustani – Indian
65. Sadhna – The ritualistic practices
66. Gharanas – Traditional musical households
67. Raga Magh Malhar – Traditional musical notes of classical Hindustani
68. Taan Haati Chingar – A note of Hindustani classical music resembling the call of elephants
69. Nawab – A Muslim Ruler
70. Khvab – Dreams
71. Choga – Traditional dress of the Muslims
72. Achkan – A traditional upper garment worn by male Muslim gentry
73. Sherwani – A traditional upper garment worn by males
74. Shawl – A square or oblong piece of woven or knitted fabric used especially as a covering for the head or shoulders.
75. Mehfil – A musical gathering
76. Shayar – An Urdu poet
77. Salaam – Reverential gesture
78. Gayaki – A style of rendering Hindustani vocal music

79. Kachauri – A snack made of flour
80. Lathi – A stick
81. Kamasutra – A sexual treatise of ancient India
82. Izzat – Honour
83. Murlimanohar – A form of lord Krishna
84. Agni-pariksha – Test by fire
85. Kholis – A small dwelling, often in the slums
86. Pharratedaar – Very fast
87. Bhabi – Sister-in-law
88. Bazaar – Market
89. Filmwallahs – Film people
90. Bhang – An intoxicating drink of traditional weed
91. Bachoo – A condescending remark, meaning 'childlike'
92. Mughlai – Food attributed to Mughals
93. Biryani – A mix of rice and meat cooked in the oven
94. Kababs – A meat recipe cooked in special oven
95. Desi – Traditionally Indian
96. Haveli – A traditional palace like building
97. Lehenga – A traditional skirt worn by women
98. Aachar – Pickle
99. Naan – Traditional bread
100. Guru – The preceptor
101. Machan – A seat prepared atop trees for the hunters
102. Mishmi – A tribe in North East India

103. Kund – A pool of water for ritualistic bath/ablutions
104. Makar Sankranti – The Capricorn transit, an astronomical phenomenon and a festival
105. Karma – The result of accumulated actions
106. Puran – Collected traditional Hindu quasi-religious folklore

Acknowledgements

I am deeply indebted to my late parents, Mitarupa and Rishindra Krishna Dutta Chowdhury, for sowing the seeds of values in me. I'm also grateful to my sister, Dr Rupali for being a constant, albeit nudging, companion during my younger days.

I express gratitude to my teachers and my friends from school and college for inspiring me. And to my wife, Nandita, thank you for your patience and for being a ruthless critic of my work.

I extend my thanks to the Nu Voice Press team—Tanvi, Navya, Abhishek, Vedika, Jasodha, Archita, and many others—who have tirelessly contributed to the final outcome of *Unbound Love* in numerous ways.

I remain ever grateful to Avdhoot Baba Ji for his blessings.

Thank you!

About the Author

Born and raised among the indigenous population of the Himalayan foothills in India, Ratnojyoti is a Civil Engineer and a writer.

His writing captures the dreamy ambience and the pristine human values of the mountains, where life is simple and closer to divinity. He lives in Silchar, Assam.

Unbound Love is his novel with autobiographical shades, especially in the early and middle sections of the book.